I0718562

Nightmares of Caitlin Lockyer

DEMELZA CARLTON

DEDICATION

This book is dedicated to Johanna.
Never underestimate the power of dreams.
Especially when they follow you to the toilet.

ONE

They took her away from me.

I mumbled a protest through the haze of pain and exhaustion that had turned me into little more than a zombie. I'll never be able to watch a zombie movie again without remembering this night, I thought.

"It's all right – we have to move her somewhere else to take care of her. She's hurt worse than you," I was told. "We need to treat you, too. There's a gunshot wound in your shoulder."

I couldn't remember how long it had been since I'd last slept, so it took a few seconds to register what she'd said. Gunshot wound. My shoulder. Oh yeah, it hurt. I couldn't help her 'til that was sorted. Hospital staff would take care of her until I was okay.

The pain began to dull as a local anaesthetic took effect. I turned to look at the mess of blood my right shoulder had become. The smell of disinfectant jolted my brain out of sleep and most of the way to alertness. All that blood and it was barely more than a graze. A few stitches would sort that.

One of the hospital staff held a clipboard while she spoke to two police officers just out of earshot. She nodded, looked grim and came over. She started firing questions at me.

"Name?"

"Nathan Miller."

"What happened?"

"I was shot."

"By whom?"

"A homicidal lunatic with a gun and bad aim."

The next question came tersely. "Her name?"

"Caitlin Lockyer."

"What happened to her?"

"Looks like someone tried to kill her."

"Was that you?"

"No, it was the homicidal lunatic and his mates, for all I know."

"What's your relationship to her?"

"Friend." What the hell, I thought. She'd probably agree with that, for the moment, at least.

"There. Done." The nurse stitching up my shoulder was cheerful, glad to be finished with me. "Now I'll show you to your room – just overnight. . ."

"I want to see her."

"She's still in Emergency."

"I want to see her," I repeated.

"Only family are allowed. She's in a critical condition. . ."

"Which is why I want to see her."

"But you can't. . ."

"Take me to where she is, now."

Nurse Grim was reluctant, but Caitlin wasn't that far away. Instead of a normal Emergency Department curtained cubicle, they'd put her in the room for child patients, with cheerful pictures and mobiles on the ceiling. Small though she was, I hadn't made the mistake of thinking she was a child.

Nurse Grim stopped to speak in a low voice to an orderly outside. I accosted a nurse on her way out of Caitlin's room.

"How is she?"

"She's fighting us. Calls out for someone and tries to get up. We can't do anything for her unless she calms down."

I glanced inside and saw someone with a syringe, advancing on her. "Please – don't hurt her!" I blurted out.

The orderly blocked my path. "You're not family. . ."

"I'm the one she's calling for."

"You said your name was Nathan Miller, and. . ."

"But she doesn't know that." I pushed past him.

The syringe-wielding nurse stared at me, her mouth open. Caitlin struggled to sit up and grabbed the syringe from the distracted nurse. "Don't let them hurt me again!" For an instant, I saw her face. Her eyes had hell in them.

I approached her slowly, looking deep into her tortured eyes, avoiding looking at the injuries that caused her so much pain. "I'm here. We're in a hospital and they're trying to help you." I kept my voice calm and steady.

She sagged back against the bed as she took this in, her eyes never leaving mine. The syringe rolled across the floor as it slipped from her fingers.

"So. . . tired," she managed to say, "but. . . scared to

sleep. What if. . . I wake up. . . you're gone and I'm still. . . there. . . with them?" She didn't look away, even as her eyes filled with tears. "Please."

"I'll be here. When you wake up I'll be here. Here, in hospital with you," I promised recklessly, forcing myself to smile as I reached to touch her hair.

"Thank you," she murmured, closing her eyes.

I waited until I was sure she was asleep before I said anything else. "You cut her hair off. She won't like that." Her long hair was now a short, dark cap that curled slightly around her ears.

"She didn't," came the nurse's voice behind me. "That must have been what woke her up. But we couldn't leave it — it was matted with blood and sand. We had to clean the wounds on her back. I've never seen so many ulcers, especially ones that bad. It's a good thing she's unconscious for this, because those must really hurt. . ."

She talked as she worked. I tried to keep my eyes firmly fixed on Caitlin's sleeping face, so I didn't see the extent of her injuries, but occasionally my eyes would stray to the subject of the nurse's running commentary. Every time I wanted to close my eyes in horror at the thought of what Caitlin had been through, but I didn't. Instead, I dragged my eyes back to her face.

When the nurse had finished with her now-cooperative patient, she said, "Now I'm taking her up to her room. . ."

"And I'm taking you to yours," an orderly behind me chimed in.

"If you think you're taking us to separate rooms, you've got another thing coming."

"The police want you under guard. . ."

"And she won't feel safe without some sort of protection. We'll share."

As they wheeled her bed out, I followed, along with a police officer I hadn't noticed earlier.

"Can I have a word with you?" he asked abruptly.

I shrugged. My eyes were on Caitlin, asleep on the hospital bed.

"Look, you found an injured girl on a beach and got her to hospital, probably saving her life. That sort of thing can get you a medal. But there are a few suspicious things that just don't add up. You were walking down a beach in winter at 2 am. You got into the ambulance with her. She refused all medical assistance until you were there. There was a dead body on the beach, not far from where you found her, shot with the gun you were holding. And she was last seen three weeks ago, speaking to someone in a car just like yours."

I shrugged again. "Look, I've already told two different officers this, but I can tell you, too, if you like. I couldn't sleep so I went for a drive, then decided to take a walk on the beach. I saw a couple going for it near where I'd parked my car when I got back, so I decided to take a longer walk and come back a bit later.

"When I returned later, they were still there and I tried to keep my distance from them, but I heard her telling him to stop. When I gathered he wasn't stopping and she was getting increasingly upset about it, I went over and asked if they were all right.

"She asked me to help her and the guy told me to fuck off. He pulled a gun out and started waving it around and threatening me. I dived for the gun and got into a fight with him. I managed to knock the gun out of his hands and I didn't see where it landed.

"The next thing I knew, there were gunshots and I threw myself to the ground, but he didn't. She'd gotten hold of the gun and shot him. I'm lucky she didn't hit me, her aim was so bad.

"I told her that he wasn't going to hurt her again and tried to take the gun off her, but she wouldn't let go until I promised they wouldn't hurt her again. So I did."

I took a deep breath and went on.

"I rang an ambulance and waited with her. The police turned up, someone got mixed up and figured I was the one responsible, possibly because I was holding the gun.

"They let me carry her to the ambulance. Then one of your guys shot me, or tried to, but he only grazed me and managed to shoot her instead. The last thing she said before she passed out was, 'You promised. . .'" I gritted my teeth, remembering what she'd looked like as she said it. "I got in the ambulance because I was carrying her, I stayed because I'd been shot and I'd promised.

"She's been beaten and worse by the dead guy, then when I tried to help her we both got SHOT by the police who were supposedly trying to help her. About the only person who hasn't hurt her is me, so she doesn't trust anyone else. Damn it, your guys shot her!

"And yes, I'm staying. I found some random girl on a beach, fought off her attacker and helped to get her to hospital, while getting shot in the process and winding up in hospital myself. So I'm sticking around because I want to know she's okay. If you were in my place, I imagine you'd want to know whether you'd wasted your time, too." I let out a breath I hadn't known I was holding.

He looked unmoved. "You have no witnesses to confirm your story before the police showed up? Anyone you told you were going for a walk, anyone who saw you?"

I nodded toward Caitlin. "She saw me." After thinking a moment, I added, "My doctor knows I have trouble sleeping. He gave me something called Temaze, but I only use it as a last resort."

"And how do you explain that your car was seen when she disappeared?"

I narrowed my eyes. "My car? I drive a red Mercedes. I know it's an unusual car, but I bet it's not the only one in Perth. You know it was my car? Someone saw the licence plates of my car?"

The cop looked abashed. "Okay, no, we don't know what the number plate was. We don't know it was your car. But it is a hell of a coincidence, all the same."

I took a deep breath and laughed. "Look mate, do you think she'd trust me if I was the guy who'd raped her?" More soberly, I continued: "Hell of a coincidence — more like someone's trying to set me up for this."

He looked indecisive for a moment, before replying in a low voice, "If someone's trying to set you up, they'll need to set you up with accomplices. Her medical report says that she's been raped repeatedly by at least four of them, probably including the dead one on the beach. And judging by her injuries, they've been at it for at least a couple of weeks. Three of them are still out there. When she wakes up she might be able to tell us who they are. But I never told you."

TWO

Red Mercedes.
They had a red Mercedes.
Hit me, pulled me in, drugged me.
Eyes like saucers. Pervert.
Sorry. Oh God, so sorry.
Let me go, you bastard.
Fighting the drugs.
Clawing at my throat.
Fighting the darkness.
The pain in the darkness.
Fight them.
Don't let them win.

THREE

I woke in daylight and glanced at my watch. Early afternoon. My shoulder ached and more besides. It must have been time for more pain medication. Please, please let there be more pain medication.

A smiling woman set a tray of lunch on the table next to my bed. She returned to the trolley for Caitlin's lunch, which she placed hesitantly on the table beside her.

"One of the volunteers should be along shortly, with the book and magazine trolley. Your roommate's on the front cover of today's paper – you might want to keep a copy for her."

I thanked the woman.

"When she wakes up, can you tell her I've given her today's and tomorrow's menu, so she can pick what she wants? Yours is on your tray, too." She lowered her voice. "The ice cream is really good."

I smiled and thanked her again as she left, my eyes straying to Caitlin. I slid out of bed and made my way over to her.

She was tucked tightly in her bed, still asleep, her face and hair all that showed. She looked as if she hadn't moved since we were brought here early this morning. With the amount of sedative she'd been given last night, she wasn't going to be awake for lunch today, nor dinner – I figured her first hospital meal wouldn't be earlier than breakfast tomorrow. I had until then to work out what I wanted to say to her when she woke up.

I headed past her, to the bathroom we shared, before I went back to sit on my bed to eat lunch for breakfast at lunchtime. I didn't taste any of it, from the first bite 'til I'd finished the ice cream.

When did I last eat? I wondered, realising that I couldn't remember. No wonder I'd been hungry. I'd last had a drink more than twelve hours ago, a sip on the beach, before I gave the rest of the can to Caitlin.

Almost without thinking, I pushed myself off my bed and settled into the visitor's chair beside her, so I could see her face. For the first time, I felt self-conscious that I was only wearing my shorts. They were the only item of clothing I had left – I'd handed the rest over to the police, her blood on everything else. I'd have to call my sister today and ask her to bring some fresh clothes, before Caitlin woke up. I didn't want to frighten her any more than she had been already.

"You'd have to be the first pretty girl I'd rather woke up to me fully clothed than in just my underwear," I told her. I laughed quietly.

Caitlin neither replied nor moved, she was so deeply asleep.

"I never wanted to see you hurt. I'm sorry I didn't help you sooner," I began hesitantly. No, that wasn't the first thing I wanted her to hear – reminding her of what had happened to her. I stared into space, my eyes focussing on her untouched meal tray. "Do you want your ice cream?"

When she didn't respond, I helped myself to the little cardboard tub, lifting the lid with a slight sucking sound. The ice cream had already started to melt in the warm room.

In between bites, I voiced the things I could say to her when she woke.

"Hi, remember me? I was oblivious to you getting hurt, so you're in hospital now." No. Could I sound more callous if I tried?

"I'm Nathan, I stole a shirt from a corpse and stuck it on you." Lovely.

"I wish I'd never seen you and then neither of us would be here. I wish none of this had ever happened." True, but still not something I should say to her. If I hadn't seen her, she might be dead now instead of in hospital.

I scraped the bottom of the cardboard container for the last melted drops. "I'm sorry – I finished your ice cream. When you wake up, I'll owe you one." I stood up and took the empty container to my meal tray.

All that I'd said should have been funny, given my dark humour, but I had no laughter left. I only felt empty. Not even my stolen ice cream could help to fill that void. What kind of person stole a sleeping girl's ice cream?

I made it to our shared bathroom before I threw up – her ice cream, mine and probably most of the lunch I hadn't tasted. When I was done, I rinsed my mouth and left the bathroom, closing the door hard behind me.

I returned to my own bed and stretched out on top of the covers. I folded my arms behind my head and stared at the ceiling for a moment, before I spoke again.

"I'm sorry, Caitlin. I'm so sorry."

My eyes started to water, probably from staring at the room light, so I closed them.

FOUR

Dark. Pain. Cold. Tears.
Screaming for them to let me go until my throat
hurt and my voice was almost gone.
No one.
No reply, no light.
More pain.
Bitter tears.
Alone in the dark when I needed HELP.
I remember lying down, sobbing.
Cold, rough, hard concrete.
Dusty. Made me cough but no one heard.
Cold and alone and hurting in the dark.
Pain.
Relief that no one had heard me, that there was
no reply.
Not alone was worse. Oh hell. . .

FIVE

"Go away – leave me alone!" Caitlin cried in panic.

I woke with a shock in the middle of the night. She was screaming and struggling to get away from someone – but there was no one else here.

I sat on the edge of her bed and shook her gently, but she didn't wake up. She was locked in a deadly struggle with the people in her nightmare.

She screamed abuse at me as I panicked and let go of her. There was nothing I could do.

Gradually, her struggles gave way to helpless tears. "Please help me. . . you promised. . ." she whimpered.

I tried to tell her I was here, that she was safe now, that there was nothing to worry about, because she was in the very best of care, but she kept going like she never heard a word of it. Her whispered, desperate pleas continued as I pressed the button to bring a nurse. It felt like forever before a nurse arrived.

I heard her in the corridor, talking to another nurse.

"You go on down to tea, Judith. I'll just see to this one and I'll join you. It's that girl who came in last night – the one with the police guard. I heard one of them's pretty hot."

The other nurse thought this was funny. "You mean the young one who looks like Matt Damon? I heard he's her boyfriend. If she needs a nurse, it's probably because he isn't there to help her. Have fun, Carol."

Sick of waiting, I spoke. "If you're the nurse, come here."

The nurse entered the room and sized me up, her look openly curious.

At another time, I might have found her obvious approval gratifying. I know I would have liked what I saw. I would have responded by verbalising the invitation in her eyes. Maybe I should have. I know I wanted to.

Later.

All those fleeting thoughts dissolved in my irritation that her attention was on me instead of Caitlin, whose sobs made my chest ache in sympathy.

"She's having nightmares and she won't wake up. Is there anything you can give her to help her?"

"I can't," she told me flatly. "What she's on, and the condition she's in – hell, she's so sedated she shouldn't be able to have nightmares. She won't be waking up for a while."

"I see." I kept my voice equally flat.

"Please. You promised," Caitlin sobbed. "No, don't let them. . ."

"Who's she talking to?" the nurse asked.

"Me. She wants me to help her." It came out bitter. Because I couldn't stop her nightmares.

The nurse looked like she wanted to ask something else, but I didn't want to explore this any further. I let my eyes wander over her body. When I lifted my eyes to her face, I gave her a look that plainly said, "Damn, not bad." I hated myself for raising her expectations, knowing I was only going to dash them again in moments. She looked flustered, and I took the opportunity to get rid of her.

"If there's nothing you can do for her, then I guess you're better off going back to the nurses' station, or wherever else you're needed." I flashed her my most charming smile, feeling cheap for not following it up with anything else. "Go to tea, Carol." Which Carol did, without hesitation.

I stayed by Caitlin, where I promised I'd be, Nurse Carol's words running through my head. *She won't be waking up for a while.* Caitlin wouldn't miss me if I went downstairs for a few minutes. Not if she wasn't waking up for a while.

I'd be back before she woke up. Perhaps I could make up for my curt dismissal of Nurse Carol and offer to pay for her tea.

Caitlin was weeping quietly now, oblivious to me. I stood up and moved away from her toward the door, thinking of joining Nurse Carol for tea, coffee or anything else she cared to name. Maybe getting to know the shapely Singaporean girl better. . .

"No. . . please. . . don't leave me!" Caitlin's voice grew louder and more panicked with each word. "You promised!" Swearing softly, I sat down beside her again and she was silent.

Swearing a bit more, I realised there was only one way I was going to get any more sleep tonight.

I grabbed a sheet and pillow from my bed and carefully cocooned her body in her own sheet. I squeezed in behind her, so I was half under her pillow and up against the headboard. If she hadn't been so small, I wouldn't have fitted.

So, I didn't get to have a drink with Nurse Carol, but I got the consolation of sleeping with Caitlin.

I stuck my pillow behind me to cushion my head from the cold, laminated surface of the headboard and spread my sheet over myself as best I could. My last thought before I fell asleep was that, under better circumstances, with a bigger bed and less clothes, I'd be happy to climb into bed with Caitlin, so maybe this wasn't so bad after all. . .

Ah, who was I kidding? It was a bloody nightmare.

SIX

Hold her for me.
No. . .
Hold her still.
No. . .
Don't touch me!
Hold her down, I said.
Touch me and I'll kick your face in!
How are you going to do that with him holding
you down?
I said. . .
No!

SEVEN

Movement and sound in the room startled me awake. I mumbled something vaguely threatening and opened my eyes.

Nurse Carol was smiling, standing beside the bed, reaching toward my lap.

Wow. The hot nurse was back. Yes, please!

But of course she wasn't here for me. She brushed aside Caitlin's hair and checked her temperature. When she was done, she smoothed Caitlin's hair back down over her ear, just as it was before. Her fingers rested on the pillow beside Caitlin's head for a moment before she pulled them away. Caitlin's pillow lay across my lap, hiding my eagerness. Thank God.

Nurse Carol walked away from me to pick up the clipboard that held Caitlin's medical chart. She started flipping through it, carefully writing down her observations, her lips moving soundlessly.

More than disappointed, I opened my mouth to say

something to draw the nurse's attention to me.

I closed my mouth quickly when Carol's eyes shifted from the medical chart in her hands to my face. "It's good that you care about her so much. She'll need all your help and support when she wakes up."

What the hell could I say to that? I'd be a callous, lying scumbag if I said I didn't care whether Caitlin recovered or not, but she made me sound like the girl's boyfriend if I didn't say it. So I said nothing.

She tucked Caitlin's chart back into its pocket at the end of the bed. "You shouldn't be in her bed with her, though. One of the other nurses will kick you out if I don't."

Hey, if she had a better offer for me, I'd be there. I looked up at her and thought about saying it, but decided I couldn't. Not yet.

I cleared my throat. "She sleeps better when I'm here." I smiled ruefully. "So do I, because she's quieter, too."

Carol smiled at me. "Well, you can't say I didn't warn you. I hope you get some sleep, for the rest of the night." She took a deep breath. "Take good care of her. We all want to see her make a full recovery."

"So do I," I admitted, wanting to say more.

While I was working out how to ask her out for later, she left.

My chances with Nurse Carol crashed and burned. All because I got into bed with Caitlin.

I shrugged and settled back to sleep, Caitlin's head still pillowed in my lap.

Maybe later, when this job was over, I'd ask Nurse Carol to come join me for a drink. Maybe if I asked nicely, she'd even wear a nurse's uniform, one heaps sexier than the one she wore to work. . . hell yeah! Sweet dreams, here I come.

EIGHT

Breathing in the dark.
Not just mine.
Help me. Get me out of here.
Holding my breath.
Breathe in, breathe out.
Approaching, closer.
Too dark to see.
Breathing faster.
Are you going to hurt me?
Sharp intake of breath.
ARE YOU GOING TO HURT ME?
Almost panting.
Too close.
No. . .

NINE

"You're mad," my sister told me, handing me the bag of clothes I'd asked for. "You find some random girl left for dead on a beach, promise you'll protect her from someone who hurt her who's already dead, only to find out he has mates, so you're going to stick around to protect her from all of them, too? It could be years before the police put them away – if they ever find them! What are you going to do, stay with her for the rest of her life? Marry her?" She snorted with laughter.

I shook my head, rubbing at my bleary eyes in the hope that it would wake me up. Caitlin had woken me with her screaming more than once last night. "I promised I'd be here when she wakes up. She's been out for longer than I expected, is all. She's been through more than anyone should ever have to and I'm not going to do that to her – just go home and let her wake up alone."

Chris was quick to notice the gaps in my explanation. "How do you know what she's been through? She's barely been conscious since you found her!"

"I don't," I admitted. "But. . . she has nightmares. . . even with the drugs they're giving her, and they sound pretty bad. And. . . I saw what she looked like when I found her. It wasn't pretty." I suppressed a shudder, but she noticed anyway.

"How bad is it? Can I see her?"

We were in the lounge at the end of the ward. It was only a short walk back to Caitlin's room, but still I hesitated. "Don't touch her," I warned. If she touched her, she'd scream again and I couldn't handle it. I just couldn't.

"Wh. . ." She started to ask a question, but she looked like she was having trouble deciding which to ask first. Why she'd want to touch her, why she couldn't, or even what in hell I was thinking. Instead, she shrugged and followed me back to the hospital room.

She thought I was crazy. She could be right.

The guard outside the door looked askance at Chris. I nodded to him and he let her pass unchallenged. Chris didn't acknowledge the police officer at all.

She stopped just inside the door and stared, looking puzzled.

I looked closely at Caitlin, trying to work out precisely what Chris was staring at.

It couldn't be the bruises on Caitlin's pale face. They'd faded to faint shadows now. She looked as beautiful as the first day I'd seen her.

Caitlin's hands rested by her face on the pillow, each finger individually bandaged and splinted, an IV line slipped between the gauze. The bandages extended down her wrists, like long, white gloves. She wore a hospital-issue nightgown and she'd managed to kick the bedclothes off in her struggle against her nightmares, so everything the scanty nightgown didn't cover was on show. White dressings were stuck to her back, with more on her legs, particularly her ankles and her thighs. Bruises covered her exposed skin in a disturbing rainbow of dark colours.

Before I could stop her, Chris crossed the room and grabbed Caitlin's sheet. She yanked it up to Caitlin's chin, covering her up almost completely. Her eyes turned to me. "You need to take your own advice."

I was annoyed at my sister. "It's not like that. Have you ever known me to take advantage of a girl, without her permission?"

Chris frowned deeply, her eyebrows almost meeting. "She's not like any of the girls you usually bring home. She's younger, more fragile. . ." She stopped, looking lost for words, before her tone changed abruptly. "How in hell did this little girl survive all that?" She waved a hand over Caitlin's body, encompassing everything now covered by the sheet.

"No one knows," I told her shortly, sitting heavily on the visitor's chair by Caitlin's bed. "But when she wakes up, it's one of the first things I'll ask her."

"Yeah, well, I hope that's soon." She paused and looked at Caitlin again. "Or you'll have to adopt her."

TEN

Kissed me.
Two of them.
Pinned me, forced me, kissed me.
Why?
Because I can.
Nothing you can do to stop me.
First one smelled and tasted bad.
Rough. Hurt me. Told me what they'd do later.
Fear. Cold.
Wanting to cry.
Won't show weakness.
Stuff you.
Second one. . . didn't want to let go.
Called me beautiful.
Oh God. Sorry. . .

ELEVEN

A week without sleep and I was having trouble focussing. I couldn't sleep in Caitlin's bed with her, she'd scream the place down if I slept in my bed or anywhere else, and I couldn't wake her up. I swear I was so exhausted my eyes kept closing of their own accord, but it was only a matter of time before she had another nightmare and woke me.

"Help me, get me out of here!" Caitlin screamed.

I tried calling and then shouting her name, begging her to wake up.

"You promised. . ." Caitlin sobbed.

I tried talking over her, saying whatever came into my head. I may as well have talked to myself. She was oblivious to whatever I said.

"Let me go, you bastard!" Caitlin's hoarse voice hissed as I crossed the room to the bathroom.

I saturated a face washer with cold water from the bathroom basin and squeezed it out so that it dripped onto her face and neck.

She started to cry. Her voice was a raw whimper. "Please. . . so cold. Give me my clothes back. Or a blanket. Get me out of here. . ."

I picked up her medical charts, trying to decipher her doctor's scribbled terminology in the hope that it would put me to sleep. The word *hypothermia* caught my eye on the first page and I looked more closely at the hieroglyphics surrounding it. I remembered how cold she'd been on the beach, too cold to shiver in air that was close to freezing.

Oh, shit.

I got a towel from the bathroom and dried every droplet off her skin. I wrapped her up in her hospital-issue blanket and hugged her 'til her tears dried up, too. Dawn came before sleep did.

I called my sister and asked her to get me some earplugs. I tried them the very next night. I got to sleep fine but Caitlin's nightmares just got worse until she was screaming so loud the earplugs were useless. It took forever to calm her down.

"Please, don't let them. . ." Caitlin begged, over and over. Her words echoed in my head even after she lost her voice.

The earplugs were in the bin before the sun rose.

I prayed to any deity who'd listen that Caitlin would wake up and the nightmares would stop.

"Oh God, please, stop. . ." Caitlin sobbed.

Yes, please, stop.

No deity heard me. Her cries for help were more heartfelt, more urgent and delivered in a far more desperate voice than mine. Even I listened and I couldn't do a damn thing for her.

I don't deny I was desperate to leave. But the more I heard of her nightmares, the more I realised the horror of what she'd been through. I wasn't cruel enough to leave her here alone when I'd promised her I'd stay 'til she woke up.

"Please. . . you promised. . ." Caitlin's voice was a pitiful moan.

I wanted to tell her how sorry I was for not helping her sooner.

I turned the TV on, to find it was Disney time. Close to the end of it, I guessed, because Prince Charming was about to kiss some girl in a long, impractical dress and make the whole world perfect again. She woke up and was so pleased to see this perfect stranger in her bedroom that she fell for him, instead of calling the police.

Wouldn't it be nice if the world worked on Disney principles. . .

I couldn't begrudge Caitlin one kiss, in the faintest hope it would help. Hell, it couldn't hurt, could it?

I shook my head and laughed at my own misguided idea. Sleep deprivation makes you think of stupid things.

I dozed fitfully until the sun went down and woke to screaming.

Some hours later, in desperation, darkness and insanity, I kissed her. I pressed my lips to hers for a second – nothing more She froze for that second, then called me names and tried to claw my eyes out. My heart sinking with guilt, I closed my eyes and held my hands up in surrender, backing away slowly. I didn't dare touch her again, let alone try to fend her off.

What kind of scumbag kissed a girl without her permission as she slept? A lower form of scum than the bloke who stole her ice cream. Kids' cartoons had no concept of rape. Prince Charming was never up on an assault charge, no matter how much the sleazy bastard deserved it.

I pressed the nurse call button. There was nothing I could do to calm Caitlin down this time.

They had to reset three of her broken fingers and there wasn't a scratch on me. I kept my own fingers crossed that the nurses didn't ask me how or why Caitlin had ripped through the dressings on her hands. By some twist of fate, they didn't say a word to me at all. Good thing, too, because I wasn't sure I had the guts to admit to anyone what I'd done.

I paced up and down at the end of her bed 'til the nurses were done. When Caitlin's fingers were firmly wrapped once more, the nurses left.

Caitlin was quiet for a few moments and I lay down on my own bed to try and get some sleep.

"Let me go, you bastard!" she hissed through gritted teeth, but with considerable venom.

"You keep fighting them, even in your dreams," I mumbled in her direction, closing my eyes. "Whatever you do, angel, don't you let them win, no matter what."

"Keep fighting. Don't let them win," she murmured softly.

I sat up in surprise, looking at her, but her eyes were still closed.

Come on, Caitlin, wake up. It's my turn to sleep.

But still she slept.

TWELVE

Waking up in the dark.
Drugged blur. Couldn't see. Head hurt.
Tied up.
Cut myself free, dizzy when I stood up.
Angry voices in the dark.
Open door and light.
Running, pushing past him in the doorway.
Too dizzy. Dark again. Falling.
His hands on me.
I'll bite.
He laughed.
They're going to hurt me. . .

THIRTEEN

"I have a few more questions." The police officer who came into Caitlin's room was familiar. Was he the one who'd started interrogating me the night we arrived in hospital, before giving me information? Or was he a hallucination, the unwanted child of sleep deprivation?

Caitlin hadn't slept well last night, either. Caitlin never slept well any night. She slept and screamed but didn't wake up. I was forgetting what it was like to sleep at all. My eyes itched from fatigue.

I responded cautiously, "Okay."

"Has she woken up yet?" He leaned over Caitlin's bed, looking closely at her face. He reached out, as if to shake her shoulder.

"Don't touch her," I blurted out, wincing.

His hand stopped, curved not far from her. "Why not?"

"She'll scream." I shuddered. I couldn't stand it when she screamed. I clenched my hands into fists so he wouldn't see them shaking.

He looked at me for a moment, taking in my fists and the look on my face. He shrugged and seated himself in the visitor's chair by Caitlin's bed, angling his head toward me. "What do you know about the dead man you left on the beach?" His eyes were on me, his expression expectant.

My brain felt slow and tired. "He was hurting her. He was a big bastard with a gun. He and I got into a fight. . ."

"No," he interrupted. "You told me this already. What do you know about him, except for the few minutes before he died?"

I thought for a moment. "When I checked to see if he was dead, I took his shirt and put it on her. I figured she needed it more than he did and he owed her that much. That was after he died."

The grey shirt had been sticky with blood and it had wicked up the red like sweat, making the white Adidas logo stand out even more. There'd been half-healed welts on the man's back and chest that I'd wondered about, but the police officer probably knew more about them than I did. I only know what I saw. When I'd pulled the dead man's shirt over her head, it had left pink streaks on her face where his blood mingled with her tears. I remember feeling satisfied that I'd forced the lifeless bastard to help her when he was too dead to do anything about it, after all the pain he'd caused her. . .

"But did you know anything about him, before that night?" the officer pressed.

"No, I didn't know him." I paused, irritated. "I'm not sure I would have wanted to, either."

He stretched his legs out in front of him, his arms above and behind his head. He looked at the ceiling, sounding thoughtful. "He owned a holiday house not far from where he died. When his wife heard what had happened to him, she was very distraught. She thought he'd gone for a walk along the beach." He sighed. "She was little and pretty, with short, dark hair. Her name was Laura."

I snorted. "Some walk. I wonder if she knew what he was really doing."

"Who knows?" He smiled at me and stood up, looking at his watch. "And now, I have to go. Thank you for your assistance."

He strode out of the room, giving a brief nod to the guard outside before continuing down the corridor to the lifts.

I shook my head. The dead bastard had a wife and her name was Laura. Who would have thought?

FOURTEEN

Not again.
Too heavy. Couldn't breathe.
Hurt me.
Couldn't scream.
Hurt me again.
Gasping, sobbing. No air.
Crushing weight lifted.
A breath. Another.
Why a reprieve?
Touching me.
NO. A scream. Mine.
Hurt me more.

FIFTEEN

"Fuck me, but you took your precious time helping her, didn't you? Could you have let them fuck her up any more without killing her?"

I rubbed my eyes wearily. I hadn't grown a conscience that liked to swear and shout at me. The angry voice could only belong to my boss. Actually, he was my boss's boss. I'd only met him once before and I couldn't remember his name, but I did remember that arguing with him was a bad idea. If I didn't answer, he'd get to the point eventually.

"The boys in Canberra are breathing down our necks on this one, because of the high media profile. We've organised round-the-clock guards for her, and no one even gets her room number unless they have ID and they're on her list of friends and family. We need her and we need her to stay safe. If you want to catch the guys who did this to her, we need to know everything she can remember," he told me, keeping his voice low. "Names, descriptions and what they did to her, with any dates and times she can remember."

"When she wakes up, I'll ask her," I said.

"Fuck, Nathan, the police will be asking, too, and if you want to get to them before the local police do, you need to know everything before they do. You've got to do better than just fucking wait. You need to be her fucking best mate."

I sighed. "So, that means I have to stay with her? The hospital's going to discharge me today. How do you expect me to convince her she needs some random stranger around all the time without her suspecting, when she wakes up?"

He smiled. "I'll take care of the hospital and arrange to have you stay for as long as necessary. The local police are already cooperating with you, right?" He paused and I nodded. "As for the girl – make yourself useful. Be your usual charming self and give her a hand when she needs one. Her hands look like they'll be out of action a while. Your charming personality worked on that receptionist – what was her name, Christie?"

Shit, Christie. Christie the receptionist had turned out to be religious, waiting for marriage and her true love before she'd let anyone in her pants. Even down on her knees she'd been a disappointment. After she'd spilled all she knew and everything she wouldn't swallow, I hadn't seen her again. I'd been glad to give her up. I cleared my throat.

"Christie the receptionist was nowhere near as. . . traumatised as Caitlin. That's not a fair comparison." Oh hell, I thought, I almost called Caitlin damaged. And she was – covered in blood and bruises and beaten and broken and. . . "This one's not going to be won over by a bit of charm and a smile."

"This one's a shitload better looking than that receptionist, or so I've heard. A bit of an incentive, maybe?" He lowered his voice. "Look, the police are going on about how she was raped by more than one man. You're going to have to be honest with me on this one. You didn't. . ."

I waited, but he didn't tell me what he didn't want me to do. "I didn't sleep with her. Is that what you mean? She wasn't offering and I'm not interested if she isn't willing." I winked. "It's not as much fun if she doesn't enjoy herself."

"Or at least pretending she is," he replied, distracted.

I forced a laugh. "Not with me. No need, mate." I winked again, but my cheer felt hollow. There was no need when this was one girl I'd never sleep with. Oh God, what I'd give for a decent night's sleep without her. . .

He sighed, looking wistful. "Yeah, that's why you're the one who's pumping her for information. Don't let the police find out if you do decide to fuck her." He got up to leave. "Let me know what you find out. And don't let anyone fucking kill her."

SIXTEEN

Don't touch me.
Don't touch her.
Don't. . .
Can't stop. Must. . .
Shouting. Shots.
Hurts.
No.
Can't stop. Must. . .
Hurts.
Can't get up.
Must. . .
Red light. Blood.
Scared. Slipping.
Stars.
Dark. . .

SEVENTEEN

Caitlin slept peacefully, for the moment. As the bright sunlight streamed through the window into her hospital room, I was incapable of sleep.

I felt I owed her some explanation and it was easier to tell her when she was asleep. I hesitated, not knowing how much to tell or how little. Maybe if I spoke my piece now I could resist telling her when she was awake and asking for answers. Or maybe I'd never have to tell her.

"She'd gone shopping and we didn't even know she was missing until hours afterwards," I blurted out before I realised what I was doing. "It was weeks and she wouldn't answer her phone, no one had seen her.

"Then there were the envelopes. No return address, just printed labels on the outside and inside. . . zip-locked freezer bags with bloodied cloth and skin, cut with a jagged knife. Sometimes every day, or more than one every few days. I wouldn't let Chris check the mail – I put a lock on the letterbox so she couldn't. . ." My voice died as I remembered again what I could never forget.

"It must have been over a month before her body turned up, dumped at the base of some sand dunes. Near where you were." I swallowed convulsively, but continued. "For more than a month, they'd just hurt her, until they killed her." A memory I didn't want. One that plagued my dreams.

I looked at Caitlin, wondering who her envelopes had been sent to. Nothing had been found at her house and she still lived at home with her father. Had they even sent them? Or were the cuts on her body something someone did just for the hell of it? I tried not to think about it. My thoughts went back to Alanna, as they always did.

I sat in the chair next to her bed, my closed eyes seeing only pictures of the past. "Alanna was my sister, my twin, but we were so different. She was always so cheerful, so determined to succeed and make a difference. She'd help someone when no one else would bother. The next thing you know, everyone would be helping *her*. She stopped to help a woman push her broken-down car off a busy road outside Uni once. The two of them could barely budge it, then a Council truck pulled over and the whole road crew helped her get the car onto the kerb. I was stuck on the other side of the road and six lanes of traffic, so I saw the whole thing. I wouldn't have believed it if it was anyone else, but Alanna. . . it's just who she was.

"We were at a party once, and everyone was drinking. A normal Uni party after the end of exams. A girl she didn't know was so drunk she passed out and hit her head as she fell. A room full of drunken med students and no one seemed to know what to do. Alanna just stepped in and took charge. She knelt on the floor next to the girl. She sent one person for ice, another to call an ambulance, someone else to find the friend the girl had arrived with. By the time the ambulance arrived, she had the girl's name, contact details of her next of kin and everything. There was nothing for the ambulance officers to do but get the girl to hospital.

"Alanna was such a fighter, she would never have given in to them. Never stopped fighting, never let them win. So they broke her and they killed her. How could anyone do that to her?

"I wanted to hunt them down and hurt them for what they did to her. But the police didn't arrest anyone and they could still do it again, to someone else!" They'd do it to Chris next. My parents would never give in. I gritted my teeth, trying to force the thought out of my brain. "Please wake up. I need to know how to find them before they can get to Chris. She's the same age as you and I can't let it happen again. Not after. . ."

I looked at Caitlin, serene in sleep. It was hard not to see the corpse I'd thought she was.

I didn't get there in time. I'd let it happen to her.

I looked away, at a mercifully blank wall.

"I'm sorry, Caitlin. I never wanted to see you hurt. Not like this. I should have helped you sooner."

Once again, I lay back and closed my eyes. I couldn't look at her any more, but the image of her on the beach seemed burned into my retinas, eyes open or closed.

Shit. Sleep felt like a dream I barely remembered, while this was a nightmare I couldn't wake up from.

EIGHTEEN

Took my clothes.
Tried to fight.
Threatened me.
Scared. Froze.
Cried.
Couldn't fight.
So cold.
Shivering and cold in the dark.
Two of them.
One laughing, one clinical.
Wanted someone to help, rescue me.
Superman?
No one else, only me.
Tears. Cold. . .

NINETEEN

I paid little attention to the nurse in the room until she started to pull the curtains closed around Caitlin's bed, blocking my view of both of them.

"No," I said suddenly, hoisting myself off my bed and pushing the curtains open again.

The nurse glared at me, anonymous to me now that her name badge was obscured by the curtain she held clenched in her hand. "I'm changing her dressings. Even if she has to share a room with you, she's entitled to some privacy."

She yanked the curtain shut again and I heard the rustle of latex and cardboard as she pulled out a pair of gloves. "Caitlin did her first practical placement for medical school in this ward and we all know her. She won't want some sleazy bastard staring at her as she sleeps." Her voice was low but loud enough for me to hear it.

I stepped into the area by Caitlin's bed, inside the curtains. "You know the last thing she said, before she passed out in the Emergency Department? She reminded me that I'd promised not to let anyone hurt her again." I stared back at the nurse. "Until she wakes up and tells me otherwise, I'm just keeping my promise. I'm not letting her out of my sight while you're here."

She raised her eyebrows and let out a snort of breath, but she didn't say another word to me. Pointedly ignoring me, the nurse snapped on her gloves and started opening the first of the large stack of dressing packs on Caitlin's bedside table. The first dressing she pulled off Caitlin's wrist revealed an open, ulcerated wound that looked painful.

That's where they tied her up. There was rope gouging into her skin, caked with her blood.

The nurse swabbed it with disinfectant. For a moment, the raw wound was hidden again as the disinfectant fumes stung my eyes and they started to water.

Caitlin tossed restlessly as soon as the nurse's hands touched her, mumbling something I couldn't hear. My eyes still burning, I had to move to her bedside to discern the words. "Please. . . you promised. . ." she whimpered.

At that, I cropped into the chair by her bed. I couldn't remember the last time I was this close to tears – primary school, perhaps. The disinfectant fumes didn't help. I tried to speak, but no sound came out. I cleared my throat and tried again. "It's okay, Caitlin. You've been hurt." My voice shook, but I made myself continue. "We're trying to help you get better."

The nurse snorted again, louder this time. "You're in hospital as a patient now and all of us on the clinical team here are doing our best to help you get better. Your roommate is sleazy and, if I were you, I'd wake up fast so you can ask for a room transfer."

I'd like you to wake up, too, I thought but didn't say.

I tried to focus on the nurse's hands, not the wounds she was treating. No matter what the nurse thought, I didn't want to stare at Caitlin's bare skin as she slept. Conscious and consenting was one thing, but she was neither, and she wouldn't be until she recovered, if ever. It took a real fucked-up bloke to look at her in her current state and feel anything but pity, sympathy and the fist-clenching desire to cause some righteous pain. Which I couldn't do a fucking thing about until she woke up and told me how to find them.

The grumpy nurse gently rolled Caitlin on her side so she could reach some the dressings on her back. The first one she pulled off revealed more nasty-looking ulcers and a patch of scraped skin. She reached for the eye-watering disinfectant wipes again as I winced and wanted to look away.

I wished that Caitlin was wearing more than her hospital-issue nightdress. Normally, that meant she'd be showing a whole lot of skin, but there were so many dressings on her that she seemed swathed in white, like a badly beaten angel. She may as well have been an angel fallen to Earth, she had so little with her. The police had taken all her clothes, so the hospital gown was all she had. I felt guilty for wearing the clean t-shirt my sister had brought.

It seemed an eternity before the nurse was finished, but I didn't take my eyes away from her until she left, without saying another word.

Released from my vigil, I squeezed my eyes shut. My head in my hands, I tried to knead the livid images out of my forehead with my fingers. Under every dressing on Caitlin's body were wounds that screamed of repeated abuse, over and over again during the weeks they had her.

Not for the first time I wondered how anyone could force themselves to look at that every day, job notwithstanding. I didn't know how I could stand to watch a nurse bare her every cut, bruise and break again tomorrow, or force myself to sit through this every day until she woke up.

How did she manage to survive, driving herself to keep going as those sick bastards inflicted countless wounds on her body and mind, time and time again?

Fuck. I didn't know. Wake up, Caitlin, so you can tell me the answers. Fucked if I knew.

TWENTY

The door was open.
Someone calling me a little bitch.
Attacked him.
Hit me.
Hit the floor.
Blood, pain.
Pushing me down, on top of me.
Bound my hands.
Broke my fingers.
Screaming. Pain.
Couldn't see for tears.
He had a knife.
Cut my clothes off.
Tried to kick him.
Couldn't see, too dark.
He caught my legs.
Pushed them down, apart.
Unzipped.
Oh God please no

TWENTY ONE

Any time Caitlin was quiet, I closed my eyes and tried to sleep. But it was a hospital and there were always doctors and nurses coming to check on her. Once there was a med student, too.

I tried to ignore them and kept my eyes closed, but I couldn't help listening.

Maybe it was the sound of her voice – cute and young, but serious, too, like she really cared about her patient. "She's probably pregnant. With rape a possibility it's best to know as early as possible," she argued.

My heart contracted, as if I were crushing it in my own clenched fist. Hadn't Caitlin been through enough? She needed to recover from her ordeal and one day learn to forget. She didn't deserve a lifelong reminder, a child belonging to one of the bastards who'd hurt her. She'd have scars enough as it was.

"No, she isn't. We checked twice. Both were negative." The other voice was calmer but sad.

I breathed a sigh of relief.

"Like I said, it could have been a mistake or too early to tell."

The sad voice sighed heavily. He sounded Irish. "Or she was very early into the pregnancy and she miscarried. But that would have been before she was admitted. . ."

There was blood everywhere. Her eyes were open, staring at the stars in the sky. I'd thought she was dead.

"Do we know for certain she was raped?"

Another sigh. "If she was awake, I could ask her. But she's a seventeen-year-old girl who's been through hell and a lot of pain, given how long she was missing and the state she's in now. I'd say it's pretty much a certainty. I've left a note in her file and I'm leaving it at that. There's no need to ask her or even mention it. She's definitely not pregnant."

"I'd ask, Dr Lannon, just to be thorough. What if. . ."

"Did you see her when she came in?" he demanded.

Blood and bruises everywhere. So cold. Twisted, broken fingers. Haunted eyes. Screaming. . .

"Have you been here when she has nightmares?" he pressed.

Endless screaming, wanting to run. . .

"No, I've just read her file because she was on my patient list today." Her voice sounded subdued.

I'd never seen such a long list of injuries. Line after line of damage.

"This girl was beaten and raped repeatedly for weeks then left on a beach to die. It's been all over the news. Would you want to be the one to remind her and make her relive all the gory details?"

No, but I didn't have any choice. I had to ask her. I

needed to know.

A pregnant pause. A quiet, "No, Dr Lannon."

"Besides, she'll tell us everything we need to know when she wakes up. She's a med student," said Dr Lannon with satisfaction.

Even the fucking doctor knew more about her than I did.

"Do you know her?"

The doctor laughed. "She stole my parking spot on her first day on prac here."

A sharp intake of breath. "What did you do?"

"I parked somewhere else and told her what happens when you steal a doctor's parking space." Dr Lannon sounded amused.

"What?"

He took a deep breath, no longer laughing. "A midwife I met when I was an intern told me I'd be at that doctor's beck and call, running paperwork to the airport with medical evac patients and the like." He paused and sighed. "But that was a country hospital, a long time ago. Here, she'd probably just get me coffee."

Caitlin's medical chart clacked as it was dropped into the slot at the end of her bed.

"Did she buy you a coffee?"

Dr Lannon laughed again. "No, my wife would kill me if I let strange girls buy me coffee."

"Which country hospital were you an intern at, Dr Lannon?"

Footsteps leaving.

"Albany Regional." I heard the voices fade away down the corridor. "I'd feel more comfortable if you called me

Aidan. I still look around for my father whenever someone says, 'Dr Lannon,' though it's been me for six years now. . ."

I drifted into sleep, trying to shut out the images of what Caitlin had looked like when I found her. Instead, they blended into a nightmare that I couldn't run from.

When Caitlin's scream woke me, it was almost a relief.

"Angel, it's all right. I'm here. Wake up, angel. It's over," I said as I settled into the chair by her bed, hoping her nightmares would keep me awake for a while.

TWENTY TWO

Cold and alone. Sand.
Couldn't feel anything anymore.
Stab of pain.
One of them, hurting me.
Too much pain.
Too weak to fight any more.
Saw a gun. Time to end it.
Gunshots. Screaming.
NO.
Won't let them hurt me again.
Promise?
Angel.
It's all right. I'm here.
Wake up, angel.
It's over.

TWENTY THREE

"Hello?" Caitlin tried to sit up, struggling against the sheets that tucked her tightly in the bed. She looked around, bewildered, stretching her hands out as if reaching for something. "Where are you?"

Relief flooded through me. Finally. "I'm here, Caitlin. I haven't left." I stood up so that all she had to do was look up to see me.

Her eyes focussed on me, but she looked troubled. In concern, I reached for her hand. Too late I realised that I might hurt her. As my fingers grazed the gauze, I snatched them back. She looked at her hand in wonder at my touch as if she'd felt it through the bandage.

"I'm not dead, am I?" she asked in hushed tones.

I almost laughed but caught myself. She looked as if she might cry if I said the wrong thing. "You're doped up to the eyeballs and wrapped up like a mummy, but you're alive. Very much alive – and in hospital, where you should be."

"What happened?" she quavered.

I was at a loss for where to begin. I didn't know how to describe what she'd been through – just thinking about it was enough to give me nightmares. "You were hurt. . ."

She started to shake her head, then grimaced as this caused her pain. "No, I know that. There was lots of yellow with cartoon animals on the ceiling. . . but now I'm here and Winnie the Pooh is gone." She glared suspiciously at the ceiling.

If I were Winnie the Pooh, I'd be hiring a bodyguard, I thought, hiding my smile. She looked as if she was ready to put him on a hit list.

Her eyes fixed on me again, her voice firmer and more urgent. "What happened?"

This time I didn't hesitate. "You fought the nurses. You were so scared. I think they gave you something to make you sleep – you've been asleep for a while."

She swallowed as if remembering was an effort. "I called for you. You weren't there. They said that you were being treated somewhere else. I wanted to get up to find you, but they wouldn't let me. I mustn't have tried hard enough. . ."

Horrified at the memory, I cut her off. "You did too much as it was – if you'd done any more, we might have lost you. You came so close, Caitlin. . . hell, I was scared." She looked shocked. Embarrassed at having said it, I looked out the window – anywhere but at her. Careful. I had a job to do here and couldn't afford to make any mistakes.

I waited for her to say something, but she was strangely silent. "Caitlin?" I asked, worried, looking back at her. Oh, fuck. Work could wait. She was far more important than any job. Seeing the tears cascading down her face and how hopeless she was at hiding them, I burst out, "Don't cry, angel. It's over."

That did it. She clung to me, sobbing, and I just held her, letting her cry herself out. After what seemed like forever, when I figured she'd cried herself to sleep against my shirt, she pulled away, hiccupping.

"Thank you. I think. . . you saved my life." Biting her lip, hesitating, she turned her eyes on me. "Who are you? I. . . I barely know you." She looked as if she might start crying again, her tears held back only by a force of will. I'd seen enough of her tears to last me into my next lifetime – or maybe just an eternity in hell after the end of this one.

I answered immediately, all of my prepared beginnings forgotten. "My name is Nathan Miller. I found you lying on the beach. I just brought you in to the hospital."

At this, she looked at her hands, bandaged up to her wrists, the IV drip taped to her already swollen right hand. "Nathan Miller," she murmured quietly, before taking a deep breath and closing her eyes. "Nathan," she breathed, her eyes still closed, as if my name were a new wine she were tasting, focussing on the feel of the word on her tongue.

I found myself holding my breath, unsure of what to say to this girl, a near stranger. A hysterical thought occurred to me. If there were a wine with my name on it, what sort would it be? I didn't know enough about wine to imagine it. One with a high alcohol content that came with a hangover in the morning, that's for sure. But what would she do? Would she savour the taste and take another sip, or spit it out with a shake of her head and refuse to let it pass her lips again? What was she thinking? I desperately wanted her not to reject me, this girl I barely knew. This girl I couldn't tear my eyes away from.

She moistened her lips with the tip of her tongue before her mouth curved upwards in the slightest smile. "Thank you. You chose to keep your promise. . . Nathan." She opened her eyes slowly as she said my name, her tone caressing, those big dark eyes fixed on me as she tilted her head the tiniest bit to one side.

How did she do that? One moment my head was full of questions about what she'd said before my name, then it was wiped blissfully blank. All I wanted now was to hear her say my name like that again. All I could think about was what I wanted to do to her to elicit that kind of response. I wanted. . . Fuck, no!

There was no way in hell I could want a girl who was in hospital after being beaten and worse. A girl whose piercing screams woke me when anyone touched her, even in her dreams. I'd have to be a real sick bastard to want that.

A sick bastard who's going to fucking forget he'd ever entertained the thought of wanting Caitlin, that's for sure, I promised myself.

Her eyes no longer held mine, focussing first on her white-swathed hands, before moving to her lap, surveying the whole length of the bed. She looked up slowly, biting her lip, taking an inventory of her hurts.

Knowing that her injuries were far worse than just those covered by the white bandages I could see, I swallowed and tried to speak. Better late than never. "I'm so sorry, Caitlin. If anything I did hurt you, I'm sorry."

Now she looked puzzled. "You. . . didn't. You were. . . shot?" She looked at me, struggling to remember. She reached out, touching her palm lightly to the place where the bullet had grazed my shoulder.

Through both the bandage and the fabric of my shirt, I barely felt her light touch, but the contact felt electric, as if there was nothing between her skin and mine. As if she'd touched a nerve that fed directly into my spine, a tingling that was far from painful.

Hastily, I answered, "Yes. So were you. But. . . it could have been far worse if you hadn't distracted him. Thank you. I may very well owe you my life."

She gave a tiny smile in reply, still looking troubled, but her next words were interrupted by a fit of coughing that left her breathless and exhausted. I shifted the pillows behind her so she'd be comfortable as she sank back into them. I carefully pulled her sheets and blankets up to cover her again, conscious of her eyes on me.

"Will you still be here in the morning when I wake up?" she asked in a small voice.

Of course. Where else would I be? I'll lose my job if I'm not, I thought but didn't say. "Would you like me to be?" I asked instead.

She nodded hesitantly, her eyes fearful.

"Then I'll be here," I said with a smile.

"Thank you," she responded softly, closing her eyes.

"Nathan," she murmured a few seconds later, almost as an afterthought, as she drifted into sleep once more.

I stood and moved to my own bed, intent on going back to sleep, too.

Brilliant. I'd made her cry, compared myself to a hangover in a bottle and nearly propositioned her. Maybe the next time I stuck my foot in my mouth I'd do her a favour and fucking choke on it.

My eyes snapped open as I realised. I turned to look at her, but she was asleep. I lay back on my pillow, now wearing a smile on my face.

However badly I'd handled this, she still wanted me to stay 'til the next morning.

TWENTY FOUR

I woke to swearing, then a heavy thump accompanied by more swearing. I opened my eyes and looked automatically at Caitlin's bed beside me. It was empty.

I stood up quickly, close to panic, before I saw her bandaged hand rise into view and clutch ineffectually at the sheets. They slithered off the bed as I watched, taking the blanket with them. The swearing intensified but it was somewhat muffled. I realised I knew the angry voice and I'd never been so relieved to hear it.

"What's wrong?" I asked as I walked around the bed to where I could see Caitlin, thinking that she'd probably just fallen out of bed. Instead, she lay face down, her feet closest to the bed, as she struggled to get up with her damaged hands. It looked like she'd tripped and fallen flat on her face, before she'd pulled the bed linen down on top of herself.

I knelt down to pull the blanket away from her head, thanking whatever helpful deity had made the linen fall so that it covered most of her.

Caitlin was both angry and frustrated. "I can't walk and I can't get up."

"Here, let me help you." I made good use of the blanket and sheet to keep some separation between her body and mine, tucking the whole mess around her as I picked her up.

"Thank you," she said quickly, biting her lip, still looking a little flustered.

"What happened?"

She hesitated a moment before she spoke. "I got out of bed, tried to take a step and it hurt. Then I fell." She frowned. "I can't walk if it hurts that much."

"Perhaps you should stay in bed and rest then," I suggested.

"But I needed. . . I was trying to get to the bathroom." She wouldn't look at me as she said it.

Understanding her embarrassment, I offered casually, "I can carry you in there, if you like."

"Thank you." Her gratitude was fervent.

I looked from her to the bathroom. Oh, shit. This time I'd have to do it with just her and the skimpy nightie. She'd scream for sure.

I lifted her up and quickly carried her to the toilet in the ensuite bathroom, conscious of the hospital-issue nightdress she still wore and the amount of skin it didn't cover. I couldn't put her down fast enough, praying with every step that she wouldn't scream.

I almost shuddered with relief when I let go of her, but I tried to control myself so she wouldn't see my reaction and take it the wrong way. Even injured, Caitlin was still one hell of a temptation – pretty in all the right ways.

Wrong ways, I told myself as I turned my back and walked to the bathroom doorway to give her some privacy. She was damn fine in all the wrong ways and it'd be really great if she had some clothes to cover up with so I wouldn't be tempted any more than I had been already.

After a moment's thought, I called back over my shoulder, "If you want, I could ask my sister to drop by your house the next time she comes in to see me and she could pick up some of your own clothes for you to wear." Please say yes, please say yes. . .

She was silent for a moment before she replied, "Thank you, but I think with all the dressings and stuff, plus the trouble I'd have putting on or taking off clothes, I'm better off with hospital issue."

Shit. "Fair enough." I nodded, trying not to think of her wearing a backless nightdress with no underwear. Especially once the dressings came off. I'd just have to control my thoughts better. That's it. Not difficult at all. Hesitantly, I added, "Let me know when you're done and need my help again."

"I. . . I'm not done, but I may need your help." Her voice faded to a mortified whisper. I glanced over my shoulder and saw her pawing uselessly at the toilet paper dispenser, unable to grasp anything with her bandaged hands. She bit down hard on her lip in an effort to stop herself from crying.

Oh, fuck. This was just painful to watch.

"Did you know," I asked her as I crossed the bathroom quickly, ripping a wad of toilet paper out of the dispenser and pressing it into her upturned hand, "that you looked just like a kitten batting at a new toy just now? It was very cute." I smiled gently, my eyes on her face to gauge her reaction to my poor attempt at a joke. And not look at what she was doing with the toilet paper.

For a second, she looked hurt, then she looked up and met my eyes. A small smile slowly spread across her face. "Meow," she said, holding up her 'paws'. "I feel about as weak as a kitten, so the comparison is probably right." She sighed. "Now, I would appreciate your help one more time, because I think you're right. I need to rest in bed a bit longer."

"At your service." I took a deep breath and braced myself. I carried her back to bed and attempted to tuck the sheets around her again. I'd never been so relieved to see a girl covered up. Casually, I mentioned that she could ask the nurses for help when she needed it – after all, that was why she was in hospital. I prayed she'd take the hint and let other women help her. Anyone but me.

She looked down at her lap, not meeting my eyes. "I know, but I feel uncomfortable asking some random stranger to help me with something so personal. . . and I don't. . . like. . . anyone touching me at the moment." She shuddered.

Shit. I was on bathroom duty indefinitely. Was there any chance I could ask for her to be catheterised so I didn't have to. . . fuck, that wasn't something I should think about, either.

I took a breath and let it out. She didn't need me to make her feel worse. She felt bad enough as it was. I tried to be funny. "And the last time you asked a random stranger for help, you ended up in hospital with him and now you can't get rid of him — he even followed you into the bathroom." I smiled, attempting to make light of it.

She looked up but didn't smile. "After you saved my life, got shot and even helped me wipe my. . ." She blushed, unable to finish. "I don't think you qualify as a random stranger any more. I'd like to think you're a very good friend, even if I don't know you very well."

"And here I thought you were going to call me an arse wipe." I shook my head in mock sadness, feeling nothing but uneasy relief.

TWENTY FIVE

"Good morning, here's your breakfast."

The ladies who served the hospital meals always seemed too cheerful to be real. The sleepless nights with Caitlin had meant they usually woke me from an uneasy doze, only serving to heighten the impression that their bright smiles were a hallucination. Yet here was one, smiling first at me, then at Caitlin.

"I heard you were awake, hon." The woman winked at her. "I wasn't sure what you'd like, so I picked out the best of this morning's breakfast menu for you. I'll give you your menu, too, so you can order what you like for tomorrow."

Jokes about bad hospital food aside, I'd soon learned that they didn't apply to this place. I was most of the way through my eggs before I thought to ask Caitlin about her breakfast.

Swallowing the last mouthful of egg, I asked her, "So, what's the best of this morning's breakfast menu?"

When she didn't reply, I looked over at her, only to see

her breakfast was still covered. She concentrated on keeping the glass of orange juice between her bandaged hands firmly enough to lift it off the tray. She managed to take a mouthful of juice before slowly and carefully returning the glass to the tray.

"Caitlin? How's your breakfast?" I asked, realising that, aside from the juice, her tray was untouched. She stared down at the tray, her lips pressed firmly together. She couldn't even feed herself, I realised. And she was trying not to cry about it but she wouldn't ask for help, either.

I took a step toward her, leaned over and pressed her nurse call button.

"Hey!" She turned her tear-filled eyes on me, suddenly angry.

"You need someone to help you with your breakfast," I told her gently.

"I was managing fine!" She reached for the orange juice again, but only succeeded in knocking the glass off the tray and onto the bed. "Oh hell." Her tears spilled over, too, streaking down her cheeks as she tried clumsily to climb onto her pillows without using her hands, to avoid the spreading pool of orange on her sheets.

I hesitated a second before I offered, "Please, let me help." This time I didn't wait for an answer. I lifted her out of her bed and transferred her to mine. I pushed my breakfast tray away from her and dragged her breakfast-laden table over. She turned away from me, reaching for a tissue that she couldn't grasp.

I reached over her for the same tissue with markedly more success. I carefully wiped every trace of tears from her face before I helped her blow her nose. It wasn't until I walked away from her to put the tissues in the bin and wash my hands that she spoke.

"Thank you," she said in a small voice. I didn't say anything.

When I returned, I sat next to her on the bed, pulling my tray onto the table beside hers. I lifted the cover off her plate to find she'd been given the same as me.

"So, do you want those eggs?" I asked her.

"Just the thought of being fed like a baby makes me lose my appetite," she stated in the same small voice, not looking at me.

"Because I wouldn't mind them, if you're not eating them," I continued, as if she hadn't spoken. I picked up her cutlery and started to cut them into bite-sized pieces. I slid one piece onto the fork and waved it in front of her. "Last chance."

She took it. She chewed thoughtfully with her eyes closed for a moment before she swallowed and looked at me.

"More?" I asked blithely, loading up the fork again.

"Please," she answered with a hesitant, watery smile.

I helped her to eat as much as she could, occasionally taking a bite of the remains of my breakfast. She ate the eggs and some toast, but she wouldn't touch the cereal.

I offered her my orange juice, as yet untouched, in place of her lost one. She threw her arms around me in a hug as unexpected as it was clumsy, considering the orange juice was part of it.

"Thank you so much, Nathan," she murmured in my ear. Then she gasped and pulled away from me, suddenly very interested in her near-empty breakfast tray.

I turned to see what had startled her and saw the now-forgotten nurse I'd summoned with the call button.

"She shouldn't be out of her bed." The nurse glared at me as she spoke. Her name badge read *Judith*.

Oh, Nurse Carol's friend, I thought. Who told her I'm Caitlin's boyfriend. Before she called me a sleazy bastard. Right. . .

"We had an accident with some orange juice. Until you can get someone to change the sheets, I'm sure she'll be perfectly comfortable in my bed." I gave the nurse a smile that said, I know there's more than one way you can take that and they're all true.

More than a little flustered, she mumbled something about linen as she bundled up the orange sheets and left in a hurry.

TWENTY SIX

Waking again in the dark.
Hurting. Hungry.
Cold.
Didn't want him to touch me.
He had food and a blanket.
Blanket was rough, scratched tender skin.
Horrible to be fed by a stranger, my hands
tied.
Wouldn't untie me.
Food was dry, stale cereal, hard to swallow
with a dry throat.
Drink spilled and burned.
Fighting it.
Hurting.
Wanting to give up, for it to be over.
NO.
Whatever it takes to stay alive.
Keep fighting. Don't let them win.

TWENTY SEVEN

I left Caitlin for a couple of hours to get some clothes from home. She'd assured me she wouldn't need me 'til her next meal.

Full of misgivings for leaving her alone, even with one of our guys on guard outside, I resolved to be as quick as I could. My car was in the car park, exactly where Chris said it would be. I didn't know how Chris had gotten home afterwards – I was certain she'd make me pay for it when I saw her next. As I unlocked the car, I said a silent prayer that she'd be at university today instead of at home.

It was like they were watching me.

I parked my bum in the driver's seat and shut the door just as my phone rang. I answered with a hello, but that's all I managed to say before the interrogation began.

"She's awake. Michael called in his report already and you haven't. What has she told you?"

ASIO wasn't omniscient, no matter how much they'd like to be. Michael had probably called the minute I left

Caitlin's room, bored of guard duty with nothing to report.

Forgetting my sister, I thought of the pretty girl with the haunted eyes I'd reluctantly left watching TV not fifteen minutes ago. "That she doesn't want anyone touching her, she doesn't like breakfast cereal and her recovery is going to take a while."

A snort. "Breakfast cereal? What kind of fucking help is that? We want intel — we want to know where they are. We want to know who they are and what they did — not her fucking favourite foods! What the hell's wrong with you?"

Where do I start? I wondered. "I'm trying to build up some trust with her. She's hellishly traumatised. She's only been awake a day and she's had to deal with some pretty crippling injuries. I'm getting what I can but it'll be a few days before I can get anything useful out of her." Just let her recover a bit first.

"We don't have time to wait for her to feel perfect again. We need to know how to find them and soon. Before the police. Today, Nathan."

I felt uneasy. If I stuffed this up, I'd have to leave and someone else would have to start over. It'd be even harder for anyone else, if Caitlin told them anything at all. And who'd take care of her if I left? I had to do this. "I'll try," I conceded grudgingly.

An angry grunt. "Don't forget we broke protocol to allow you in on this one, Nathan. You're in hospital with her because of your special skill set, nothing else. We can easily pull you and get someone else."

"No one else would get as much out of her as quickly as I can," I replied instantly, knowing it was true.

"Then fucking do it!" He hung up.

I started the car with a sigh and a turn of the key, my heart heavy. I took my time driving home, selecting and packing a heap of clothes to take to hospital, then driving back to Caitlin. I delayed a little more, stopping at the supermarket for some supplies.

When I reached her floor, Michael hurried toward me, a finger to his lips. He grabbed my arm to stop me from going to Caitlin. I shook him off angrily.

He started to explain. "You know that friend of hers, Jo, who comes in every morning? The one who asked for updates from the nurses on Caitlin's condition?"

I nodded curtly, not saying anything. I'd seen the girl, who was on Caitlin's short list of approved visitors. She'd come into Caitlin's hospital room, glared at me for a few minutes and left again. I hadn't thought much about her until now, but already I was worried.

"We think one of the nurses tipped her off that you'd gone out. She's just arrived – and I don't think you should go in just yet." Michael looked nervous. So he bloody well should. He'd left Caitlin alone with a stranger.

I stared at him. "If you think I trust some girl I don't know with Caitlin's safety. . ." I tried to keep it quiet, but I was pretty pissed off.

Michael had both his hands up, gesturing to tell me to lower my voice. He looked scared. "Word from the boss is to listen – see if she tells her anything she hasn't yet told us. You can hear her from the doorway – close enough to get to her quickly if you need to," he said in a low voice.

Reluctantly, I nodded once. Together we walked back to Caitlin's room.

". . . At least you're looking better," I heard Jo's

unfamiliar voice say. "Where's your gallant hero this morning? Off polishing his sword?" She paused a moment before continuing. "Oh, come on. The half-crazed look in his eyes, full of guilt for what he did to you, and the anguish he's causing you now by sticking around? You're barely a shadow of yourself – what did he do to you?"

Incensed, I wanted to storm in and evict the little idiot, but Michael shook his head, signalling me to wait.

"Caitlin, please! You cry at the drop of a hat, and there *he* is, saying nonsensical things like, 'It's all over now,' when it never will be, not until you get rid of him." She paused again. "The bruises on your face are fading. You're starting to look almost normal now. At least he isn't hitting you any more."

Fucking BITCH! Like I'd ever do that. Not Caitlin. Not ever.

I looked at Michael. "This is what he wants us to hear?" I hissed. "I don't need to listen to this bullshit."

He was grim. "He said wait. We wait and listen to whatever Caitlin says. The other one doesn't matter."

The fuck it didn't matter. Like Caitlin would trust me if she thought I'd hurt her.

A long pause, as if Jo was waiting for Caitlin to reply, but I heard nothing before she spoke again. "It's lucky that he found you when he did."

"Hmmm?" Caitlin sounded confused.

"It's incredibly lucky that he was walking on that bit of beach just after you were dumped there. It couldn't be a coincidence – he knew you'd be dumped there, didn't he? He was one of *them*."

Finally, I heard Caitlin's voice. "I was lucky he was

there," she agreed half-heartedly.

"It's all right, you can tell me," Jo encouraged. "I know he was one of *them*."

Caitlin sounded confused again. "One of them?"

"One of the ones who hurt you," Jo explained, as though to a child.

Now she was upset. "Nathan never hurt me!"

Fucking right I didn't.

I took a step toward Caitlin, ignoring Michael shaking his head behind me.

Jo's voice had dropped lower, so that I could hear her speaking but I couldn't discern the words. Growing worried, I moved closer to the door until I heard Caitlin's voice again. My knuckles were white as my fingers gripped the door frame.

"No!" She was vehement. "He never did anything like that. He couldn't do that to me. . . He would never. . ." I could hear the tears in her voice.

This was fucking useless. We wouldn't get any information out of her like this and it was only going to take longer 'til I did.

"You didn't always see the face of the man who was hurting you, did you?" Jo demanded.

"No, wait – " Michael started to say as he grabbed my shoulder, but I shook him off.

There was no fucking way I was going to let some girl upset Caitlin like this – no matter how good a friend she claimed to be.

I stormed into the room and, sure enough, Jo had made her cry. I strode straight to Caitlin to give her a hug. I glared at Jo over Caitlin's shoulder as I asked her just loud enough for Jo to hear, "What did she do to you?"

Jo glared back at me for a moment, before she turned on her heel and left.

Good riddance. Fuck off, bitch.

I soothed Caitlin as best I could, all the while thinking that there was no way I'd ask her anything upsetting today. Her so-called friend had made her cry enough. No, my boss's fucking stupid idea had made her cry enough. If he'd only let me do my job and stayed out of it. It was going to take me all day to undo the damage he'd done. She'd done. Both of them had done.

Today was for her. I'd give her whatever she wanted in an effort to make up for my absence in the morning. I kicked my bag across the floor to my bed, hearing the crackle of plastic before I remembered.

"Hey, I brought contraband," I said to Caitlin.

"Hmm?" she asked, a single tear sparkling on her cheek as it slid down.

I knelt on the floor and unzipped my bag. "I owe you ice cream, so I thought I'd get the best."

I pulled out a tub of ice cream – one of the expensive ones that seemed to only come in one-litre tubs. It'd probably melted while I'd waited, but I told myself it was the thought that counted. If she liked it. If she didn't, I'd eat it myself.

Caitlin bit her lip, trying to wipe her last tear away. "I don't remember. Why would you owe me ice cream?"

Oh, fuck. I hesitated before deciding to tell her anyway. "When we first got here, you were asleep and not going to eat your meal. I did something really horrible." I took a deep breath, trying to make it sound worse than it was. "I'm really sorry. I stole your ice cream."

She looked as if she wanted to laugh, but she didn't. Her big eyes turned grave. "That's okay. I'm sure that will go some way in helping me forgive you."

I laughed, but not for long. I wondered how serious she was. Oh well, if this sweetened her up, I'd be laughing again before long. I tore open the tub and dug a spoon out of the bag. "Ice cream?"

She gave me a tiny smile. "Yes, please."

I crossed the fingers on the hand I held the tub with while I plied the spoon with the other, making sure the cardboard hid my bid for luck from Caitlin.

I'd have to ask her again soon, whether I liked it or not. Just not today.

Maybe tomorrow.

TWENTY EIGHT

Still dark.
Tied up.
Rope on wrists, legs.
Someone else there?
Help.
Water.
Let me go!
Coughing.
Can't.
Help me, you bastard.
Tears.
Rope burns, blood.
No.
I'm going to
Sorry.

TWENTY NINE

"Time to change your dressings. Let's see how you're healing up!" Nurse Carol sounded more cheerful than I'd ever heard her. I wondered if it was because Caitlin was awake, or whether the shapely nurse'd had a hot date the night before. It sure hadn't been a night with me.

Caitlin's eyes on the nurse showed her relief. "Hi, Carol. Of all the wards to bring me to, I ended up here."

Carol's voice was brassy-bright. "Of course. We had to fight for you, but we traded a couple of sporting injury patients to the other wards to keep you."

Caitlin coughed out a painful little laugh. My throat ached in sympathy. "You just wanted fewer names to learn at handover."

"You know it. Actually, while you were asleep there have been some very interesting men in the ward keeping guard over you. I almost thought about asking them to pull out their weapons. . ." Carol blushed as she said it. Her eyes travelled to me and quickly looked away. I wondered if she included me as one of those *interesting men.*

"I have guards?" Caitlin asked, her eyes widening.

Oh, shit. Hadn't I told her?

I struggled to remember, amid all the things I'd said to her while she was asleep and in the brief time she'd been awake. I couldn't remember if I'd told her that her room was guarded.

"Sure, a different police officer every day, like some sort of desk calendar. They make sure you don't have any unwelcome visitors. Plus. . ." Carol's gaze strayed to me and Caitlin's followed.

I stared into Caitlin's eyes for a moment, wishing I could work out what she was thinking, but I didn't know her well enough for that. The depths of these windows into her soul were dark to me. I sighed and looked away first.

"I thought you had a new man, Scott. How does he stack up against the desk calendar guys, or is he out of the picture now?" Caitlin asked.

Oh, the hot Singaporean nurse had a boyfriend. I bet I could've made her forget him easily, if I'd tried. A pity that I hadn't. Inwardly, I shrugged. I had enough to think about. The nurse wasn't a priority.

"I'm still with Scott, but that doesn't mean I can't look." Carol cleared her throat. "So, where do we start?"

"What does it matter? I guess it's time for me to see what they've done to me," Caitlin said, sounding resigned.

I heard the sound of adhesive gauze parting from skin and stared fixedly out the window. The strong smell of disinfectant stung my eyes. There was a small spider in a dense web in the corner, its legs and underside up against the glass. I tried to count every leg, every joint. . .

"Oh hell. That looks bad," Caitlin struggled to say.

My eyes darted to her. She stared down at her lap and I caught a glimpse of the mess the bullet had made of her leg.

"A skin graft over that would help hide the scar," Nurse Carol said gravely.

Caitlin's voice sounded weak. "But where would you take the graft from? Everywhere is. . ." Her voice faded as the tears took over.

I crossed the room, hesitating as I approached her. I didn't want to see that leg wound, but I didn't want her to cry, either. Shit, now that she was awake, it wasn't as simple as before. She might not even want me here.

Carol looked up at me for a moment, before her eyes returned to Caitlin. "Hey, that's the worst of your wounds. The rest are healing up nicely. You'll see." She worked to cover the bullet wound up again as I watched. The next piece of gauze the nurse removed uncovered a series of shallow cuts that looked like someone had tried to carve letters into her leg. Now that they were healing, I could see the shapes of the scars.

I swallowed, trying not to say anything.

How could they. . .

I gritted my teeth so hard it felt like I'd break them. I didn't relax until the nurse smoothed a dressing over her leg.

I breathed again, sure the wound on her other thigh couldn't be worse. My eyes flew to it, expectantly. Nurse Carol ripped the dressing off.

"Oh God," I burst out before I could stop myself. I could feel my jaw lock open, too horrified to close.

Both of the girls regarded me with consternation. Caitlin

lifted her arms up, as if she was considering asking for a hug. Her hospital gown showed the dark, damp splotches where her tears had landed. Darker blue on blue. I didn't wait for her to ask, rushing the last few steps to comfort her.

I squeezed my own eyes shut as she cried into my shirt.

Plastic and paper crackled as Nurse Carol covered up the livid letters that spelled CHRIS in jagged lines across Caitlin's thigh, matching the crossed-out ALANNA on her other leg.

THIRTY

Hurting. So cold. . .
Go away. Let me sleep.
End this.
Don't hurt me any more.
Buzz OFF!
Keep fighting. Don't let them win.
Knew the voice. Didn't say that.
Not when they hurt me.
Wasn't THERE.
He's dead.
Saw him get shot.
Can't be him.
Must be. . . a dream.

THIRTY ONE

Caitlin's screams woke me again, so I lumbered out of my bed and over to hers before I was fully awake. Taking care to make sure her crisp cotton sheet was between us, I folded her into a comforting hug. "It's okay, I'm here. . ." I murmured. "Keep fighting it, don't let them win. . ."

I waited for the screaming to become sobbing before she calmed down enough to lie still again. When I was sure it was over, I gently let her down onto her pillows and stumbled back to my bed. The vinyl floor was cool beneath my feet.

"Nathan?" Caitlin's voice was quavery.

Shit. It wasn't over yet. No sleep for the wicked. "It's all right, I'm here," I began wearily, sliding my hand down her back to lift her into my arms again.

She gave a shudder and pulled away from me, sitting up on her own. "What are you doing? Why were you touching me when I woke up?"

Oh, shit. I crossed my arms over my chest, suddenly

wide awake. "You've been having a lot of really bad nightmares and you wouldn't wake up. You. . . were screaming. Screaming for me to help you. You. . . don't scream as much if I. . . hug you." I sounded like the worst kind of deviant, watching and touching her while she slept.

"How often have you. . . hugged me?" Caitlin asked cautiously.

I didn't want to answer, but it was better if I did. The nurses would tell her, anyway, if I didn't. "Whenever you had nightmares, until you stopped screaming."

Her round, dark eyes held a lot of things in their depths: betrayal, sadness, panic. She didn't say anything, but her eyes said plenty.

"I did it because I couldn't wake you up. I promised. . . I promised I wouldn't let them hurt you and they were hurting you in your dreams. I couldn't just sit by and do nothing." I spoke faster than I'd intended. Shit. It was like I'd told my boss, charm and a smile wouldn't work on Caitlin. I was fucked.

She bit her lip, still not saying a word.

"That's all, I swear! The same as tonight. It helped you to calm down, stop screaming and settle back into a peaceful sleep." I swallowed. Except the one time I went too far and kissed her, when she let me know just how much she didn't like that. Shit, don't even think about it.

Her voice was soft and she spoke slowly, as if considering each word. "That explains. . . some things." She didn't explain anything. Her big eyes studied me. "Nathan, could you do me a favour?"

If she let me stay like I was supposed to after this monumental fuck-up, I'd do just about anything. "Sure," I replied.

"Next time I have a bad dream, can you please wake me up first?" Her eyes were pleading.

I smiled broadly. "Sure," I said again, turning on the charm just a little in relief. "With pleasure."

She shrank back against the pillows, her eyes wide with fear once more. "But please don't touch me."

I felt my heart shrink in response. I wanted to comfort her, but I didn t know how to do it without touching her. I stared at her for a moment, before closing my eyes, nodding wearily as I headed back to bed.

I got the message, all right. I was more useful asleep and on the other side of the room. I wasn't going to argue with that.

THIRTY TWO

In the evening, I sat in the chair beside her bed, watching some programme that Caitlin found more interesting than I did. It seemed to be about some women who agonised over their inability to have a perfect, long-term relationship with a man, in between trying men on the way they tried on clothes. It was funny, if nothing else. More than once, I saw a watery smile float to the surface of Caitlin's expression, before it sank to the hidden depths again.

I ached to see her smile properly or even laugh. I found my thoughts drifting to what I could do to lift her spirits. I decided to go to the gift shop downstairs and pick up some chocolate. I stood up, opening my mouth to tell her I'd be right back.

The phone rang on the bedside cabinet between us. We looked at each other, surprised, before she started to reach for it.

She's going to realise she can't pick it up, then she's going to cry, I thought. Quicker and closer, I hit the button that put the call on the phone's hands-free setting.

"Hello?" I answered quickly, before she could react.

An older man responded in a heavy accent, sounding confused. "Ah, I was looking for Caitlin Lockyer? I'm her father."

My eyes went to Caitlin, questioningly.

She nodded as she spoke up. "Hi, Dad. I'm here."

"I've only just checked my messages — we've been out of range of all but satphones for the last month. The police got a hold of me just as we left, to say they'd call me if they had any updates, but it didn't seem that they did. Your friend Jo left a message for me to say you'd been found, but you were in hospital. What happened?"

I took a step toward the door, trying to keep my voice as low as possible. "Did you want me to stay, or will you be okay if I. . ." I gestured toward the corridor beyond her room.

Caitlin shook her head, looking unconcerned. "Go, go," she mouthed, waving her hands as if she were pushing me out the door.

I went, smiling and nodding in what I hoped was an understanding way. As she started to tell a very abridged version of what she'd been through, I listened to her tone. Careful, as flat as she could make it, Caitlin barely sounded distressed at all as she recited, "Some men pulled me into their car, knocked me out and took me somewhere dark. They. . . hurt me. Someone found me, took me to hospital." Here she paused, as if she needed something to give her the impetus to carry on.

I hesitated, wondering if I should turn around and go back in.

I heard the murmur of her father's voice, but not the words, as I was too far down the corridor. I stopped and strained to hear her reply.

". . . I wasn't out alone after dark. It was broad daylight – I was shopping for Jason's birthday present," she said, sounding resigned. Her voice dropped lower so I couldn't hear more.

Who was Jason that she needed to get him a birthday present?

Forgetting the chocolate, I returned to her room. I debated whether I should go back in or not and decided to do something I'm not proud of. I stood beside her open door, out of her line of sight, and listened to the whole conversation.

Her father's voice was the next I heard. "Will you be okay if I take this contract? It's a whole three months with an exploration drilling rig, but they've offered me so much money I don't want to turn it down."

Three months? She'd be alone in her house for three months and there was no one there now. I needed to get our remote surveillance guys in and out of there before she got home. I'd call them as soon as she was asleep. Work would be happy I had something to report, even if it was just intel on her house.

"Sure, Dad, I'll be fine," she murmured. "I'm still going to be in hospital for a couple of weeks and it's not like I can't cook when I get home. Take photos, okay? Something cool. You know I like to see what you're up to, even if I have to wait 'til you're home to see them."

"Bye honey – they're calling my flight, time to go again."

"Bye, Dad," she said softly. I heard the dial tone as he

hung up, then her deep sigh. I ached for her.

I wanted to see her smile again. Now more than ever.

I skipped the lifts and ran down the stairs to the ground floor gift shop. I was going to get her the best chocolate they had. I wished I'd asked her what she liked. . . but everyone liked chocolate peanut brittle, surely.

If she didn't, I'd eat it and go back to get her something else.

Or should I just buy a bit of everything that looked good? I figured that could work.

I checked my wallet to make sure I had enough cash.

"That's a lot of chocolate," the woman with white curls in the gift shop said with a smile. "Are you trying to impress a lady?"

I allowed myself a proper smile. "Perhaps," I replied with a wink.

She looked a little flustered. "Well, I'd be impressed," she said defensively, looking away so she could put my purchases in a bag.

I thanked her and ran up the stairs, two at a time, back up to Caitlin's room on the second floor.

I dropped the bag of chocolate on Caitlin's bedside table with a grin, turning to see her reaction.

She was fast asleep, tears sparkling on her eyelashes in the last rays of the sun, and I didn't have the heart to wake her. The empty pill cup on her table told me she'd be out for a few hours, so maybe it was a good idea for me to try and get some sleep, too.

As I relaxed into my pillow, I wondered who'd given her the pills and helped her drink the water to wash them down. I figured it was probably the nurse who administered them. I shrugged and slept.

THIRTY THREE

Wrists bound in rope and blood.
Cutting.
Hurting.
Twisted.
Lost.
Too cold.
Oh God. Broken.
Too dark.
So much blood.
Too late.
Heart frozen.
Do it.
Give me death.
End it.

THIRTY FOUR

I woke with my heart beating against my ribs for escape

Who gave her the medication she took last night? Why did I go to sleep without finding out, making sure she was okay, checking to be sure. . . Who was on guard? Shit, I couldn't even remember his face. Was he there for the phone call and all the time I was gone? Was he still here so I could ask him? Fuck, what if I'd fucked up and let them get to her? I held my breath, hoping and praying my dread was unfounded.

Please, let her be okay.

In the dim light filtering in from the corridor, I could see Caitlin shift restlessly in her bed. She whimpered as if she was in pain or trapped in another nightmare. I breathed again. I wanted to hug her, I was so happy to see her alive, but I remembered. Even if she was having a nightmare, I wasn't stupid enough to do it again.

"Caitlin, angel, wake up," I said, sitting up. "It's a dream. Only a dream. Wake up."

I stood up and stretched. The ache in my muscles reminded me how much I wanted to visit the gym. I wondered if the hospital had one for staff. Fuck. Focus. Wake Caitlin and ask her.

I repeated the same words, a little louder. I crossed the room to be closer to her.

"Angel. Caitlin, it's a dream. Only a dream. Wake up. See? I'm here, just like I promised, and you're safe, I swear.'

She didn't seem to have heard me, still struggling against her sheets and the scary men in her dream. Her scream shattered what was left of my sleepiness, like a screen of clouded glass. I stumbled, swallowed, and told myself I was made of sterner stuff than the scrambled eggs I expected for breakfast. I took the last step that left me standing beside her bed, my shorts flush against her sheets.

I reached over her and hit the switch by her bed. In the flickering beam of the fluorescent light, I saw her eyes flutter. "It's a dream, angel. Wake up. It's me, you're in hospital and everything's going to be fine. . ."

A head-shake, blinking, as Caitlin slowly sat up, her face sinking into shadow. "Nathan?"

I broke into a smile. "That's me."

She slowed her breathing from a panicked pant to something closer to calm. "I'm. . . safe in hospital with you. Right?"

"Yeah," I replied, yawning. I wanted to go back to sleep, but I wouldn't manage it until I asked her what I should have found out last night. "Who gave you your afternoon meds?"

She thought for a minute. "Judith. . . no, Carol. Carol was on last night. I said I was having trouble sleeping so she found me some milk in the handover room fridge. I was out like a light." She didn't meet my eyes.

"You must have been tired," I responded with a smile, trying hard not to think of her crying herself to sleep without me yesterday. Taking medication without me checking to make sure it was safe. I felt guilty already and no amount of chocolate would make up for it. I'd been lucky, was all. I couldn't afford to fuck up like that again. It could cost her life, my job and Chris. . . I closed my eyes, trying to clear my head before I opened them again.

"I won't keep you up. You need your rest to heal." I turned away and padded across the vinyl back to bed.

"No, wait," Caitlin said softly. I stopped. "Would you please sit by me for a little bit, 'til I calm down properly? I just want to get some of the horrible pictures out of my head. The police come to take my statement tomorrow and I can't stop thinking about all the things I have to say. . ."

Last chance. The perfect opportunity to ask. Just don't be stupid and don't go back to sleep.

I settled in the chair beside her bed, shifting so that I faced her. "Can you tell me about them? Maybe that'll help them go away faster." I didn't dare cross my fingers for luck, but in my heart I hoped.

She looked fearfully at me. "Nathan. . . I. . . don't even want to think about them. Talking about my nightmares will only bring them back."

"No it won't," I coaxed. "That's what all the psychologists and counsellors say. You wait. They'll tell you it's good to get it out and your heart will feel lighter."

Caitlin shook her head. "Nathan. . ." Fresh tears started to flow. She lifted her arms, shaking with her first sob.

I hesitated. I wasn't stupid, but I wasn't heartless, either. I moved from the chair to her bed so I could hug her like she wanted. It felt like the right thing to do, too.

"I can't, Nathan, not yet. I can't," Caitlin murmured as she clung to me and cried.

Fuck it. I stroked her hair. "It's okay. You don't have to."

THIRTY FIVE

It was a shiny red Mercedes. Not the newest.
The driver looked at me.
Friend in the back.
Saucer eyes.
Someone hit me, pushed me into the back of the
car with Saucer Eyes.
Two in the front.
Passenger, driver.
Passenger hit me, drugged me.
Sorry. Oh God, so sorry.
Fight them.
Don't let them win.
Sleep and remember.
Until later.

THIRTY SIX

"We need a statement from you, Miss Lockyer." The police officer sounded almost hesitant. After last night, I was, too. "I understand this will be upsetting for you, but we need your assistance to catch the people who did this to you."

Caitlin bit her lip and nodded, her eyes downcast. Her hand reached for mine and I held it carefully, mindful of her fingers.

The police officer cleared his throat. "Mr Miller, I'll have to ask you to leave or at least step outside."

Unwillingly, I rose. I tried to let go of her hand, but I couldn't. Somehow, she'd twined her fingers through mine and couldn't, or wouldn't, let go. She emitted a strangled sound as I tried to detach her gauze-shrouded fingers, so I stopped. I looked hard at Caitlin, but her eyes remained fixed on her lap. Her face grew paler the longer I looked.

"No." The firmness in her voice surprised me and the police officer, too.

"I'm sorry?" He looked confused. "You won't give a

statement yet?"

Caitlin looked up, her brow furrowed. "I'll make a statement now, but I want Nathan to stay."

The police officer cleared his throat. "Mr Miller is a suspect in this matter and we'd prefer that your statement is made privately, so you feel safe and don't hold back information. Your statement will remain confidential."

Caitlin's eyes locked on his and her voice hardened. "Detective, I will *never* feel safe until I know every one of those bastards can't touch me again. And I will never feel safe alone with a police officer, after one of them shot at me. Nathan. . . Nathan shouldn't be a suspect in this. He never. . . He didn't. . . He's about the only person who hasn't hurt me." Her voice was firm through most of this, but wavered toward the end. Her eyes filled with tears, which spilled down her cheeks. She reached for a tissue with one bandaged hand, then the other, unsuccessfully.

I reached over and pulled a tissue out of the box, holding it out for her. Caitlin turned her sad eyes to me, her useless hands held out in front of her. "Please," she whispered. I hesitated a second before I carefully wiped her tears away.

She turned back at the police officer. "I can't use my hands and I can barely stand, let alone walk. I feel so helpless, one of these pillows would probably be an effective weapon against me." She gave him a sad little smile. "I know I need to make a statement so you can catch the people who did this to me, no matter how upset talking about it will make me feel. I'll do it, however many tears it takes, but please don't make me do this alone." Her voice faded to a whisper. She looked pleadingly at the police officer, then at me.

I spoke first. "If you want me to stay, I'll be here for you."

The police officer looked hesitant, as if he wanted to agree but knew he couldn't.

She laced her fingers through mine before turning her tear-filled eyes back to the police officer, her voice barely louder than a whisper. "I don't know how long it will take before I'm strong enough to tell this story without someone to support me. I don't even know if I can. I want you to catch them and I want to help you do it. I want to know they can't touch me and that I'll be safe as soon as possible. Please – I feel like I have so little courage left. Let me tell this story before it's gone. I don't know when I'll be brave enough to attempt it again." She held his gaze for a moment, before bowing her head in defeat. She looked so small and vulnerable all of a sudden.

I found myself moving almost automatically to comfort and protect her. The words were out of my mouth before I could think. "I promised I won't let them hurt you again. They won't touch you – you will be safe."

The police officer cleared his throat. "I think that if you'd like to make your statement with him present, under the circumstances, you can do so. Provided, of course, that Mr Miller doesn't interrupt or interfere in any way."

I felt her whole body relax in my arms. "Thank you." Her voice was fervent with relief.

"Can you tell me what you remember?" the police officer asked carefully.

Caitlin sat up, resting against me, both of her hands in mine. I felt her stiffen as she closed her eyes.

"I remember they had a red Mercedes. They hit me, pushed me into the car, made me breathe something that knocked me out in the back seat. It was dark when I woke up. It was always dark and. . . they hurt me. I remember pain and cold in the dark. And then Nathan – telling me it was over, that they weren't going to hurt me again. The next thing I remember is waking up here." Her eyes opened, looking as lost as when she'd woken here and called for me.

The officer looked stunned. "That's all you remember? Don't you remember being shot?"

"No," she whispered, then cleared her throat and resumed in a more normal voice. "I have. . . dreams. . . nightmares. . . and sometimes I see things that make me remember. Bits come back, but they're only ever bits. I should write them down, but I can't yet." She held up her bandaged hands.

"I'll do it," I found myself saying. "I can bring in my laptop, you can tell me what you remember and I'll type it in for you."

I earned a suspicious look from the police officer, but Caitlin looked relieved.

"Thank you," she said as she crumpled. She fell mostly against me, so it was a small matter to twist my fingers from hers and shift her so that she rested on her pillows. Her eyelids fluttered a little, but she didn't open her eyes.

The officer stood up. "Well, if that's all you have to say today, I'll be going. Until next time, Miss Lockyer."

"Mmm hmmm," Caitlin murmured quietly, her eyes still closed.

He nodded to me and I returned the curt gesture.

He left, but I watched Caitlin. She hadn't shown any

warning signs of feeling faint. I wondered if I should call a nurse.

The door clicked shut behind the man and I saw her go from rigid to relaxed.

"Do you want me to call a nurse?" I tested.

Caitlin breathed a sigh so deep it made her sink further into the pillows. "No, it's okay. I just need to rest."

"You absolutely do," I replied. "Rest and heal. Tomorrow I'll bring in the laptop and you can tell me everything you remember."

She sucked in a breath but she didn't reply.

THIRTY SEVEN

Dark. Laboured breathing.
Couldn't see.
Touch.
Skin on skin.
So cold.
Moaning. Coughing.
Can't find a blanket.
Cold.
Need warmth.
Blood.
Silent scream.
Can't.
Die. . .
Help.
Need to run.
Can't
Oh God

THIRTY EIGHT

"Pervert. Sorry. Oh God, so sorry." Caitlin rubbed her cheek against her shoulder. A smear of tears turned the cotton from light blue to dark. "Let me go. . ."

If I'd thought having to listen to her nightmares was bad, writing her memories was worse. I've never seen anyone cry as much as Caitlin did those first two hours.

"No reply, no light. More pain, bitter tears. Alone in the dark when I needed *help*." Her voice broke into a sob on the last word, but she hiccupped and continued. "I remember lying down, sobbing. Cold, rough, hard concrete. Dusty. Made me cough but no one heard. Pain. Relief that no one heard me. . ."

She sat with her eyes closed, tears streaming down her face as she fought to find the words to describe the horrors she could remember. Disjointed memories — every one of them dark.

"Don't touch me! Hold her down, I said. . . Touch me and I'll kick your face in! How are you going to do that with him holding you down? I said. . ." She swallowed painfully. "No!"

I'd keep typing until she stopped, her sobs choking her into silence. Then I'd put an arm around her shoulder, she'd cry into my shirt for a while, she'd sit up, hiccupping, and she'd start again, presumably where she'd left off.

"Too heavy. . . couldn't breathe. . . hhhurt me. . . couldn't scream. Hurt me again. Gasping, sobbing. . . no air. Crushing weight lifted. . . a breath. . . another. Why a reprieve? Touching me. . . NO! A scream. . . mine. . . hhhurt me more. . ."

It was like watching her throw up.

"Don't touch me. . . don't touch her. . . don't. . ." Caitlin's voice failed. I waited, but she went on. "Can't stop. Must. . . shouting. . . shots. . . hurts. . . No. Can't stop. Must. . . hurts. . . Can't get up. Must. . . red light. . . blood. Scared. . . slipping. . ."

At first, I thought I could take it, but what was coming out of her mouth and what it was doing to her made me sick to my stomach.

"T-t-took my clothes. . . tried to fight. . . threatened me. Scared. . . froze. . . cried. . . couldn't fight. So cold. . . ssshhhivering and cold in the dark. . . Two – two of them."

By halfway through, I wanted to kill them all.

"B-bound my hands. . . broke my fingers. Screaming. . . pain. . . Couldn't see for tears. He had a knife. . . cut my clothes off." She swallowed. "Tried to kick him. Couldn't see. Too dark. He. . . caught my legs. Pushed them down. . . apart. . . unzipped. . . Oh God, please. . . no. . ."

By the time she'd been at it for a couple of hours and was so choked up she couldn't do it anymore, I was ready to not just kill them, but chop them up into small pieces and burn their remains, in no particular order. Then burn the clothes I'd been wearing and take a shower in disinfectant.

I asked Caitlin if she wanted to take a look at what I'd written, to add to it where I hadn't been able to type fast enough, but she shook her head, her eyes tightly closed.

"Later," she murmured. "Another day. I can't any more today." She lay down again on the pillows and turned her face away from me.

"Did you want me to leave you alone for a bit?" I asked hesitantly, already thinking about getting a nice coffee from the cafe downstairs and the possibility of any distraction to get the last two hours out of my head. I wondered how many sexy nurses and doctors visited the coffee shop.

"Please don't." The face Caitlin turned toward me now was wide-eyed with fear. "I don't want to sleep again yet. I'm going to have nightmares after this."

You're not the only one, I thought.

I hesitated for a second before I offered, "Why don't you come downstairs and we'll get a coffee? There's a coffee shop downstairs and they had some nice-looking cakes this morning. I know the hospital staff don't let you have cake. . ."

She gave a tiny smile, looking wistful. Before she could refuse, I called the nurses' station to arrange a wheelchair and some theatre scrubs for her to wear.

As I hung up the phone, I looked down and realised I could do with a change, too, out of my salt-encrusted shirt and into a clean one. I pulled the dirty one over my head and dug in my bag for clean clothes.

I heard Caitlin make a sound behind me as she shifted between the sheets. I turned to see why. She was looking at the bathroom door, turned away from me.

"What is it?" I asked, moving closer to her.

She kept her face averted and pressed her lips together. She closed her eyes and shook her head. "Nothing," she said softly.

"Are you sure?" I asked, touching her arm.

She shuddered and shrank away from me. "Please, I. . . Let me know when you're done changing your clothes."

I looked down. It's not as if I'd suddenly sprouted a beer belly. I still had my six-pack; softened a bit by days in bed, but a six-pack I was proud of, nonetheless. I resolved to work out a bit more when she was asleep. It was as I was looking down that I realised.

Oh, shit. This much bare skin made her uncomfortable. No bloody wonder. I crossed the room to the far corner by the window and turned my back to put my shirt on, so I didn't have to see her horror. How anyone thought I could ever seduce this girl was beyond me. Not a hope in hell.

Nurse Judith came in before I could say anything else to Caitlin. The blonde nurse held the scrubs clenched in one fist as she told me, "If you want a wheelchair for her, you'll have to go to the ward clerk at the nurses' station to find out where one is." She glared at me. "Get out. I'm going to help her change."

I looked askance at Caitlin, but she sat with her head down and her eyes closed, too miserable to react.

I left the room, but stood outside the door where I could still hear. Just because this nurse hadn't hurt her before didn't mean she wasn't a danger today.

"He never leaves. The whole time you were unconscious, he barely left the room. He just kept talking to you. It didn't stop him trying to chat up the nurses, though, sleazy bastard." Judith's disapproval of me was palpable. "He sat in the chair by your bed and wouldn't leave, even when I was changing your dressings."

Caitlin roused herself enough to reply, though her voice was muffled. "Really? Why? Did he say?"

Judith sounded disgruntled. "He said he'd promised you something and he wasn't letting you out of his sight." She evidently didn't believe it.

"Then I should thank him when he gets back," Caitlin said softly.

Back. Oh shit. I strode down the ward to the nurses' station, asking as quietly as I could for a spare wheelchair I could borrow. The phone rang just as the ward clerk opened her mouth to answer me, so she pointed at one down the corridor as she picked up the receiver in her other hand.

I grabbed the wheelchair and pushed it as quickly as I could back to Caitlin's hospital room.

"Thank you," Caitlin said quietly as I reached her room. Nurse Judith glared at me as she walked out of the door before I could go in, but she didn't say anything.

Caitlin looked up at me hopefully. I lifted her into the wheelchair and we headed to the lift.

It had to be the strangest first date I'd ever been on: with a girl wearing a pair of borrowed pyjamas in public, drinking coffee through a straw, while I spoon-fed her a slice of every cake they had — a grand total of three. I didn't taste a bite of them and I couldn't even remember what they were when they were gone.

The cafe speakers played some boy band I'd never heard of, but when I asked Caitlin to identify them for me, she didn't know, either. We talked about music and movies, safe topics that stayed away from her nightmares.

I lost track of both the time and the cake. I looked down to get her another bite to find all the cake was gone. "Do you think we have time for another round before the staff upstairs realise I've kidnapped you and decide to report you missing?"

It took a moment for my horrified brain to catch up with my mouth. "Oh God, I'm sorry. I didn't mean to. . ." I looked up into her eyes and forgot whatever I'd meant to say.

Her whole face lit up as she smiled and let out a peal of laughter that drowned out the anonymous boy band.

So beautiful. Even the perky boy band agreed with me. I stared at her, mesmerised, dimly aware that other cafe patrons were looking at her, too. For that moment, I wanted. . . what I couldn't have.

She noticed people staring and blushed, looking down at her lap. "I think I've had enough cake to last me for the next month, and I'm sure I'd hate to be reported missing. Please, could we go back upstairs?" Her voice was barely audible.

I babbled thoughtlessly as we waited for the lifts. "I'm sure you were just making up for the last month. We'd have to come back and do this again to get you in credit for the next month!"

Nice. Remind her that those bastards starved her, too.

She stayed silent as I pushed her into the lift and back to

her room. As I helped her back into bed, she smiled at me again, to my surprise, although less brilliantly than before.

"Perhaps, Nathan," she finally replied. "But not before tomorrow. I'll be sick if I have any more cake today."

THIRTY NINE

Sweet smell to set stomach stirring.
Sick or hungry?
Not sure.
Dizzy and dark.
Here.
Taste and texture, teeth sliding over skin.
Crunch of apple, chewing, swallowing.
Too fast to taste. Too hungry.
Forcing food to stay down.
Water?
Cold and tasteless in a plastic cup.
No whiff of chlorine.
Not city water.
Far from home.
Far from help.
No one nearby to hear me scream.
Want more.
More food.
More water.
More help.
Please

FORTY

"No breakfast for you, hon. A cancellation in the theatres moved your skin graft up to this morning," the unfamiliar nurse said briskly as she bustled in, sticking a sign on Caitlin's bedhead that read: *Nil by mouth*. She swept out without another word.

As if on cue, one of the smiling breakfast ladies entered, a tray on each arm as she headed to where I sat beside Caitlin. I could smell bacon, burned toast and coffee, my stomach roaring audibly for all of it.

I shook my head. "She has surgery today. I won't have any, either."

Caitlin looked up at me, her brow wrinkled. "Why not?"

I tried to smile. "I don't want to throw up on the operating theatre floor," I admitted. I felt queasy already.

Comprehension broke like a wave over her face. "You mean you're coming in with me?" Her expression turned to amazement.

I wondered if I'd stuck my foot in my mouth again.

"Only if you want me there. They'll put you under and. . ."

"Oh God." She shuddered and looked like she was having trouble swallowing. "Please, I. . . I do. I didn't realise they'd knock me out for it. I'll be asleep and they'll be touching me. . ." Her voice died, horrified into silence.

My stomach settled a little as I reached out and carefully placed my hand on her arm. My little finger grazed the edge of the bandage on her wrist. I could feel her shaking as goosebumps formed under my fingers – I felt her fear. My mind rapidly clicked from conflicted to calm. I could do this for Caitlin. "I'll be there. I'll scrub up and watch over you as you sleep until your eyes open in Recovery."

She was still so scared and stiff, but Caitlin managed a weak laugh. "You sound like some sort of sick stalker out of a movie for teenagers. Is there something wrong with me that I'm relieved to have you watch me sleep?"

I joined her laughter, though mine had strength that hers lacked. "There's nothing wrong with you that time and rest won't fix after a little surgery today. You're going to be fine. I'll make sure of it." As long as I didn't throw up.

Luckily, it wasn't long before an orderly collected her to be prepped for theatre. I stayed beside her in the curtained cubicle they'd assigned her while she waited for the anaesthetist. She was already drowsy from the first set of drugs they'd given her as I'd looked on. I'd learned my lesson. I wasn't letting her take any more medication without knowing what it was and who gave it to her.

Caitlin stretched out her hand to me, looking like a bemused drunk with her slight, sleepy smile. "Will you be here when I wake up?" she slurred.

I smiled. One day it'd be nice to go the pub with her and

see how many drinks it took to make her slur like this again. "Absolutely, angel. Your own personal stalker."

"Not a stalker," she mumbled. Further mumbling followed, but I didn't understand it. Her eyelids dropped.

"Tell me that again," I said softly, not expecting her to respond.

"They did. They were watching me. Three of them. Don't know who was the bigger pervert. . ." Her voice meandered off into a sigh. I strained to hear more.

"I need space to work, mate," an unfamiliar voice said. I straightened up.

The anaesthetist had arrived.

"You can see her when she's out of Recovery, after surgery's over," he said, nodding to an orderly to start shifting Caitlin's bed.

I panicked. "No, I'm going in with her. I swore I wouldn't leave her alone. I'm supposed to guard her. . ."

He snorted. "Hope you've got a strong stomach, then. This one's a skin graft and they're not pretty. Go scrub up and don't forget your shoe covers." He waved his security pass over the door behind him and kicked it open for me.

I was torn between Caitlin and the gaping door.

He waved his hand down his theatre blues. "You can't go into theatre 'til you're a Smurf like the rest of us. I'm taking her through and I'll see you in there."

I gave in and forced myself to step into the changing room. The door closed heavily behind me, like a dungeon door that didn't open often. Feverishly, I looked around for the shelves of scrubs. It hadn't been that long since I'd done my med school pracs. . .

Stripping off as quickly as I could, I tried not to think

about having to wear the blue overalls again. I'd never expected to have to do it. That part of my life was done. Over. There would never be a Dr Miller. That dream had died with Alanna. Or on an autopsy table, when they'd asked me to identify the body of my dead sister. Oh, shit. . . I squeezed my eyes shut, trying to think of anything but Alanna.

Caitlin. I was here for Caitlin.

I struggled into the cotton clothes and found the disposables that finished off the costume. Shoe covers, cap, eye shield, mask. I put them all on and pushed the door to the theatre open. I caught the faint whiff of fresh blood and disinfectant before I held my breath. I let it out slowly, striding across the room to Caitlin's head.

"Who's he?" one masked figure asked another.

"The guard you're waiting for. Let's get this done. I want this procedure finished before coffee comes. Catering swore there'd be strawberry tarts today. . ."

Like we had yesterday, I thought as I looked down at Caitlin's sleeping face. Her beautiful eyes were closed, her hair covered by a cap, but her face was still a little worried. I reached for her hand, then thought better of it. I touched my fingers to her cheek instead. "I'm here," I murmured. "I'm not going anywhere."

I forced myself to watch the bloody procedure, as a patch of skin was cut from one part of her leg and attached over the bullet wound on Caitlin's thigh. Somehow this was easier to bear than seeing her wounds revealed – today was about helping her recover, a cosmetic patch over a gaping hole that shouldn't be there. That wouldn't be there, if. . .

Don't think about it!

Keeping my breathing shallow, I tried to ignore the smells and sounds that were the same as any other operating theatre I'd been in before Alanna died. When I'd wanted to help people, not kill them.

I shook my head, forcing myself to focus. They were almost done and she hadn't woken or cried out. Caitlin's breath was a slight breeze over my fingers.

Breathe. She's alive. Keep her that way.

I bit my lip so hard behind my mask that I could taste my own blood.

"Take her to Recovery," a male voice said from between the two bloodied hands he held up. "Wash up. Time for coffee."

Pulling the shroud of paper and plastic off my head, I followed Caitlin out of the operating theatre and down the stark, breezy corridor to Recovery. I ripped the shoe covers off, too, keeping my hand by her cheek as I hopped and struggled to keep up.

I didn't struggle for long. The orderly left her bed under a patch of ceiling decorated with cheerful stickers for children. I glared at him, but he left without a word. I dropped my disposable stuff in the bin by the entrance and paced around her bed, waiting for Caitlin to wake up. There were no visitor chairs in Recovery. You were either staff or a recovering patient.

I felt drained from standing in readiness to calm Caitlin while forcing myself to watch my first surgical procedure since I'd dropped out of university. Since Alanna had died. Since I'd sworn I'd hunt down the bastards who'd hurt her and. . . Caitlin. Right now, my primary concern was Caitlin. There was nothing more I could do for Alanna. Take care of Caitlin.

I waited and watched, seeing slight movements as the drugs wore off. Caitlin woke up sooner than they said she would. Even the doctors underestimated her.

"Stop smiling at me," Caitlin mumbled. My eyes flew to her face. She glared at the ceiling. My eyes followed hers to the Disney characters I knew she despised.

"Death to Winnie the Pooh?" I asked.

"Death and hell afterwards, for enjoying my pain," she replied slowly. She shifted so that she could see me. "You're all dressed up like the theatre staff. You didn't perform the procedure, did you?" Her eyes were wide with worry.

She didn't trust me. My heart hurt. Such a simple operation could have been done by an intern, if I'd finished my degree. "No," I replied. "A qualified surgeon did your skin grafts. I watched to make sure you were okay, just like I said I would."

She relaxed. "How did it go?"

I smiled. "The doctors patched you up and you snored."

Her brow wrinkled. "I don't snore. What else?"

I laughed. "The doctors are having strawberry tarts with their coffee today."

She looked wistful. "I wish I could join them."

"I can get you one as soon as you're cleared to go," I offered.

"A doctor or a tart?" Caitlin asked, starting to smile.

I stared at her, lost. Surely she couldn't be making fun of me.

"You'll get a doctor to give you the all clear and then I can buy you cake. . ." I began.

Her breathy laugh shut me up. "Thank you, Nathan,"

she said softly, closing her eyes. Somehow, I still felt like she was laughing at me.

"Any time," I replied. I meant it, too.

FORTY ONE

Four of them.
They all said they were called Chris.
All sounded different.
Hurt me differently.
Too dark to see them.
Didn't see their faces.
Only the voices.
Different voices, different hands.
Four different pricks who could only get a girl
by force in the dark.
Wanting to hurt them back. Kill them.
Couldn't get free.
So tired. . .
Enough of my nightmares for today. You promised
me cake, Nathan.

FORTY TWO

"Want to watch some TV?" I asked Caitlin. We were done with breakfast. I'd helped her in the bathroom while the trays were cleared away. I wasn't game to even mention the laptop. After her marathon effort two days ago, she'd agreed to try to tell me more yesterday, but it hadn't been long before she was too tired to talk.

She nodded and I hit the power on the remote. I flipped through the channels, hoping we wouldn't get stuck with any kids' shows.

"Oh, wait," she said suddenly. "That didn't look too bad." I blipped back to the one she indicated, with a bunch of people sitting in a helicopter. It looked familiar. "That one."

I settled into the chair beside her bed. "Is that. . . *Jurassic Park*? I haven't seen that since I was a kid."

Caitlin nodded, a slow smile appearing. "Nor have I." The smile faded fast.

"Do you want to watch this?" I asked her, my fingers

poised over the remote. I'd take all-day cartoons if it meant she wouldn't cry.

She looked resigned. "Sure. It'll be fine." Her eyes were already on the screen. She folded her arms across her chest, pressing her lips together.

I stared at her for a few minutes, just waiting.

"What?" she asked finally, turning to me.

I nodded at her crossed arms. "It doesn't look like you want to watch it. What's wrong?"

I think she held out for another minute before she relented. "The first time I saw it as a kid, I had nightmares about velociraptors for weeks."

"Have you seen it since?" I probed.

"No," she admitted. "But even the thought of them still freaks me out."

I fought to keep the laughter out of my voice. "So you don't like this movie because you think you might have nightmares after watching it?" I tried to keep my face expressionless.

"Yes," she replied defensively.

"Nightmares worse than the one you told me about yesterday?" I asked gently, my eyes not leaving hers.

Her face hardened. "No. Velociraptors sound like a picnic after. . . what they did to me." Her voice faded from fierce to a barely audible whisper. She swallowed. "Bring on the dinosaurs. Watching them eat people will be fun." Her expression was fierce.

I laughed. "Even the bloke on the toilet?"

She struggled not to smile, but she gave in with a breathy laugh. "Yes, even when the T-Rex eats the man on the toilet." She laughed properly. "There aren't enough scary scenes in toilets."

I grinned back. "Yeah, because the world needs more crappy horror scenes."

We both settled back to watch dinosaurs eat people, even the T-Rex with the toilet. I heard Caitlin's musical laughter again at that part and smiled to myself. Maybe she was finally recovering from her ordeal.

As the movie progressed, my thoughts turned dark once more. If Caitlin was more scared of the men who'd hurt her than a pack of vicious, intelligent dinosaurs, then I needed to know what she knew, so I could hunt the bastards down.

I resolved to try again later. I'd set up the laptop and ask her to tell me more as she cried and cried and. . . I tried to be a heartless bastard. Yeah. . . no.

It could wait until tomorrow. Let her be happy for today.

Oh, wait. No, not tomorrow either. The next day. Tomorrow'd be her eighteenth birthday and I didn't want to spoil it by upsetting her. The day after tomorrow, then.

Two days of peace wouldn't be too much of a delay. It's not like the hospital was going to be overrun with velociraptors or vicious bastards, plus she'd been in surgery yesterday. She deserved a rest. She'd been unconscious for almost two weeks — what more could happen if we waited another two days?

FORTY THREE

The second I stepped out of the lift I heard Caitlin's voice. I'd gone downstairs to get some flowers – it was her birthday, after all, and I didn't know what else to get her.

I sprinted down her ward to the sound of her screaming. Another nightmare – and I wasn't there to wake her from it. I hadn't been gone long, but I'd wanted to wake her with the sweet-scented flowers. Liliums, the florist had called them. Ah, fuck, who cared what they were called? My feet pounded on the carpet as her screaming grew louder. Where in hell was her guard? Fuck, Navid had been standing guard by her door when I left, drinking his coffee like his life depended on it. . .

I skidded into the room to see the nightmare had become more real than it should have. She fought someone real. Someone I'd never seen before. Someone who should never have been allowed in.

"Leave her alone!" I ordered, striding over to her. I threw the flowers into the sink, barely registering that there was already a bunch there.

In shock, he let go of her and Caitlin fell harmlessly back to the bed. I saw her eyes snap open, disoriented and scared.

He was still too close to Caitlin, his eyes not leaving her.

"What did you do to her?" I thundered, taking another step toward him. He started to back away, so I spared a glance at Caitlin.

She blinked, lying there, stunned. Then she saw him. Her eyes widened in shock.

She didn't invite him — she was as surprised to see him as I was. I needed to get him away from her and out of here, so she'd be safe again. "Get away from her!"

"I didn't mean to scare you. I wanted. . ." he began, but I cut him short with a fist to the face that he didn't see until it was too late. He was piss-weak, though, going down like a sack of surprised potatoes. I don't think he'd ever been in a fight before. He climbed awkwardly to his feet, backing away in the direction of the door.

He looked at Caitlin. He saw something in her face that hardened some sort of resolve in him. Instead of leaving, his face firmed up and he tried to fight me. I dodged a few wild swings that didn't connect as I waited for the opportunity to lay this idiot out on the floor for the second time. This time, he wouldn't be getting up again. Right. . .

I was forced to stop mid-swing as Caitlin stood between us. Oh, God, she shouldn't be out of bed yet. She was shaking and I reached out to steady her at almost the same instant he did.

"Don't you dare touch me." She lifted a face contorted with fury. He immediately tore his hands away.

He edged away from her. His eyes jerked from her hands and wrists to her ankles and feet, slowly dragging his gaze up to her thighs, his horror growing as he stared at her rainbow of bruises. The sheer sight of her was enough to incapacitate him, the useless idiot.

Movement caught my eye and I saw a trickle of fresh blood pool beside her foot. A scarlet flower blossomed on her nightdress. The skin graft. She'd ripped her stitches. I needed to get her off her feet. Oh God, how much was this hurting her? How was she still standing?

"I want nothing to do with either of you if you're going to fight like animals. Get your hands off me!"

Her screech was directed at me. I only tightened my grip on her. I wasn't letting go – she'd fall without support. She was already visibly sagging with the effort. Or the blood loss. Or the pain.

Oh God, Caitlin! Don't do this.

"Not until you're back in bed. You can yell at me or him to your heart's content from there. I know how much pain this is costing you." The last part was spoken in a low voice in her ear as I lifted her in my arms. She curled up in pain – I could feel every muscle as tense as she could clench it – and she didn't relax when I set her down on her bed. She looked like she wanted to scream at how much it hurt and it took every bit of her self-control not to.

"I can get you more pain medication. I'll call a nurse – you don't need to hurt like this," I said urgently, praying he hadn't done anything else to her before I'd arrived.

I ignored the bloke behind me, all of my attention focussed on her, waiting for her reply.

She turned away from me to speak to him, as if I didn't

exist.

"Jason." She sounded almost hypnotised. "Something else. . . scared me. . . and I was just shocked to be woken up." Her voice had gone deathly quiet. Tears flowed down her face, but still she sat, rigidly upright, her eyes on him. She stretched out a hand to him, every finger bandaged and splinted.

I turned so I could see his expression. His eyes were just about popping out of his head and he looked green as he gasped out, "Oh my God, what did they do to you?" He turned and fled.

"No. Jason. . . wait!" she called after him, but I doubt he heard her. When he didn't come back, she dropped back down on the pillows, her eyes closed. No more tears escaped her iron control.

I crossed to the door of the room in time to see him stumble into the toilet at the end of the ward. I heard him retch as the door swung shut behind him.

"He left in a hurry," Navid said beside me, inclining his head toward the nauseous numb-nuts.

I stared at him. "Where were you? How the hell did he get in to Caitlin's room?" I hissed, as quietly as I could so Caitlin wouldn't hear me.

He shrugged, far from fazed. "Call of nature. He's her friend — that girl Jo's brother. He's on the list. Of course I let him in. She had him there, you'd disappeared and I've been up all night because my son's teething. I've had two coffees already this morning. I needed to take a piss."

I wanted to break the calm expression on his face, but I knew he was a better fighter than me. I'd had one sparring session with him in the gym and I'd sworn never to do it again. Not ever and not now, either. Shaking my head, I headed back to Caitlin.

"Is he coming back?" she asked, her eyes still closed.

"No, he looked pretty sick," I answered.

She sat up and shook her head. "He shouldn't have come. He faints at the sight of blood. What was he thinking. . ."

It's not as if there's that much blood, I thought sourly. Bloody wanker. He wouldn't have been any use to her on that beach. I tried to ignore the thought that followed it. I'd been shocked when I saw how badly injured she was, too. I couldn't get away from her fast enough.

But I'd promised. . .

I wanted to hug her tightly, wishing I could forget. I opened my arms, offering.

"No," Caitlin said, her hands up like a mime artist, showing me an invisible wall that I couldn't penetrate. Her face was set. "I said don't touch me." She took a deep breath. "What in hell did you think you were doing?"

"I swore I wouldn't let anyone hurt you! He was touching you and you were screaming!" I replied, louder than I meant to. I didn't regret punching the idiot. I wish I'd knocked him out with the first blow.

"You swore you wouldn't let *them* hurt me again. That doesn't mean you pick fights with my friends." Caitlin sounded angry as all hell. "He never hurt me. My *friends* don't hurt me." She glared at me. "Right?"

My hands itched to wrap around the neck of her green friend and choke the life out of him, but I swallowed painfully before I replied, "I'll never hurt you. I was trying to protect you. You know that, right?" Shit. She was going to kick me out for trying to keep her safe.

Her expression softened the tiniest bit. "I know, but you're wasting your effort. Save the violence for the bastards who really deserve it."

I didn't trust myself to say a word. I nodded fervently and looked away. My eyes landed on the bouquets in the sink. "I'll go get some vases for your flowers." I grabbed them.

"Flowers?" Her question came out entirely devoid of emotion.

"Flowers," I repeated, holding them out. "Happy birthday, Caitlin." Dragging my heavy heart with me, I left.

FORTY FOUR

Forced kisses. A violation.
The breath of a cruel mouth on mine.
Smell of stale old beer. Like a pub the morning
after a party.
Pathetic and mean.
Taste of ash.
Dry hard lips.
Dry tongue, rough and forceful.
Discarded.
No.
Passed to another.
Now what?
Arms closed.
Steel.
Trapped.
Going to hurt
No

FORTY FIVE

"Today we'll take the dressings off your hands. Your fingers should have almost healed up by now." Nurse Judith sounded really pleased at the prospect. She started pulling the curtains around the bed, the rings scraping on the rail. "You, out."

I looked up to find the nurse glaring at me, jabbing her finger at the door.

I was sitting fairly comfortably in the visitor's chair beside Caitlin's bed. We were watching a Simpsons rerun on her TV and every time she laughed my heart felt a little lighter.

Caitlin had barely spoken to me in three days, except when it was absolutely necessary, but this morning it seemed like she'd decided to forgive me a little. At least, she'd thanked me with a smile for helping her with breakfast. I still held out hope that she'd be happy to have me here in hospital with her — maybe having her hands healed and whole would help. Hell, it'd make me feel better to know she was less helpless.

I stood up so that I could look down on the grumpy nurse.

She had no excuse to kick me out this time. Baring Caitlin's hands was hardly R-rated, especially as I'd seen them in a far worse state than they'd be in today. In a month, her fingers had almost healed straight. I wanted to be there to celebrate with her, if she'd let me.

I glanced at Caitlin to see if there was the slightest chance that she agreed with the nurse. If she didn't want me here, that was different.

Caitlin looked at me fearfully, her eyes widening as panic seized her. "No, I want Nathan to stay," she managed to say. Her eyes said *please* when her mouth was silent.

With a slight nod to Caitlin and a shrug to the blonde nurse, I sat down again. Caitlin leaned closer to me and I placed an arm lightly on the pillows behind her, around but not quite touching her shoulders, ready to take it away if she objected. To my surprise, she relaxed into my embrace as she held out her hands to the nurse. "Do it," Caitlin said, swallowing hard. I felt her tense as the nurse took hold of her right hand, the one farther away from me.

The nurse freed Caitlin's hands as if she were eagerly unwrapping a fragile gift while wanting to preserve the paper. She peeled the gauze away with deft fingers and pulled off the splints. I almost didn't realise when Caitlin's fingers were bare. I thought I was looking at another layer of bandages. Pale, thin and white, her fingers were like brittle, petrified sticks of driftwood.

Nurse Judith's hands were as pale as her complexion, but they looked in the pink of health beneath Caitlin's damaged digits. I ached to hold Caitlin's delicate hand in mine, but I couldn't say why.

"Okay, let's see how well you can move these. Just bend them, one at a time," the nurse coaxed.

I held my breath, my eyes on each finger as it curled up like a salted slug before straightening again. Her thumb looked fine, as did her index finger. . . only her middle finger provoked a grimace of pain as Caitlin tried to curl it into her palm.

"Good," cooed the nurse, nodding her approval. "Well, four out of five healing perfectly is good. You might have trouble with that middle one, but I'm sure you won't need it. You might even be nicer to us nurses. . ."

Caitlin's face broke into a beaming smile as she flipped the finger at the nurse.

Nurse Judith looked put out. "Maybe not."

Caitlin laughed. "I'm always nice to nurses, except when they tell me I'm not going to recover. I'll be fine. You'll see."

The nurse sighed. "Yup, another arrogant doctor." She held out her hand and Caitlin placed her left hand in the grumpy woman's clutches.

She rested her right hand on the sheet, where it blended in like a pale spider. I fought the urge to take her hand in mine as she wiggled her fingers absently.

"And the other hand?" Nurse Judith asked expectantly.

Both Caitlin and I looked at her fragile left hand. This time she bent all her fingers at once, like a spider curling up to die, before spreading them out straight. Some of them didn't straighten completely. "Some stiffness," she mused. "But better." She placed both hands side by side in her lap.

"Physio with finger exercises next. Won't that be fun!" She moved her fingers, simulating typing on a keyboard.

Soon she'd be able to type up her own nightmares. She wouldn't need my help and I'd have to ask her to tell me before she sent me away. Soon. I didn't know whether to be happy for her freedom or sad for mine.

"Here, I'll help you wash your hands," I heard Nurse Judith say, bringing my mind back to the two women in front of me.

The nurse carefully wiped Caitlin's hands with a face washer from the bathroom and helped her dry them on a towel. She threw them both into a bag for dirty linen in the corner and leaned in closer to Caitlin. "Do you want me to go see if I can get some bubbly from the kitchen?"

Caitlin shook her head. "I don't believe there's any alcohol for drinking in a hospital."

Nurse Judith winked. "There is – for the candlelight dinners in the maternity ward. I'll go get you some and you can toast having your hands back!"

She headed out of the room.

I shifted out of the visitor's chair and perched on the edge of Caitlin's bed. She had a big smile on her face as she looked down at her hands.

I couldn't help smiling – I'd never seen her look so happy. "Congratulations," I said.

She lifted her eyes so she smiled at me. She held out her hands as if she was drying nail polish. Her hands were trembling a little and I reached out to take hers in mine.

Words couldn't describe how relieved I was that her hands had healed okay. I wanted to shake her hand, but even the slightest pressure of my fingers had her trying to pull out of my grasp, so I stopped. Lightheaded, I did something silly. I touched my lips to the back of first one hand, then the other. Her hands were warm and moist, like I imagined her lips would feel after she'd just had a sip of coffee.

Caitlin laughed, breaking into my reverie, her eyes puzzled. "What was that for?" she asked.

I forced a smile, trying to make my tone light. "I'm not sure. It just seemed like the right thing to do."

And now what I wanted to do most was kiss her properly, but not on her hands. There's a stupid idea. I let go of her and turned away to look out of the window. I looked in vain for the spider in her corner web, but all I saw was the image of Caitlin's ghostly hands spread across my vision, finally free.

FORTY SIX

I remember waking up and it was dark.
Still groggy from the drugs, I couldn't see.
My head hurt.
I was tied up.
My body resting on cold concrete. I felt bruised, not knowing how long I'd lain there.
Shifting. Something harder by my hip.
They didn't. They did?
They missed it. Let me keep it.
Stupid.
Thank you.
Must reach it to free myself.
Painfully twisting, trying to reach my pocket.
Need something sharp.
Shoulders burning, straining, reaching. . .
Fingertips found plastic.
Now for something sharp.
Tiny scissors, slow but safer than a knife.
Didn't want to risk hurting my hands with the big blade.
Slicing strands, sawing. . . then my hands were free.

Slipping the card back into my pocket. Just in case.
Dizzy when I stood up.
Angry voices in the dark. Shouting at Chris.
A door opened and there was light.
I ran for it, trying to push past the standing shape in the doorway.
Room swirling into darkness again. I was falling.
His hands on me.
He caught me, so I didn't fall.
Helping.
He offered me food and water.
Something for the pain.
Help.
But not enough.

FORTY SEVEN

Caitlin sat at the window, her hand a pale spider on the glass, her eyes scanning the lake and the gardens below. She sat so long without moving that I thought she'd fallen asleep, until she spoke. "What's the date, Nathan? It's September, isn't it?" She didn't look away from the window.

I admitted that I didn't know the exact date, but that, yes, it was September.

"The last time I was outside in daylight it was still winter. Now it's spring." She heaved a big sigh and turned her dark eyes on me. "I want to see the flowers."

I'll bring you any flowers you want. I'll fill your room with them – as long as I can keep you safe.

I looked at the bin in the corner, which now held the remains of her birthday flowers. Mine had outlasted Jason's, but only by a day.

"I don't know if it's a good idea to leave the hospital yet," I hedged. "Maybe after you've been discharged – it can't be long."

"The gardens downstairs are still hospital grounds," she stated. "And I've seen at least two patients walking around in them. I think they were smoking."

"So you want to go downstairs and inhale lots of passive cigarette smoke?" That was the least of my concerns. I was worried about the difficulty of keeping her safe in the grounds, with their winding paths and spots where you were invisible to most eyes. "What if one of the smokers is actually one of your attackers waiting for a second chance?"

"Then I'll have to run them over," she said softly, her voice muffled. "Anyway, only one of them smoked and he's dead."

I lost interest in what she was saying, watching in fascination as she struggled out of the hospital gown and into her borrowed surgical scrubs. Her hands were paler than the rest of her skin between the dressings, but the dressings were far fewer than they'd initially been. Her back looked smooth, the curve of her shoulders down to her spine unmarred by any gauze now. There were scars, of course, but these were starting to fade. She let out a whimper as she pulled the V-necked shirt over her head. I tensed, waiting. I knew something must have hurt her, but she seemed determined not to ask for help.

I watched as she arched her back, pulling the pants on over the patch on her thigh where the stitches had been removed only yesterday. She whimpered a little more, then gritted her teeth and dragged the pants up to her waist.

She saw me watching, but didn't say anything until she'd finished. "You could have averted your eyes. It's considered polite."

"I could have, but you should have asked me for help," I

returned, keeping my voice even. "If you'd wanted privacy, you could have changed in the bathroom, or closed the curtains around your bed." She wouldn't admit that she couldn't do either of those, I realised. Nor would she ask for help. I wished I'd done what any normal person would have and looked away, instead of waiting for her to stop and ask me for help. Then maybe I wouldn't have felt like such a pervert, watching an injured girl struggle to dress herself. I wanted to apologise.

Caitlin wasn't listening. She eyed the wheelchair outside her room, much further than she could walk unaided. She stood up carefully, clamping her mouth shut. She took a step, her face white from the effort, but her eyes spoke volumes about pain. My heart felt crushed like a Coke can – I could almost hear the sound of it crunching in her clenched fist.

Don't do this to yourself, angel – it's painful to watch.

I gave in, standing up and moving to bar her way before she took another step. For a moment, she looked up at me, determined not to be cowed, but the pain was too much for her and she closed her eyes as she crumpled. I was ready; I had my arms around her, supporting her weight, before she could hit the floor. I lifted her and carried her back to where she'd been sitting on the edge of her bed.

"You don't need to fight me," I said softly. "I'm not here to hurt you. Save your energy so you can recover for when you do need to fight."

She was still pale, shaking where she sat. Even as she opened her eyes, they looked down and wouldn't meet mine.

I sank to a crouch in front of her on the floor. "If you

don't recover, they win."

She stared at me. "I'm getting better."

I dropped my voice lower, aiming to be persuasive. "If you let me help you, you'll get better faster. And it won't hurt as much, either."

"I'm not asking for your help. You know I won't." Stubbornly, she pressed her lips together and looked away.

I couldn't charm her. Maybe I could shock it out of her. Not like I'd get anything any other way.

"Who helped you before, Caitlin? Who brought you food, water, medicine? Someone helped you survive." I kept my voice low, so only she could hear me.

She looked back at me, shocked, swallowing convulsively, before closing her eyes. Her voice was barely more than a whisper. "Someone who didn't wait for me to ask. Someone kind. Someone. . . I haven't talked about."

Stubborn little thing, I thought, jubilant that she told me more than anyone else and uneasy that she could remember so much. How much more had she remembered that I didn't know? "It's polite to wait 'til you ask. But even if you're not going to ask, I'm still going to try to help you. I won't let them win."

Her eyes were still closed, so I couldn't tell what her reaction was. Yet my eyes never left her face.

"I want to go outside." Her voice surprised me. Something in her expression said I couldn't stop her.

"And how are you going to get there?" I asked.

She looked across the corridor. "I'm going to reach that wheelchair, then I'm going to use it to go down in the lift and outside."

"What if you fall again?" I asked her.

She bit her lip. "Then I'll crawl."

I believed her. But the mental image of her crawling commando-style across the floor was pretty damn funny.

"How will you push the wheelchair?" I struggled to keep a straight face.

She held out her hands, which shook slightly even as she tried to hold them still. "I can use my hands a little. It's downhill from the front entrance to the gardens, so that should be easy."

"How will you get back up the hill to the hospital?" I asked her.

She lifted her chin. "I'll wait until someone offers me a hand."

"What if no one else is out there to make the offer?"

She bit her lip again. "Then I'll wait for security to come looking for me."

At the thought of her waiting in the garden until security came looking for her, I laughed. I couldn't think of her doing anything more senseless when it came to her own safety – and Caitlin wasn't that stupid.

"Or you could ask me to come with you," I suggested as I lifted her from the bed and over to the wheelchair.

"Thank you," she said softly, looking down. Hesitantly, she placed her hands on the wheels and I held my breath. I didn't want her fragile fingers getting hurt all over again, struggling to handle a wheelchair. I couldn't keep up this show of indifference. If she went without me, I was damn well going to follow her to make sure she stayed safe.

Caitlin looked up at me, smiling impishly. "So, are you coming?"

My face lifted with a smile, taking my heart up with it.

"Sure," I said. "The downhill path goes all the way through the garden to the lake. Someone's going to have to be there to fish you out."

She stared at me in disbelief.

"You'll see." I shrugged, starting to push her down the corridor to the lift.

I was bloody glad she couldn't see my face, because I couldn't keep the grin off it. She trusted me more than anyone else and she still wanted me around.

FORTY EIGHT

When we reached the lake, Caitlin started to laugh. I helped her sit on a bench by the edge of the water. She stretched her bare foot out but we were too far away for her toes to reach the murky brown surface. She pulled her foot back quickly, her toes lightly brushing the grass beneath the seat.

"So, are you going in?" I asked her, nodding at the water.

She laughed a little more. "No, it's cold and dirty. I'll leave the lake for the ducks and the fish." More soberly, she continued, "And I'm not sure if I should even consider swimming yet. I'd probably have to recover more before I could swim, or even go in the water." She stared out over the lake, her fingers resting on the cotton covering the transplanted skin on her thigh.

I sat beside her in silence, waiting for her to break it.

"Oh, look!" she cried suddenly, pointing across the lake.

I could see ripples on the surface, but nothing remarkable, and I said as much.

"Ducklings – look, four of them!" She pointed again, counting them for me. I could barely discern something small and brown on top of the ripples. She looked at me hopefully. "Can we go to the other side of the lake to see them better?"

I lifted her back into the wheelchair and pushed her to the paths on the other side of the lake, where they became the maze I'd been trying to avoid.

As we reached the far side, we could see the little ducks climbing up beside the waterfall that fed the lake, into the garden bed above. Full of misgivings, I took her further along one of the paths, into the gardens where the ducklings had disappeared.

Around a corner we found a small pond, hidden from view by manicured hedges, where an adult duck swam with a whole family of ducklings. There must have been at least ten of them.

Caitlin dropped to her knees beside the pond and sat motionless, entranced by the small fluffy things floating on the surface of the water. I stood near her, mesmerised by the smile on her face as she watched the ducks. I still had enough presence of mind to look around every few minutes, worried for her safety.

I heard their voices before I saw them.

"I give it another hour or two. Then it's pretty much getting dark – when I give up 'til tomorrow," one drawled.

"So if I stay five minutes longer than you and I spot her, I get her all to myself," the second taunted.

"If she comes out. All the hospital will say is that she's in a critical condition – no visitors – but it's been weeks. What makes you think it'll be today?"

"Why today or any other day? No one's critical for weeks. Either she's dead or she'll be discharged any day. Bet you a beer it's today." Two sounded bored. I heard the repeated scrape and click of a lighter, but he was too far away for me to smell the smoke from his cigarette.

"Okay. Bet you a coffee she's not as pretty as all the pictures. . ." One of the voices faded as he moved down the path away from us.

"Angel," I leaned down to say in a low voice beside her ear, "are you ready to give press interviews yet?"

"Hmm?" She looked up at me in surprise. "Interviews?"

"There's a press crew around, waiting for you. I heard them talking."

She went pale, her smile evaporating. "I don't want to, oh hell, not yet."

"Time to go back inside, then." I held out my arms, ready to help her up.

She looked wistful. "We're pretty well hidden here. We could stay and hope they'll just go away."

Against my better judgement, I gave in, with conditions. "If they do see us, I'll get you inside as fast as I can."

"Okay." She looked up at me with inviting eyes, her eager smile back. "Oh, come on, they're so cute. Take a look at the baby ducks. I've never seen ducklings this close before."

I watched the ducklings scoot around the pond for a few moments, before turning my attention back to her. She looked so happy, as if there were nothing else on her mind at all. As if none of this had ever happened.

I looked around again, more as a precaution than any feeling that it was necessary. Sunlight glinted off something.

It took me a second to realise it was a camera lens.

"Time to go, angel," I told her. "Look, they're taking photos of us."

I lifted her back to the wheelchair and started to push her up the shortest path to the hospital entrance.

"Wait!" I heard the shout behind me. "Please, I just want to ask a few questions!"

"Do you want to answer them, angel?" I asked her, walking as fast as I could with her.

"No." She sounded scared.

I broke into a run as we approached the doors, trying to get her to the lifts before they could follow us. I caught the eye of the security guard as we sped past. I jerked my head in the direction of the reporters following us and he nodded, moving to the entrance to bar their way.

We made it into a lift just before the doors closed and travelled back up to her floor in silence. Too out of breath to say anything, I helped Caitlin back to her room and into her bed before I collapsed into the chair beside her.

I grabbed for the water jug, sloshing water into a glass and gulping most of it down as I struggled to catch my breath.

"Why would any reporter want to interview me?" Caitlin asked, bewildered.

I looked up from my glass to her, wondering if she was joking. "The missing girl back from the dead? When anyone else would have died? You're a real-life Harry Potter — look." I rummaged through the pocket of the laptop bag and pulled out the newspaper I'd kept from that first morning in hospital. An old photo of her, taken before she went missing, smiled from the front page, above the headline *CAITLIN FOUND*. The article itself was short, telling how her body had been discovered on a south-west beach early that morning where she'd been left to die, before she'd been transported to a hospital in Perth where she remained in a critical condition.

Caitlin looked at the article, still puzzled.

"This is all the press has on you," I told her. "The police won't tell them anything else. They want an interview with you, but the hospital won't give out any more information, either."

"But. . . I don't want to talk about it. Why would they care about me?"

I laughed. "Because you're news. They've had almost daily features with lots of pictures of you while you were missing, hoping someone would come out with information that would help the police find you. Now someone's found you and they want to know all about it." I paused. "It probably helps that you look good in photographs."

"What will they do now, when they took photos but didn't get any answers?"

"Print the pictures and make something up." I smiled broadly. "We should read the paper tomorrow." And I'll keep that one, too, I thought but didn't say. "I'll go speak to security and make sure you don't get any visitors or phone calls you don't want."

FORTY NINE

"Well that's fucking useless. You and her on the front cover of *The West* – what's the point trying to hide her now? And you've learned. . . what, exactly?"

I winced, wishing I hadn't called in my report. But it was better than receiving an angry phone call when tomorrow's paper had my picture in it. "She's told me what she remembers, but it's all vague and hazy. There were four men who hurt her, she heard the name Chris, the red Mercedes, being tied up in the dark, repeated abuse, the names cut into her skin. . ." I swallowed, finding it hard to continue.

"Most of that we already knew before she woke up. New info, Nathan – what has she told you to help us find them?"

"They held her outside the city, somewhere outside of any town – the water they gave her to drink wasn't chlorinated city water. She didn't hear any sounds from outside, so it was well insulated or isolated," I said quickly, trying to tell every tiny detail. "I think she knows a lot more, but she needs someone to help her remember it. That takes time and. . ."

"Well, you're out of fucking time now. Unless she spills her guts to you in the next hour or two, it's time for a change of plan." I heard a slurp, as if he was drinking coffee.

"What change of plan?" I asked uneasily.

"None of them are stupid enough to come after her in hospital. So she's going home. Maybe they'll target her there." He sounded completely unfazed. "Better than a month of close surveillance with nothing to show for it, which is what we have now."

"You're going to leave Caitlin unprotected and use her as *bait* for those bastards?" I blurted out, horrified.

"Now, no name-calling. They're fucking potential terror suspects. The girl would be dead anyway if it weren't for your intervention, and by all accounts, including yours, she's pretty damn damaged anyway, so it's a small risk compared to what else and who else could be at stake if we don't get them." I heard his business-like tone but it sounded pretty fucking callous to me.

"She's not damaged. She's recovering. You mean I saved her life only to risk it again to catch the. . . *potential terror suspects* who tried to kill her the first time? I can't ask her to do that. . . she'll never agree to be bait in a trap. Especially not if it means they'll get near her again!" I barked into my phone. Some hospital visitors carrying flowers looked at me in alarm, before hurrying off down the ward.

"Fuck, Nathan, you're not stupid enough to think we're going to tell her, are you? She'll go home and we'll just keep an eye out for anyone suspicious approaching her house. We'll send a team in and we'll have our suspects!" He laughed. I wanted to smash his phone through his teeth. Maybe calling in reports wasn't such a bad thing, after all. I'd hate to find out what ASIO would do to me for punching my superior in the face.

I tried to keep my voice down, but it was bloody hard. "And what if our team is slow and doesn't get there in time? What if they reach Caitlin before we can stop them?"

He'd stopped laughing. "That's a risk we'll have to take. If she won't tell us what we need to know, then she's more valuable as a possible target than as a source of information. Don't make this personal, Nathan. She's not your sister. She's a girl you barely know."

I lost it. "Yes, sir, I know Caitlin's not one of my sisters, because Alanna died in a lot of pain at the hands of your *suspects* and Chris will be next if we don't find them. Caitlin's the miracle girl who managed to survive, despite everything they did to her. We owe her for any info she can give us on the suspects – I owe her, if she can help me keep them from Chris." My voice broke. "Please – let me stay with her for another week or two, in case I notice anything the surveillance guys don't pick up. Maybe. . . maybe she'll tell me more and we can still go with the original plan, finding out where they are so we can arrest them before they reach her."

"What'll you do if I say no?" He sounded amused, but it wasn't fucking funny.

"I'll. . ." Obey orders and let Caitlin die? Ignore my orders and protect her anyway? Beg you to change your mind? Shoot her myself because it's more humane than what they'll do to her? "I'll take personal leave and do what I can on my own time."

There was silence, then another slurp. "You have two more weeks, tops. But you tell her nothing about who you work for or that she's under surveillance. I want her to look scared and worried, like an easy target. You'll have to use every bit of your charm on this one, if you expect her to let you live in her house." He took a deep breath. "Fuck. Good luck keeping her alive, Nathan. It'll be bloody bad press for our department if we manage to accidentally kill the girl on the front cover of tomorrow's *West*."

Oh, shit. My charm wasn't worth shit with Caitlin. And she'd never survive without me. "I'll do my utmost," I swore, desperately hoping it would be enough to keep Caitlin alive.

"You do that," he said before he hung up.

I let out a long-held breath, wondering what the chances were of me not fucking this up. Slim to none, was my best guess. And I was betting with Caitlin's life. The stakes were far too high for me, and I couldn't even tell her what I'd done. Fuck, I wouldn't want to, either. If I failed, she'd kill me.

FIFTY

She'd had her fingers free for two days, so they discharged Caitlin that afternoon, before any more press turned up. I offered to give her a lift home right away and, rather than have to call anyone else and wait longer, she accepted.

Now that her stitches were out, she could walk a little, but I was the one who walked alongside the unfamiliar nurse pushing her wheelchair. She was slow, but I kept pace with them until we reached the outside doors. I saw Michael take up his position on a couch in the foyer. He nodded to me once before turning his eyes back to Caitlin

Secure in the knowledge that she was under surveillance still and she'd be safe 'til I returned, I asked Caitlin to wait while I brought the car to her. She nodded and shifted to a seat by the door, before the nurse whisked the wheelchair back inside. I set off across the car park, my swift strides carrying me quickly across the tarmac. Surveillance or not, I didn't want to leave Caitlin alone for long.

I pulled the car up under the portico at the entrance, but

there was an ambulance in my way. I could see Caitlin sitting on the bench beside it, looking little and vulnerable. She stared at the paving below her dangling feet, for the bench was too high for her toes to touch the ground. She wore clothes I'd hurriedly bought from the nearest supermarket and they didn't fit her. Even the cheap pair of thongs hung from her feet, a few centimetres of green foam rubber clearly visible past her heels. An abandoned waif in oversized clothing, looking as lonely as if she'd been left there for good. My heart ached for her as I waited and watched.

Michael caught my eye and nodded again as he stood up. He stuck his magazine under his arm and marched out of the hospital, without another glance at Caitlin or me. His watch was over for the day – now it was my responsibility to get her home, before the next surveillance shift started at her house.

I waited patiently until the ambulance officers headed off. I drove into the space they'd sat in, right in front of Caitlin. From forlorn to frantic, the change was as sudden as cutting the car's engine. I stopped and she panicked, lurching to her feet and nearly tripping as she tried to retreat inside the hospital foyer.

I got out of the car, running around to her. "Caitlin, what's wrong? What are you doing?"

She shook her head. "They're not going to take me back. I'll die first!"

I looked around wildly, scanning the car park for any sign of danger, but I saw none. What had she seen that I'd missed?

I approached her slowly, but she shrank away, backing

up against the window beside the automatic doors. "I won't get into their car again. Not you – you can't take me back!" Her eyes were huge with horror.

Their car? My car. Oh, fuck, I forgot about the car.

I stood in front of her now, shaping my expression into a smile to mask my desire to smack myself in the head for being so stupid. "It's not their car. It's mine."

"No – I trusted you!"

I started to understand the extent of her terror.

Through the glass behind her, I saw the hospital security guard speaking to the receptionist as she pointed urgently at us. He turned to look and started toward the entrance, looking grim. He wasn't the guard who'd been on duty that morning, keeping the reporters from Caitlin. This was a new bloke who didn't know me or her, and this scene looked bad from any perspective. Oh, shit.

Every instinct went against it, but I forced myself to back away from her, my hands up in a gesture of surrender. Behind her, one security guard had become two and the newcomer knew me on sight, not least of all from his help that morning. I could see him speaking urgently to the first bloke, his hands waving wildly as he shook his head.

The helpful one. . . I struggled to remember his name. I knew I'd spoken to him before and he'd had a distinct accent. . . Sam? No, Sean. The dark-haired Irish bloke.

Sean the security guard looked enquiringly at me and I gave a slight nod, which he returned, walking away. His colleague looked grumpy, but headed away, too.

Right, that sorted security escorting me off the premises and leaving Caitlin with no one else to watch over her. I still had to get her into the car and home.

Looking at Caitlin again, I pointed at the bench. "I'm going to sit down. If you want, you can join me," I told her evenly, as I took careful steps to the bench and plonked my bum on it.

She was slower to move, but it was only a few seconds before she slumped down heavily on the bench next to me. I regretted letting her stay on her feet so long — she looked pale and clammy already.

"This is my car. It's been my car since I turned twenty-one and my parents bought it for me for my birthday," I said steadily. Yeah, they'd bought me a blocky, conservative car that said I had money but couldn't take off fast, for that wouldn't mean a smooth ride in the luxury bloody sedan.

It had a comfortable back seat, though, that'd seen some use. . . I shut that thought down before it went any further.

Focus. Caitlin.

She stared at it, licking her lips nervously. "They had a car just like this one. They pulled me into it and drove me there. . . and. . ." She gulped back tears, not wanting to finish her sentence.

"Check the number plate, if you like. Then you'll see they probably just had the same car as I do." If you know the number plate, now's the time to tell me.

She shook her head. "I never saw the number plate. I wouldn't know."

"Would you like to check the car? I'll pop the bonnet and the boot and open all the doors. If you find any of them, I will happily beat the crap out of them for you, with the tyre iron, even," I offered cheerfully. Behind my back, I crossed my fingers, desperate for any luck I could get.

She let out a held breath and laughed, a little nervously,

but it was a laugh, nonetheless.

"But. . . you swear you don't work for them?" She smiled as she spoke, as if she felt silly even voicing the words.

I did my best to take her question seriously, clearing my throat before I replied, "No. And even if I had, I'd say that arrangement would have ended about the time one of them decided to try and kill me on that beach where I found you." I paused and held out my hand. "Would you still like a lift home?"

Don't get into cars with strangers. No one knew that better than Caitlin. God, I wish I had half the courage it took her to do it again after what happened the first time.

Her breath hissed through her teeth as she gave me a frightened smile. "Yes. Could you help me to the car, too, please? I think I've had about all the walking I can take today."

FIFTY ONE

Waking up on sand. Don't know how I got there.
Not dark anymore. Stars. Clouds.
Moon. West over the water.
My hands. Not my hands. . .
Trust me.
So cold.
Indistinct voices.
Couldn't focus.
Don't remember.
Don't remember shouting, fighting.
No warning. Gunshots, more than one, in quick
succession.
It's over.
Bright lights, strangers. Scared.
Police shouting, warning, shooting. . .
One shot.
Me, screaming.
Why don't I remember?

FIFTY TWO

Caitlin glanced at the back seat as I lifted her through the passenger side door. I didn't follow her gaze. I knew no one had left underwear or anything else incriminating there. The last girl who'd lain on my back seat hadn't been wearing any underwear. . . I cut that thought short. This was hardly the time.

I turned my eyes back to Caitlin's worried ones. Guessing her thoughts, I told her, "You have a window that you can open if you want to – and a door you can leave by if you decide you don't want to be in the car. Just give me a bit of warning on the freeway – so I can pull into the emergency stopping lane before you get out."

I shut the door for her and strode to my own side of the car, sliding into the seat easily as if nothing was wrong.

Caitlin clicked the seatbelt into place and clutched at it with white-knuckled fingers of fear. "Saucer eyes," she murmured. She closed her eyes, as if struggling to remember something.

I started the car, trying harder to forget. The first time I saw her.

The red car parked on the side of the road, windows down. A spiral of smoke wafting out of the open window, the smell of the cigarette carried away on the winter wind. Watching, as they did the same.

There were plenty of people around. Commuters in suits, tradesmen in fluorescent shirts from the construction site nearby and casually dressed students on their way to university. The intermittent clicking from the crosswalk lights to the east. A ranting religious man handing out flyers, trying to save people from the end of the world. Couldn't save her.

A moving curtain of darkness in the light breeze, turned to deep red wine in the sunlight. It was her hair I saw first, drawing my eye to the rest of her.

She walked close to the kerb, a cheerful smile on her face, her loose hair rippling and catching the light. She wore a blinding white t-shirt that proclaimed she was an angel. The faint outline of her nipples punctuated the word through the cotton in the cold wind, calling the proclamation into question. An angel, but an earthly one without wings, unless they were attached to her feet. Her every step was fluid, graceful, as if she were dancing through the crowd of people, from paving stone to paving stone. I stopped watching them. I only had eyes for her. I thought she was the most incredible girl I'd ever seen and I wanted her, my angel, like I'd never wanted anyone or anything else before. God, even the memory was torture, seeing how much she'd changed.

What did I want to do to her? Hell, anything she asked me to. She was that stunning.

Of course they saw her. Of the hundreds of people walking down the Terrace, they had to pick her. Someone spoke to her, before getting out of the car. She said something else and opened the back door. For a moment, Caitlin's face lit up with a beautiful, heart-stopping smile as she leaned down to speak to someone inside.

I was mesmerised, caught up in half-formed fantasies about what I wanted to do with this girl. Precious seconds that I couldn't afford to lose. Seconds that could have cost Caitlin everything.

Caitlin's smile slid into a look of horror as she hit her and pushed her in. For a moment, her dark eyes held mine and they screamed HELP. But her lips didn't move or make a sound, sunlight catching on shiny lipstick the same colour as the scars on her wrists now.

The flick of her dark hair before it swung out of sight. The slam of the door behind her. The blur of the driver running around, closing the driver's side door and starting the engine. The roar of it revving as the flash of orange indicated they were going to move.

A cigarette butt thrown out of the window. Sparks on the paving as the mirror-tinted glass blocked my view, sliding smoothly up like a Mercedes window should.

I'd wanted to step in, stop them and help her, no matter what I was supposed to do. But I was too slow emerging from my daydream into her nightmare. It was too late. The car had already driven away with the angel inside who'd never be mine.

Now, my knuckles were whiter than hers, my nails digging deep into the soft leather steering wheel.

I glanced at Caitlin, but her face was turned away from me, staring out the window. Now that she was wearing a long-sleeved jumper with long pants, it was hard to tell she was injured at all.

"You look so much better in clothes," I blurted out, before I realised what I'd said. "Oh hell, I didn't mean. . .' I almost said that I hadn't been fantasising about her naked, but that wasn't entirely true. I'd been remembering just such a fantasy, the first time I'd seen her. I'd since seen her wearing nothing but blood. I'd give anything to forget that night.

She still didn't look at me, as if she hadn't heard.

I reached over and touched her cheek. My fingers came away wet with tears. I swore, then took her hand. "Caitlin, it's over. They can't touch you any more." I paused. "Or are you upset that I was checking you out?"

She laughed through her tears, wiped her eyes and met mine. "I'm going to be all right." She was forceful, more to herself than to me. "Please, can you take me home now?"

FIFTY THREE

Sneezing. Searching through a full bag for a
tissue.
Felt the spider-crawl of someone's eyes on me.
A woman, staring out of her car window.
Walking past her.
She got out of the car.
I looked at the car to avoid looking back at
her.
Bright red paint, shiny wheels. Nice car.
I looked up at her face.
Her friend. Wanted to talk to me.
Opening the door, from bright sunlight to
darkness.
HELP ME. Eyes met mine and understood.
Too late.

FIFTY FOUR

The only conversation in the car was the English accent of my GPS directing me dispassionately from the hospital to Caitlin's house. My part in the conversation was to listen and do as she said.

Caitlin stared out the window for the whole trip. When we pulled into her driveway, I had to call her name a few times to get her attention.

"Mmm?" she said, sounding far away.

"You're home," I said softly. I unbuckled my seatbelt and opened my car door.

My shoes scuffed and scraped the concrete driveway. I was too tired to lift my feet further as I crossed slowly to her side of the car. I had her door open before she'd even taken off her seatbelt.

Her expression was troubled. Even though her eyes were directed at mine, she didn't seem to see me. She looked lost in a memory.

I touched her now-dry cheek. "You're home," I

repeated.

"Home," she murmured, as if she couldn't remember the meaning of the word. She blinked and her eyes cleared, focussing on me. "Thank you, Nathan."

She let me help her from the car. I slammed the door behind her.

"I will never like this car," she said quietly, still looking troubled.

I tried not to laugh. I never had, either. Maybe it was time to buy something new.

She started to take slow, deliberate steps to the front door. I froze for a second before I rushed to help her. She couldn't make it from the car to the door by herself yet, even with the strong pain medication still in her system.

I helped her extract the spare key from its hiding place and unlocked the front door, holding it open to let her inside. I followed her in and dropped her meagre bag of belongings on the tiles, alongside Alanna's laptop.

Her eyes followed mine to the bags on the floor.

"You can use my sister's laptop for as long as you need to," I said and she nodded.

We both stood in the entry, suddenly awkward.

She wanted to be alone. She was finally home.

I knew all this, but that didn't stop me from asking her anyway. I wanted to stay to watch over her, to make sure she was okay.

"Do you want me to stay?" I asked, as she spoke.

"Did you want to have dinner here, or do you have something planned at home?"

We both laughed, nervously.

It was fucking stupid to drive her in that car, knowing

the memories a Mercedes held for her. The last thing she wanted was to have me in her house reminding her of the atrocities committed against her. She needed to forget.

I jumped in before she had time to invent an excuse to support her refusal. I already knew I didn't belong here. "You should probably have a rest, maybe even a couple of hours' sleep, and I'd stop you from doing that if I stayed. I'll leave you to it. . . Here's my phone number. If you need me at any time, feel free to call." I handed her a scrap of paper, on which I'd hastily scrawled a number. "How about I see myself out?"

She smiled and looked understanding, as I dragged my feet back to the door.

Unable to resist saying something, I finished with, "I'll stop in tomorrow to see how you're getting on."

She smiled and thanked me — as if she meant it.

As I walked out the front door, I had this mad urge not to go, to stay and just sit in the kitchen while she slept. She had surveillance cameras all over the house and Navid or someone else nearby, keeping watch. There was no need for me to be there.

I made myself get into the car again and pull out of the driveway. For a second I thought I saw her silhouetted in the window, but I must have imagined it.

Sleep, Caitlin, and stay safe. Please.

FIFTY FIVE

Waking up in the dark, hurting and cold.
My face wet with tears.
Screaming for them to let me go until my throat
hurt and my voice was almost gone.
No one. No reply, no light.
Cold. Rough. Hard. Draughty.
I was lying on concrete.
I didn't know where I was or who they were.
Someone else breathing in the dark.
Would they hurt me or help me?
Who was it?
Had I imagined it?
Not sure what was worse – cold and hurting,
alone in the dark, or hot and in pain, with
some prick hurting me more?
It was always dark.
And out of the dark came
Fuck.

FIFTY SIX

Blood and bare skin; sand and screaming; struggling and shots.

Oh God, Caitlin!

My sleep that night was plagued with nightmares about what she'd looked like when I found her, thinking she was dead. That they might get to her again while I wasn't there. I worried that she wouldn't survive the night without me.

I just couldn't help myself. My waking thoughts at dawn the next morning were of her. I had to see her. For weeks now, all I'd had to do was open my eyes and turn my head to see that she was okay, but now I didn't know and it drove me insane. I put it off for as long as I could, then had to drive over to her house.

I didn't have second thoughts until I knocked on her door, when I wondered how she'd react to my being there so early. Something told me she wouldn't be civil if I woke her up. I started to wish I'd waited.

Somewhere nearby, a child started to practise playing the

piano. First the slow plunking as the little fingers learned a new tune, before the monotonous drill of finger exercises. The jerkily played scales jarred with the confusion in my head. Should I stay or should I go? I wasn't sure I could go. I'd sit on the steps and wait, until I saw she was safe.

I knocked again. "Caitlin, it's me. It's Nathan," I called, hoping she'd already be awake and hear me.

She took a while to reach the door and even longer to unlock it. When I reached to open it for her, she almost fell. I think she would have if I hadn't been there to stop her. As I tried to hold her up, I could feel her exhaustion. It was as if gravity pulled her to the ground harder than it did me.

Then I saw her face – it was positively haggard. I'd only been gone a night and I wished more than ever that I hadn't left. What if they'd managed to get to her while I was gone? She'd almost knocked herself out, falling out her own front door. She was no match for anyone who wanted to hurt her in this condition.

"What happened?" I burst out.

"I can't sleep," she mumbled, not looking at me. Even in my arms she was swaying and unsteady. "The nightmares didn't go away – all night. It got so bad that I woke up and was too scared to go back to sleep again. I tried to write them down, but that only made it worse. I just have to get used to sleeping alone. . . uh, in my own bed, and at home, again."

This was my fault. I should never have left. "Come on, I'll take you to bed and make sure you sleep this time."

She was too exhausted to refuse. Her arms wearily resting on my neck, I lifted her up. It felt like the most natural thing in the world to have her in my arms again, instead of one of the stranger things I've ever done. Nothing I do with Caitlin is normal, I reflected as I re-entered her house.

"Tell me where to go," I said softly.

She pointed vaguely. Her hand looked too heavy for her wrist to lift. "My room's down the hallway. On the left."

It was an old house with wide hallways, so I didn't have to walk sideways to keep her feet or head from hitting the walls. Shouldering my way into her room, I headed straight for the big bed. I laid Caitlin carefully on it.

She grabbed my hand as I tried to straighten up, pulling me close again. "Stay. Please," she said.

"Sure," I replied, freeing my hand and sitting cautiously on her desk chair.

I watched as she smiled and her eyes slowly shut, slipping back into sleep.

A blinking blue light attracted my attention and I turned toward the desk, where Alanna's old laptop sat. With a glance at Caitlin, I lifted the laptop lid and watched the screen light up, the blinding white of a Word document drawing my eyes.

Caitlin was definitely asleep, for she didn't stir at the sudden increase in light levels, so I scrolled through some of the document. She'd been writing down her nightmares and it looked like she'd spent most of the night doing it.

I started to skim through what she'd written. Most of it was just adding details to what I'd typed in for her, but I stopped dead when I came across something she'd never told me. This I read slowly, trying to commit every word to memory.

I lost track of the days, the difference

between day and night and any sense of time. Some minutes stretched for hours when I just wanted it to be over, but it felt like I'd only just gone to sleep when someone else would hurt me and wake me up to start all over again.

I was always tired. Maybe the pain or the horror of it made me so sleepy. Sometimes I was even too tired to fight, too tired to spit the insults at them that I was thinking. Maybe they hurt me less because they didn't get much of a reaction to whatever they did to me. Maybe they hurt me more to get a reaction.

There were four of them who hurt me, all different.

One of them was there more often, a big bully who'd crush me under his weight. He was rough and strong and he probably left bruises wherever he touched me. He'd hit me or hurt me some other way with his big, meaty hands, until I'd at least whimper, before he'd start grunting his way to a climax. He was the one the others called Mike. The bastard who'd drugged me in the car.

This was what I needed, what she hadn't told me or the police. Details about what they did to her. . . hurting her. . . My mouth went dry as I started to see what she'd been subjected to, the horrifying view through her eyes in the dark.

Another one liked to break my fingers, or twist the ones he'd already broken. He liked to pinch and slap, too. He was a small, skinny bloke with a nasal, whiny voice. Torture with him couldn't have lasted more than five minutes. I heard Mike say to him once, "C'mon Pete, your five minutes are almost done!" and, thankfully, Pete had been done, too.

One of them always brought one of the others along to hold me still. He took forever and his hands were everywhere. It was like being groped by two squids. He'd make comments to himself or the guy holding me for him. I know I fell asleep more than once and I doubt he noticed. If Mike was holding me, he'd hit me 'til I woke up and he'd laugh that he and the other guys had exhausted me before it was Simon's turn. The cold fish was called Simon.

Simon's preferred accomplice he called Tom. Tom didn't say much, he just did what he came for and left. I asked him once why he bothered with me at all. He told me to shut up or he'd break my jaw. Don't remember if he came back after that.

Then there was Her. The woman who wanted me to speak to her friend. The woman who drove the red Mercedes. She hit me and pushed me in and she knew what they'd do to me. I'll kill her if I can.

Caitlin's scream was so loud it rattled the window glass. I'd been too intent on her written nightmares to realise she was trapped in a real one and needed my help.

I turned, knocking something pink off the desk as I did so. I reached to pick up the nail file from the carpet, dropping it back on the desk. Caitlin cried out again, jerking me into urgency.

I slammed the laptop shut, twisting out of the desk chair to stand up. "Wake up, angel. It's another nightmare and I'm here. You're home, you're safe. . ."

The next scream was longer and louder, drowning out my voice.

I knelt on the end of her bed. "Caitlin, it's okay, you're

safe. . ."

She started swearing, loud and panicky.

I did a bit of swearing of my own, though not as loud, as I crawled across the bed to be closer to her. I started with the reassuring litany again.

"Let me go, you bastard!" she screamed at me.

I reached out and lightly patted her cheek. Caitlin went berserk, her hands claws that homed in on my face. Arms and legs flying, screaming like nothing human, I thought she was having a fit. I scrambled off her bed and into a half-crouch on the floor, out of her reach.

She let out an agonised wail as her hands clutched at the pillow beside her. It took me a moment to realise she was saying my name.

I wished for the narrow hospital bed now, as I climbed back onto hers so I could reach her. "I'm here, angel, like I promised. It's okay. . ."

Hesitant, I touched my fingers to the hand closer to me, her nails digging into the pillowcase. When she didn't turn the nails on me, I slid my other hand under hers, lifting it between mine. "I'm here," I said.

Her eyes were open and dark with tears. She attempted a smile. "You stayed. . ." She said it like she didn't believe it, pulling her hand away to wipe her eyes.

I smiled. 'Of course I did. I said I would." I shifted and spread out, so my head was on the scrunched-up pillow she'd tried to strangle. I turned my face toward her. "Bad dream?"

Caitlin nodded, her eyes not leaving mine. She looked so vulnerable and lost. I made the offer without thinking. "C'mere." I stretched out my arms.

She stared at me a moment, but she was already moving closer to me. She cuddled up to my side, her wet cheek against my chest, as my arms closed around her. I wanted to kiss her, too, but I fought the urge. Being in bed with Caitlin was crazy enough.

FIFTY SEVEN

I woke up when the afternoon sun slanted through Caitlin's window. A lance of light that stabbed me squarely in the eye. I stretched and realised that the warm weight beside me was breathing, as Caitlin let out a little sigh and shifted against my side.

I still had one arm around her and I was bloody careful not to move, so as not to disturb her any more. I wasn't the only one short on sleep and she needed it more than me. Caitlin was still a long way from well.

She'd asked me to stay as close as I could in case the nightmares came back. I didn't doubt they would, but for now she was okay.

My heart lifted with the thought that I'd been able to help, my colossal car fuck-up of yesterday forgotten.

I looked down the length of her body, modestly clad in pyjamas with long sleeves. One ankle was bare and I could see the pink scar slicing across it. I remembered how sticky the rope had been as I'd sawn through it, how I'd had to peel it from the wound to free her. I swallowed, trying not to think about it.

I shifted my gaze further up to the fingers of her right hand, splayed across my chest. The nails were curved crescent moons, carefully shaped since Caitlin's fingers had been freed. I could still feel how the jagged edges had cut into my palms when I'd kissed her hands only three days ago.

She moved her arm further across me, her sleeve catching on my shirt and revealing the red gouge across her wrist. This scar was darker than the ones on her ankles and with good reason. The rope around her wrists had been so slick with blood it'd felt more like liquorice than nylon. It'd stuck to the scissors and they'd squeaked as I fought to free her, only to find that the rope was the least of the hurts to her hands. Her middle finger was still slightly crooked and might never be straight again, but at least the broken bones had healed somewhat. They'd healed enough for her to start documenting her own horrifying story.

I lifted my head to look at the laptop, to check if I'd closed it so she wouldn't know how I'd spied on her. I thought of emailing the whole account to myself, so I could check it for important info to use for work, but I hesitated. I wanted more than the scant outline she'd sketched out so far. I wanted everything she remembered.

Caitlin's breathing changed, the evenness broken by a long inhalation, before it was blown slowly out again. Awakening. Emails and other such violations of her trust could wait.

"So, what would you like for breakfast?" I asked, after I watched her blink, yawn and finally smile.

"Hmm?" Caitlin asked sleepily. "Breakfast? Isn't it afternoon?" She sat up and stretched, so I carefully looked away. She wasn't my angel and never would be.

The clock said it was 3:16.

"Late lunch, then?" I hazarded.

"Or early dinner," she agreed.

"Shall I go have a look at what you have in the fridge?" I asked.

Caitlin's brows dipped. "I wouldn't."

I stared at her. "Why not?"

Her voice died to a whisper. "My fridge has fur."

I laughed and stood up, holding out a hand to help her to her feet. "Show me this furry fridge." I kept a supportive arm around her waist as we headed down the passage to the kitchen.

Caitlin pulled away from me when we reached the kitchen table, sinking into a chair as far from the fridge as she could. I stopped as she did, raising my eyebrows.

"I don't need to smell it and I can't do anything about it. Not like this." she said. She waved her hands up and down her body.

"Is it really that bad?" I asked.

Her eyes were huge and heartbreaking. "Everything's been there since the day I. . . went away." Went away. What a fucking understatement.

I couldn't look away from her face. "For more than two months?"

She nodded, resigned. "That long. Be my guest," she replied, gesturing toward the fridge.

I sucked in a breath and held it, before opening the door. It didn't help. I swear her fridge smelled like blue cheese. A lot of blue cheese.

The milk was green. The crisper was black and white with fur, interspersed with streaks of red, like there was a dead cat squeezed into it. The shelves looked like there were rainbow-coloured guinea pigs asleep on them – some of them in plastic boxes. Only the orange juice looked normal. I reached for the bottle.

"Don't," said Caitlin. "I poured a cup yesterday from the other bottle and it came out in chunks. That one's older."

I slammed the fridge shut and leaned back against it. The smell lingered, but the worst of it stayed sealed inside. "So what do you want to do about it?"

Caitlin shrugged. "I don't know."

I was at a loss.

"Our cleaner just does the bathrooms, the floors and the dusting. Not the fridge," Caitlin continued.

"Cleaner?" I asked, feeling like an idiot for not thinking of it.

"A cleaner. A woman Dad pays to come clean the house once a fortnight, so I don't have to and he doesn't need to worry about it," Caitlin said patiently. "But she doesn't do the fridge and it looks like there are dead mice in there, so I think we'd need the sort of cleaner who does nasty stuff like deal with dead bodies."

I looked at her. "I think I have a friend who does industrial cleaning. Let me call him and see if he can help." I patted my pockets and realised I'd left my phone in Caitlin's bedroom. "Do you mind if I go get my phone out of your room? Will you be okay here by yourself?"

She gave a weak grin. "Go for it. I'll be fine, unless the dead mice have mutated into zombies."

Zombies. Oh God, not zombies. I fucking hated zombies now.

I forced a smile and strode back to her bedroom.

I rang Navid. "No sign of anyone watching her house," he reported by way of greeting. "Looks like domestic bliss, the two of you in the kitchen. What's for dinner?"

The surveillance cameras. Shit, he was on watch. I hoped they hadn't put a camera in her bedroom. She deserved some privacy.

I smiled and kept my voice low. "Zombie mice."

"Fuck! What the hell?"

"She has a fridge full of fur from the food that's gone bad while she was away. Can you send in a team to deal with it?" I asked, crossing my fingers.

"Mate, ASIO clean-up crews aren't for ordinary housecleaning. That's misuse of government resources," Navid complained.

"It'll be me doing it on work time if you don't send them in," I replied. "My job is to protect the valuable witness. That includes making sure she doesn't get sick from eating food from a fridge full of zombie mice."

"Fuck!" he swore. "Okay, I'll send them in. Get her out, unless you want to tell her who you work for."

I smiled for the surveillance camera. I knew he was watching. "Fuck that. I'll take her food shopping. Make sure it's clean and the team are out by the time we get back."

I ended the call. There was no point in saying goodbye when he was in a van down the street, watching our every move on the screens.

I headed back to Caitlin, who hadn't moved from her seat. Her eyes were questioning, though she didn't say a word.

"My friend can spare a cleaning team in about an hour, but it's probably best if we go out. Leave them to deal with the dead bodies so you can come home to a clean fridge. We can do your food shopping, so you can fill it up again."

"Do I have time to get dressed?" she asked.

I smiled. "Sure, if you're quick."

FIFTY EIGHT

"I want a shower," she said softly, looking up at me.

"So take one," I answered.

Caitlin looked embarrassed. "I. . . I can't. I tried last night, but I almost passed out. I can't stand up that long."

Shit.

It was on the tip of my tongue to offer to help her in the shower, but I couldn't think of any way to say it that didn't sound dirty. Not that I wouldn't take a shower with Caitlin if she was offering, it was just that. . . she wasn't. I wondered how she'd managed in hospital, on the few occasions this week once the dressings were off, before I remembered

I pointed outside through the sliding door. "How about I stick one of those plastic chairs in the shower for you to sit on?"

Caitlin smiled, looking relieved. "That could work."

I fumbled with the lock until I managed to open the door and lifted up a cobwebbed chair. I hosed off the inevitable redback spider with her puzzle web under the seat before I carried the damp chair into the shower for Caitlin.

She'd followed me slowly to the bathroom so I faced her for a moment, not sure what to say.

"Thank you," she said after a while, lifting the hem of her shirt a little so I could see her tummy. "Could you shut the door behind you? I like my showers steamy."

Oh God. Talk about dirty. "Sure. I'll go wait in the lounge room," I replied hastily, stumbling out of the bathroom as quickly as I could.

I turned on the TV and sat in the lounge room, not even noticing what was on the screen. In my head, all I saw was Caitlin in the shower. Steam curling around her as the water cascaded. . .

I heard her quick footsteps tripping across the carpet and turned in time to see Caitlin disappear into the kitchen. I stood and followed.

I found her leaning against the fridge door, her arms, hands and head in the freezer. I reached for the freezer door, opening it wider so I could see what she was doing. Caitlin pressed herself against the fridge, squashing skin against steel as I realised what I was looking at.

"Shit, sorry!" I said, turning my back and trying to get the image out of my head. Fat chance of that. Burned into my retinas was Caitlin, wearing nothing but a pair of pants, her breasts pressed against the fridge door as she pushed her hands as deep into the freezer as she could reach, her face pale with pain.

Oh, shit, the surveillance cameras. Even if I had my eyes closed, Navid was watching the screens, recording

everything. Caitlin didn't deserve to be stared at like this —
not even for her own safety.

I pulled my shirt over my head and held it out behind
me. "Please, put this on. Let me help you. . ." Cold, damp
fingers touched mine as she took the shirt. I heard the
fabric slide over her hair, her skin. . . covering her from the
cameras I couldn't tell her about.

"Are you decent?" I asked.

Caitlin sounded like she was trying not to laugh. "Yes."

I dared to turn around. My shirt came to her knees, so
wide you could have fitted two of her in it. I lifted my eyes
to her face. "What's wrong?"

She held out her hands, looking lost. "I can't. . . I can't
fasten things. Buttons and things. My fingers won't work.
Ice helps dull the pain."

I looked at my too-large shirt. "So wear a t-shirt. There's
nothing wrong with looking casual. We're only going to a
supermarket." I smiled gently. "You'll still look beautiful."

I regretted my words the instant she turned red and
looked at the floor. "I don't have a problem with my t-
shirts. I can't. . . fasten my bra."

Fuck. Now it was my turn to blush in embarrassment. I
should have seen that one coming. "I can help you with
that," I replied reluctantly.

"That would be really great," Caitlin said. She hesitated,
as if there was more she wanted to say, biting her lip until
she continued, "But. . . could you please turn around and
close your eyes while I get dressed? I'll tell you when I need
you."

I nodded. Would it have been necessary to ask anyone
else not to watch? Or just me, the pervert who wouldn't

look away while she dressed herself in hospital yesterday?

"Of course."

FIFTY NINE

Fifteen minutes later, I'd fastened my first bra. I'd taken off plenty and fondled twice as many firm breasts, but this was the first time I'd focussed so hard on those little fucking hooks, my fingers fumbling as Caitlin held her breath, fidgeted and fought not to ask me again if I'd finished yet.

I didn't have more than a split-second to admire my handiwork before Caitlin yanked a shirt over her head and down to her hips. When she turned around, I realised I was staring at her breasts and quickly shifted my eyes to her face. "Shall we go?" she said.

"Sure," I replied. I looked down for the pockets she didn't have. "Don't you need to get your wallet and phone and stuff?"

Caitlin swallowed, her eyes suddenly shimmering with tears. "I don't. . . they took. . . I don't have any. . ."

Fucking fool. I stood to hug her as her tears flowed, feeling the unfamiliar firmness of a bra between us for the first time. Caitlin had always seemed so soft before. I tried to focus. "How are you going to do food shopping without any money?" I asked reasonably.

"I don't know," was her muffled, miserable reply as she cried into my shirt.

I sat on her bed, pulling her down with me, trying to work out what to do. I could lend her the money, sure, but that didn't fix her problem of not having a phone or access to cash. I tried to remember what I'd had to do the last time I lost my wallet. "Do you have a passport?"

Caitlin sat up straighter, sniffling. "Yes."

"Do you think you have any official letters for you with your home address on them?"

"Maybe some from Uni. . ." she began, her eyes kindling with hope.

I stood. "Tell me where to find them and we'll take them to the bank. We can arrange cash and some new cards. . . maybe even get you a new phone, if we have time."

Caitlin looked relieved. "Thanks, Nathan."

Armed with her passport, some official letters and a beautifully fastened bra, if I do say so myself, Caitlin let me take her to the nearest big shopping centre – Garden City. It was too far for her to walk from the car to the entrance, so I gave her three options. "Are you riding in a gopher, wheelchair or a shopping trolley?"

Caitlin choked. "A shopping trolley? I won't fit in the child seat, Nathan."

I grinned. "I know. I figured I'd lift you into the bit where the shopping's supposed to go."

She still looked uncertain. "I'd prefer a wheelchair if we can get one, please."

As I expected, the centre had some for loan and Caitlin

was soon enthroned in a wheelchair, her feet tucked up off the ground.

"Right, which bank?" I asked.

Caitlin smiled as she replied, "Not that one."

Dealing with the bank was surprisingly easy, as Caitlin had her identification and the staff recognised her from the front cover of the day's newspaper, anyway. The photographer had captured her delighted-at-the-ducklings smile perfectly, but the pictures of me were blurred and unrecognisable. I promised myself I'd pick up a copy I could keep before we left the shopping centre.

I stuck Caitlin's money in my pocket, at her request, as we headed into the shopping centre proper for a new wallet and the rest of what she needed. A woman almost barrelled into her with a fully loaded trolley and I heard Caitlin whimper as she dragged on the wheels to stop in time.

"What the hell are you doing?" I asked the trolley woman, who glared at us as she kept going. I dropped to my knees beside Caitlin. Her hands were clasped protectively to her chest. "Are you okay?" I held out my hands for hers. She winced as she laid her fingers on mine.

"I want some gloves," she said.

I stared at her. "Gloves?"

She curled her fingers. "You know, like cyclists use."

We bought her the smallest pair of cross-training gloves we could find in a sporting goods shop, though Caitlin looked at the pale pink colour of them with distaste as she slid her fingers inside. "Better?" I asked. She nodded.

A wallet, handbag and basic pre-paid phone later, I stopped to pick up a few new t-shirts, shorts and a pair of pyjamas. Shit, I hadn't worn pyjamas since I was a kid, but

I'd have to if I stayed overnight at Caitlin's place, or she'd freak out.

I swung my bag of purchases as I asked, "Time for food shopping, or is there anything else you need?"

"No, food's good," Caitlin replied and spun her wheels in the direction of the nearest supermarket.

I followed her with a trolley as she made her selections. A couple of times, she smiled and nodded at people as if she knew them, but she didn't stop to talk.

I watched her as she rolled down the breakfast cereal aisle, placing bets with myself on what she'd choose. I was expecting her to pick one of the boxes of kids' cereal, because of how healthy the hospital food had been, but she didn't even look at the cereal. I wondered why.

When the trolley was half-full, Caitlin said she was done, so we headed to the registers to pay. I grabbed a couple of newspapers from the stand as we went past, dropping them on top of the shopping. I was careful to avoid squashing the strawberries balanced precariously on top, trying to hide my smile. I'd already earned a glare and a warning when I put my jar of coffee too close to them.

The checkout operator looked at me blankly as I handed over both newspapers, then turned to Caitlin. "Are you sure you want two papers, miss?"

Caitlin looked equally blank. "Do we, Nathan?"

I hesitated, then decided I had nothing to lose by telling her. "Well, you'll want one and I'd like one for myself, so — yes." I nodded for the shop assistant's benefit. I pointed at the picture of Caitlin that kept catching my eye. I couldn't stop glancing at it, though I had the real lady herself right in front of me. Idly, I wondered if I could contact the newspaper photographer and get a copy of the original photo. "It's a beautiful picture and I want to remember the first time you smiled, like none of this had ever happened. Because I was there."

Caitlin looked up at me, a searching smile on her face, as if she was trying to work out if I was joking.

No matter what else happened, at least she'd had one more day of happiness. And she'd shared it with me.

"Nathan?" Caitlin's voice broke through my reverie.

"Mmm?" I tried to make it sound like I wasn't miles away. I started moving the shopping bags into the trolley.

"Will you stay with me tonight?" She looked up at me with those big eyes.

"Sure, if that's what you want," I replied.

She paid the checkout operator and slipped her change into her new wallet. We headed back toward the car.

"I want you to sleep with me."

I choked. "You want. . . what?"

A light touch on my arm. The brush of three of Caitlin's fingertips was enough to stop me in my tracks. "I want you to stay and sleep with me, so you can wake me up if there are any more nightmares. Please?"

I fought to get the words out. "Sleep. You mean. . ."

Caitlin locked puzzled. "Sleep. Like you did when I was in hospital. Unless I wake you up because I'm having another nightmare." Her eyes grew huge. "You don't have to if you don't want to."

Oh God, she had no idea how much I wanted to. And more than sleep. . . Focus.

"Sure," I managed to say again. Good thing I bought pyjamas.

SIXTY

Caitlin yawned, covering her mouth with one hand. The gloves were gone. I could tell how tired she was, for she looked like a doll flung into the seat, slumped between the leather and the seatbelt with her eyes half-closed.

"Should we pick up a pizza on the way home?" I asked gently, glancing at her just in time to see her eyes slide shut.

"Mmm?" Caitlin's eyes shot open as she straightened in her seat. "Sure. I'm still sleepy, so it's best that I don't cook."

I pulled my phone out of my pocket and handed it to her. "Here, you call your local pizza shop so it'll be ready to pick up when we get there. You'll just have to tell me where to go."

She took my phone with both hands. "What do you want?"

I shrugged, slowing down to stop for a red light. "Whatever. I don't mind."

She spoke in a low voice to the pizza shop while I

weaved through the peak hour traffic, wishing the weary commuters wouldn't keep cutting me off as if they couldn't see my blazing red car. Maybe if I owned a different colour car. . .

Caitlin insisted on accompanying me into the pizza shop, though she leaned heavily on me every step of the way.

"Caitlin! It's been a while," said the woman behind the counter when we walked into her shop. "We all thought. . ."

The smile on Caitlin's lips melted me like ice cream. "Ah, you know I always come back here. You make the best pizzas. And there's a new dessert one, too!"

I looked at the menu. Apricots on pizza? Oh, wait, those were the dessert ones.

Caitlin handed over some money and the pizza woman held out the boxes with some hesitation. "I'll help carry these out to the car for you."

Caitlin smiled and nodded her thanks, turning with me to head back to the car. Once I'd carefully helped her into the passenger seat, the woman deposited the pizza boxes on her lap and stood by the door of her shop to wave goodbye. Caitlin lifted a languid hand to respond.

I kept throwing glances at her as we drove the short distance back to her house, until I finally said, "Everyone knows you, don't they?"

Her sleepy smile widened. "I've lived in this area for a while. The people in the local shops see me a lot and remember me, that's all."

The smell of pizza pervaded the car, reminding me how hungry I was, but I carried Caitlin into the house before I returned for the boxes and the shopping.

Caitlin ate on autopilot, swaying in her seat, she was so sleepy. I grabbed a slice from the box and bit into it without tasting it, deciding to put her food away for her. She could always shift it around when she wasn't so tired.

I lifted the bag of strawberry punnets first and opened the fridge. The sharp smell of bleach fumes wafted out of the white interior, the fur seared from every surface. I coughed and wrapped the bag around them, before placing the whole package into the now pristine, cat-free crisper.

Most of her purchases were frozen – packaged in portions that didn't need much preparation, I realised, as I stuck the packets in the freezer. Pre-made meals, bite-sized pieces of chicken and fish, pre-cut vegetables. Individual tubs of yoghurt, fresh fruit juice and milk all went into the pungent fridge, along with a bag of grated cheese.

I wished I'd looked more closely at the contents of her trolley while we were still at the shop. I'd have bought her steak and stuff I could cook for her. I wondered if she'd skipped meat because she was vegetarian or if she had other reasons. I stared at the slice of pizza in my hand, the same as she was eating. Between the steak strips, salami and sausage, the slice scotched any thought of Caitlin being vegetarian. I looked up, wanting to ask why.

Drooping over her plate at the dining table, Caitlin had managed to swallow a couple of slices but now she was about to fall asleep in her dinner.

"Hey!" I reached out to catch her before her face hit the plate.

"Sorry," she mumbled. "So tired. . . Should put the pizza away and sleep. . ."

"I'll fridge your leftovers," I replied, straightening up and reaching for the box. "Then I can help you to bed."

I stuck the remaining pizza in a plastic box before I slid it onto a fridge shelf. The smell was enough to make me close the door quickly.

I turned to see her barely managing to stay on her feet, her knuckles white as she held onto the back of her chair. "Let me help you," I begged, my arms out ready to lift her up. For the second time that day, I carried Caitlin to bed. And for the second time that day, she asked me to stay, so I did – stretched out on her bed beside her, waiting for her to fall asleep so I could go sleep on the couch.

I closed my eyes, listening to her breathing slow into sleep, smiling. She was safe.

I woke to a faint glow behind my eyelids, my nose full of a sweet smell. I breathed deeply, trying to identify the fruity scent that reminded me of soap. I opened my eyes. Oh, shit. I closed them again.

My face was buried in Caitlin's hair, my head resting beside hers on her pillow. She lay on her side, turned away from me, but that hadn't stopped me from sidling closer to her in sleep. I could feel the warmth of her body through my jeans, so I'd been cuddling up to her for some time. I'd even thrown an arm across her waist. Shit, I was spooning a girl I'd just slept with and sex hadn't been a part of it. Though my body definitely had ideas in that direction. Thank God I was wearing jeans instead of pyjamas. It'd be harder for her to tell what I'm thinking. Fuck, this was Caitlin! I pulled away from her as stealthily as I could, not wanting to ruin a nightmare-free night by inspiring one.

Not stealthy enough – Caitlin shifted as I did. Her body pressed along my side, she gave me a quick hug, then sat up. Her light lips touched my cheek and she whispered, "Thank you," before I felt her weight lift off the bed. Her bare feet padded on the timber boards as she headed down the hallway.

I sat up as soon as she was out of sight. I'd slept in my clothes, so I was all set for the walk of shame to my car in front of Caitlin's whole street. Ah, it wasn't the first time I'd done such a thing and last night had been better than most. Even without any sex.

Caitlin returned, her face shiny and damp, an excited smile on her face. "Would you like breakfast?"

"Sure," I replied. "Do you have any cornflakes?"

Her face fell. "No. And if we do, they're so stale they'd be inedible." She walked out, one hand on the wall to steady her steps.

Not sure what I'd said wrong, I hurried to follow her. I entered the kitchen just in time to see the bin lid close over the cornflake box. Caitlin's eyes were on the box and she looked angry.

I opened my mouth to say the first thing that came to mind. "You really don't like cornflakes, do you?"

Her hard glare turned on me. "No, I don't." She reached into the fridge and pulled out two yoghurts, holding one out to me.

"I'm right," I answered. My stomach growled a different answer. To cover the noise, I continued, "I should probably head home."

Caitlin's smile was understanding. "I know. Thank you for staying." She hesitated, then went on, "Will you. . . could you. . . please, could you come over tonight and stay again? I feel safer when you're here and I'm not alone at night." Her eyes were suddenly huge.

"Sure. I'll take you out for dinner tonight, if you like. I'll stay any night you want me," I replied easily, without a second thought.

She smiled sadly and I realised that she'd never want me. But I'd be back anyway.

I waved and wished her a nice day, then climbed into my car to pick up breakfast from McDonald's on my way home.

SIXTY ONE

I gorged on breakfast because I hadn't had hash browns in ages. I packed a bag of clothes to take to Caitlin's, then stretched out on my own couch and watched TV, calling Navid every hour for an update on her. By the fourth phone call, he answered with, "She's fine. If you're so worried, go bother her."

But Caitlin didn't expect me 'til the evening, so I didn't dare show up early. I had other plans.

It was Tuesday, when Chris had an afternoon off from university, so I waited for her to come home. I needed to know if she'd seen anything suspicious, anyone stalking her. If they weren't coming for Caitlin, they could be casing Chris.

She didn't get home until almost four, when I was starting to worry. I had my packed bag by the door, ready to go, and Chris's eyes darted straight to it as she stepped inside.

I opened my mouth before she could comment on it.

"Chris, you haven't had anyone watching you or following you, have you? After Alanna and now spending so much time with Caitlin, I'm starting to worry. . ." I trailed off.

Chris snorted. "No. Why would anyone bother stalking me?" She dropped her keys on the hall table. "What is it about that girl that has you so obsessed with her?"

My reply was automatic. "She's been badly hurt and she needs my help."

She snorted again, louder this time. "Yeah, you've said that before, but she's not unconscious in hospital now. And if anyone was going to try to hurt her again, they'd have done it by now. This is getting ridiculous. How well do you really know her?"

I hesitated for maybe a minute, but when the words came, they flooded out. "I know how many times she still wakes up at night, screaming at the nightmares of what happened to her. I know how much she still hurts from her injuries and how hard she tries to hide it from everyone. She doesn't like strangers touching her. She hates breakfast cereal, my car, anything restrictive around her wrists and asking anyone for help. I know by the sound of her screams whether she's afraid or in pain." I closed my eyes, trying to push the sound of Caitlin in pain out of my head.

Chris was silent for a moment before she spoke. "Listen to yourself, Nathan. You're not talking about a healthy relationship. What you're saying sounds seriously fucked up. Is there anything good about her? Anything the girl actually likes?"

Thank you, Chris. The images in my head turned from dark to light. "She likes strawberries, music and ducklings." And occasionally me. I felt myself smiling. I opened my eyes again.

Chris shook her head. "Strawberries, music and ducklings. You know her real well, don't you?" She pressed her lips together. "Stay away from her, Nathan. That girl isn't good for you."

I shook my own head. Stay away from her? I'd go crazy with worry in a day. "You don't know her."

Chris looked grim. "Neither do you." She turned away, picked up a sponge and scrubbed the bench so hard it looked like she wanted to take the laminate off it. "Is there anything you wouldn't do for her?" she muttered, half under her breath.

I wasn't sure if she'd meant me to hear that last bit, but I was too pissed off to care. Nothing Chris said could come between me and Caitlin.

"Yes," I snapped. "I wouldn't die for her."

Chris turned around to stare at me, her mouth hanging open. She stood there in shock for maybe half a minute before she spoke. "Well. . . well, that's good," she said uncertainly.

"Do you want to know why?" I asked steadily.

"I. . ." Chris swallowed, seemingly lost for words. That didn't happen much. Another day, I'd have felt triumph, but today there was only anger. Caitlin was the key to keeping Chris alive, but today I didn't care any more.

"I wouldn't die for her because I wouldn't be able to protect her any more. What if I missed one of the people who hurt her and my absence let them get to her? I couldn't take that risk. She's too important." I walked out of the kitchen before she replied. I'd promised Caitlin I'd be back before dark and I didn't want to be late.

". . . Fucking paranoid, delusional. . ." I heard Chris's voice say as I opened the front door.

Not as delusional as thinking that I'm safe and no one can hurt me, I thought. There are real monsters out there The worst part is that they're human.

SIXTY TWO

I stood at the garage door, wishing I didn't have to drive the car Caitlin hated so much. Maybe I should sell it and buy something so different this one would only be a distant, bad memory. I looked past it and my eyes fell on the dusty cover shrouding the car beside mine. Alanna's car, untouched since they took her. The car she'd never come home to drive again.

My feet moved of their own volition as I reached out automatically to take the cover off. I shook my head as I saw the car. I still didn't understand our parents' reasoning behind giving me the solid, dependable sedan while Alanna got the sporty convertible. She'd never had so much as a speeding fine driving this thing and there was no way she'd let me touch it.

I touched the smooth, white contours of her car, wishing she was here to say, "Don't even think about it, Nathan," as she shook her keys at me. I wished I could ask her about Caitlin, and whether she thought I was as crazy as

Chris did. Would Alanna have let me take her car, when mine scared Caitlin so much? Or would she have told me I was being stupid and to leave the poor girl alone?

I'd never know. Alanna wasn't coming back and her car would sit here, gathering dust, until we got rid of it. Unless I got rid of my car and kept hers. . .

I wiped my eyes, which were tearing up in the airborne dust from shifting the car cover. I could feel my throat choking up, too. The dust must have been pretty thick.

I found Alanna's keys and turned them in the ignition. I got nothing. It hadn't been driven in months, so a flat battery didn't come as a big surprise. I hunted around the garage for jumper leads to jumpstart her car from mine. We'd never needed them — they were still sealed in the packet. I ripped the plastic open with a pocket knife.

Hooking up the cables, I started my engine, before clipping the last clamp to Alanna's car battery. I slid into the driver's seat and shifted it back, so there was enough space for me, tossing the pocket knife into the glove box. This time, the ignition caught and as I revved the engine, I realised her little car had far more power than mine. Perfect Alanna, never a foot wrong, to the point where our parents had trusted her with a high-powered sports car when she'd turned twenty-one. God, I missed her. She'd have been able to tell me what to do.

I turned the Mercedes off and put the cables away. I climbed back into Alanna's car and headed for Caitlin's house.

Maybe half a kilometre from home, I decided to take the top off. I'd never driven a convertible before, much less a topless one, and it seemed like a really good idea right now.

Maybe the air flow would help clear my head, or even just the dust from my eyes, which were still streaming.

Five minutes later, I could barely feel my hands in the freezing wind. When I stopped at the traffic lights, I looked around for something to wrap around me to keep warm. An old, padded jacket, with a logo from an airline company that had long since gone out of business, was spread across the back seat and I struggled to put it on before the lights went green. I managed to zip it up before I took off. I wondered who'd left the jacket in Alanna's car, but I realised I'd never know. It smelled faintly of her perfume, so I knew she'd worn it in the past. Or cuddled up real close to someone who had. I laughed aloud at the thought of Alanna doing anything like that in this car. She'd have insisted on dinner, a movie or a show, before even considering suggesting he provide a luxurious bed, several dates later. The exact opposite of me.

I took the onramp to the freeway and cheered as the car responded perfectly to the accelerator. It was a heady contrast to the slow, steady speed increase of my sedan. I checked my mirrors before merging and realised my hair was standing on end, blown everywhere in the breeze that had frozen me to the bone. Caitlin would laugh herself silly – never a bad thing – if I turned up with a crest like a cockatoo, but I didn't want to take her out to dinner looking like a cocky. I spotted a cap on the floor by the passenger seat and stuck it on my head, praying it would flatten my hair or at least hide it.

As I pulled into Caitlin's street, I took the cap off and looked hopefully at the mirror, but was sadly disappointed. I stuck the cap back on and wondered if Caitlin would agree to order takeaway food again or let me use her bathroom to fix my hair. If I'd thought to get my hair cut, this wouldn't be a problem. Only skinheads and bald blokes should drive convertibles with the top down, I told myself, resolving to shave my head in the morning.

I pulled into her driveway and checked the time. Shit, I was late. Arguing with Chris and jumpstarting a car had taken more time than I thought. I saw the lace curtain at the front window move and knew Caitlin had seen me. I pulled the cap down firmly to cover my hair and took a deep breath.

Caitlin flew down the steps, a look of terror on her face. She skittered to a stop in front of my car for a moment, staring.

Cautiously, I opened the door and started to climb out. Her eyes widened further and she took off down the street. I looked around, but I couldn't see what had scared her so much.

I expected her to come back, but Caitlin kept going, as if someone was pursuing her. I broke into a run, too, determined to catch up to her so I could keep her in sight. If someone was after her, I had to stay with her to protect her.

It had been too long since I'd last gone for a run. I couldn't catch my breath, but she was visibly flagging as she reached the end of her endurance. I was amazed she'd made it this distance from the house and I worried that Caitlin would push her body too far, doing herself even more injury.

She almost tripped, then righted herself before she hit the ground.

"No, stop!" I begged her breathlessly. "Come back. You can't. . ."

I meant to say she couldn't run far, but it seemed fear had driven her to do just that.

". . . can't outrun me," I finished. That was true, at least. And I didn't want her to try.

"Come back. Please. Let me. . ."

She made a fearful sound in her throat and I redoubled my speed, desperate to catch up, stop her and find out why she was so frightened.

I reached out, desperately, trying to grab her shoulder. As my fingers touched her, she overbalanced, falling face-first onto the lawn of a stranger's house.

As soon as Caitlin hit the grass, she rolled over to face me, the tears in her eyes set on fire by the light of the setting sun. She let out a sobbing breath, her hands up as if to stop me from coming any closer.

My heart was already pounding from panic and the unaccustomed exercise. I felt it drop like Caitlin had when she'd fallen. "Angel, are you okay?" I asked, expecting the worst and hoping I was wrong.

A curtain in the house twitched and the front door opened. An angry-looking woman peered out of the partly open door, a hockey stick in her hand.

Caitlin's sobbing resolved into words. "How. . . could. . . why. . ."

I tried to smile, but it was hard. I wanted desperately to know what had scared her, but I didn't dare ask with an angry audience. "What do you think of my new car?" I asked, seeing movement around me as more of her neighbours emerged from their houses. I wondered which one held the piano-playing child. Most of them were armed with sporting equipment – I saw a couple more hockey sticks, some cricket bats and a tennis racquet. One bloke carried a massive axe that I hoped stayed on his side of the street, as far away from us as possible.

"Your. . . new car?" Caitlin managed to say.

"Yes," I replied patiently, glancing around. All of them seemed content to watch for the moment. "I know you didn't like the old one, so I figured it was time for something new." Forgive me, Alanna, but I'd drive a hot pink hatchback if it meant Caitlin wouldn't be so scared. You don't need your car any more.

She glanced around at the neighbours and lifted her lips in a forced smile. "The car's fine. Please, help me up and back to my house." She lifted her arms, looking up at me with a wide-eyed, desperate smile on her face.

I tried to lift her up, but she muttered, "Just help me walk."

"But you'll hurt yourself," I protested. "That's too far for you to walk."

Her smile was strained. "I got this far on my own, didn't I? Do it, Nathan. Or my neighbours will interfere and they're fairly protective of me when Dad's not around. Especially now. . ."

Against my best judgement, I helped her stand up, taking as much of her weight as I could as I helped her walk home, knowing I'd have nightmares about her tooth-grinding smile after this.

Her face was almost drained of all colour by the time she staggered up the steps to her front door. Even with me holding her, she was swaying on her feet. "Nathan. . .

please. . . the door. . ." she panted. She looked like she was going to pass out.

I turned the handle and kicked it open, lifting Caitlin off her feet before she fell.

"No. . . must. . ." she murmured, her eyes closed.

"You must rest," I finished for her, carrying her over the threshold like my precious bride. At least the precious part was true.

I let her down onto the couch, where she sat with her eyes closed, unmoving, for a few minutes. I stood beside her, watching. I took my cap off, not caring how crazy a cocky's crest I had any more. I ran my fingers through it absently, probably making it worse.

I waited for her to catch her breath, for her eyelids to flutter open so I could ask her what had scared her so much and take care of it for her. But they didn't. Her breathing was shallow and slow.

I knelt down beside her. "Angel," I began.

"What is it, Nathan?" Her voice was flat but calm.

"Are you okay?" I asked, desperate to know.

A pause. "Not really. I'm hurting and hoping the pain will go away if I sit still long enough."

"Oh God," I burst out. "I'm so sorry I was late. What happened?"

Someone pounded on the door. I looked at Caitlin, unsure what to do.

She opened her eyes and struggled to sit up, but she didn't move much. She nodded toward the door. "Please."

I stood and opened the door. My least favourite of her neighbours stood there, the bloke with the block splitter. The heavy axe didn't seem to be in his hands any more. I breathed a sigh of relief until I realised he'd propped it up beside the door so he had his hands free to knock. Fuck. "Can I help you?" I asked nervously. Behind him, I could see people still on their front lawns, watching.

"I want to make sure Caitlin's okay," he said, looking me right in the eye.

"Me, too, mate," I replied.

"It's okay, Nathan," Caitlin said behind me. I felt her hand on my arm and moved aside quickly, grabbing her before she collapsed. I held her to my side, trying to make it look friendly instead of forced by her frailty. "Thanks for coming to check on me, Bruce, but my friend Nathan's here to help me. I fell over and I think I hurt something. I'll be okay. I just need to rest a bit." Her body was threatening to make her rest right here on the floor if I let go. I managed a smile for her nosy, scary neighbour.

"If you say so," Bruce replied doubtfully. "If you need me for anything, all you have to do is ask. You have our number." He eyed me as he picked up his block splitter, swinging it up onto his shoulder as he walked back across the road to his own house.

I carried Caitlin back to the couch before I closed and locked the door. This time, I sat beside her. "What happened?" I repeated, urgently.

She smiled tiredly. "Nothing. I. . . nothing." She closed her eyes for a moment. "Is there any chance we can go out for dinner another night? I'm a little too tired and you look like a cockatoo."

I laughed, relieved. "Sure. I'll ring up and get something delivered."

She reached out, her hand patting my arm. "Thank you."

The patting stopped, her hand resting limply on my wrist. I looked at her in concern. Poor Caitlin had passed out.

SIXTY THREE

I waited a moment, calling her name softly, but I got no response. Even when I stroked her hair, she didn't move. I stretched Caitlin out on her side on the sofa, checking her breathing and all those things you do for first aid on an unconscious person. As I touched her legs, she whimpered slightly, so I moved away. I dug out her pain medication and placed it on the coffee table beside her with a glass of water.

Not sure how long it had been since she'd eaten, I washed and sliced up some strawberries for her. I left them on the coffee table, too.

It'd been a long time since my initial first aid training, but I was pretty sure I had one more step to follow. I pulled out my phone to call for help from an expert more qualified than I was.

"Why'd you put her to sleep on the couch? Wouldn't she be more comfortable in her own bed?" Navid asked, without so much as a hello.

"She's unconscious, not asleep," I replied, annoyed. "Look, I need to know what happened to scare her before I arrived. I'm trying to work out whether I should call an ambulance or if she'll be better off staying home where I can let her wake up normally."

"Nothing, mate," Navid drawled. I could imagine him leaning back and stretching out in his seat as he said it. "She was sitting pretty much where she is now, watching TV, before she noticed something outside. She used the remote control to turn the TV off and went to the window. She stood there for maybe a split second, then went out the front door. Whatever scared her wasn't in the house — it was outside with you. So, whatever it was, you must have seen it, too."

I racked my brains but came up with nothing. The neighbours hadn't been in sight until I started following Caitlin as she sprinted down the street. I shook my head. "I saw nothing dangerous outside. I don't know."

Navid laughed. "Maybe she's afraid of you, mate."

I joined in his laughter. "Yeah, right. Caitlin's not scared of me. Maybe I'll ask her again when she's awake. You keep an eye out, right? Make sure we have outside cameras, too, just in case." I ended the call. It felt weird not saying goodbye, but I could wave at the cameras if I wanted to.

I checked Caitlin's breathing and pulse again. Her breathing was even and her pulse was fine. It was like she was asleep instead of unconscious, worn out from walking and running too far. I wouldn't let her do it again — I'd lift her up and carry her, no matter what she said. For the first time, I noticed she was wearing lipstick, a deep, moist red that was the same colour as the strawberries I'd sliced.

I stared at her strawberries, magnified by the glass of water to an obscene size. I wanted a taste – just one – to see if they really were as amazing as I'd hoped, but I didn't dare. Not without asking Caitlin first.

I sat in the armchair beside Caitlin, wondering if I could turn the TV on without disturbing her. I decided it didn't matter – even if she did wake up, there was no way I'd let her do anything but rest.

My mind wandered as some inane TV show played in the background, the voices a vague buzz behind my busier thoughts, wondering what Caitlin had seen that I hadn't.

"Nathan?" Caitlin asked softly.

I sat up, suddenly alert. Reaching for the bowl of strawberries, I held them out to her. "Here, eat something, so you can take pain medication to help you."

She took the bowl with both hands and a smile. "Thank you." She popped a strawberry into her mouth.

I watched, mesmerised by the red on red.

Don't. Don't even think it.

SIXTY FOUR

Little bitch?
Loud shadow in the doorway.
Flipped him the finger.
Scared, determined to fight.
Biting, kicking, punching, scratching.
Half my face on fire, flying.
Landing heavily. Taste of blood, hurt to breathe. Broken ribs.
Him on top of me. Slamming my face into the floor.
Not her face. Need her pretty.
Raked my nails down his arm.
Broke my fingers. Both the middle ones.
So I could never say up yours to him again.
Fuck you instead then.
Arms twisting. Fighting not to scream.
Tied me up.
Glint of a knife in the dim light. Sliced at my clothes. Cut me, too.
Didn't care.

"It's okay, angel. A bad dream. You're safe at home."

"Broke my fingers. I have to. . . write it down, while I still remember."

"Are you sure it can't wait 'til morning?"

"No, it's a short one, I'll do it now."

"Do you need my help?"

"Don't worry about it, Nathan. You don't need to hear horrible stuff like this. I won't be long – go back to sleep. I will, soon, too."

SIXTY FIVE

"Right, time to go to your physio appointment," I said, slipping an arm under her knees and another behind her back, so I could lift Caitlin from her seat. The early morning sun shone brightly through the window behind me, casting my shadow over her.

"Put me down." Her voice was cold with fury as she struggled.

Agoraphobia, I thought, as I hesitated. She didn't want to leave the house now.

"Now, Nathan." She'd never used this tone on me before – I'd only heard it in her nightmares. I did as I was told, reseating her on the couch.

I crouched in front of her, trying to meet her eyes as I spoke. "Angel, I'm only trying to help you. Everyone's trying to help you. The doctors, the physio, even me. I want to help you – "

She hooked her arms around my neck, her face so close, looking into my eyes. She cut me off mid-sentence. "If you want to help me so much, don't carry me. Help me to walk."

"But yesterday, you hurt yourself. You shouldn't overdo it and I can't stand to see you in pain like that. . ."

"I'll walk on my own damn feet or I'm not going," she insisted.

Unwillingly, I helped her to her feet. My arm around her waist, her arm around my shoulder.

I watched her face, that look of fierce determination, then the pain she battled to hide as she took a step. I looked away, unable to watch. I was helping her hurt herself. Again. Oh God. . .

Out the front door, down the steps, down the driveway to my car. Small steps, slow steps, but she was almost there.

Maybe two metres from the car, she stopped, swung her body around and clung to me. Now I couldn't help but see the tears streaming down her face. "I can't," she gasped. ' It hurts too much."

Now I thought she'd let me lift her up and carry her the rest of the way. I leaned down to sweep her legs up, but Caitlin moved closer to me so I couldn't.

"They've taken everything from me. I can't even walk. Walk to the car!" Her voice came out sounding slightly hysterical.

I turned her around, carefully, to face the front door. "They didn't take anything from you. Look how far you've come. Tomorrow, you'll get further. You get better every day. They're not here. They can't get anywhere near you. It's like you keep saying. Keep fighting. Don't let them win now."

She relaxed and wiped her eyes with her fingers. "Thank

you." Her arms wrapped around me in a brief hug of gratitude that was over before I was aware of what she was doing.

Then she gritted her teeth, clutching my arm so hard her nails dug into my skin, and took those last agonising steps to the car.

I felt the tiny trickle of my own warm blood as it crept down my arm, but I didn't make a sound. Caitlin was hurting worse than I was and she'd pass out from the pain before she'd permit the scream to escape her teeth. How could I do any less?

SIXTY SIX

When we arrived back at her house, it was immediately apparent that something was wrong. Her front door was slightly open. I knew I'd pulled it shut and locked it behind me when we'd left, yet now it was ajar.

I left Caitlin in the car while I looked over the fence into the garage. There were no cars there, but the back gate was wide open. I wanted to go around to the back of her house to investigate, but I didn't want to leave her alone and unprotected, either. Whoever had left her front door and gate open might still be here.

As if she'd read my mind, Caitlin called, "We should phone the police. I don't want to go in unless it's safe."

I glanced back at her, sitting in the passenger seat with the door open. Her feet were on the door frame, as if she was afraid to step out of the car. She hugged her knees to her chest, her face pale and her expression frightened.

She needed me. The house could wait until I had some help, I decided as I crossed the driveway to stand beside her, pulling my phone out of my pocket. I wanted to call one of our teams, or at least Navid, but I couldn't with Caitlin so close by. So, I did as she suggested and dialled the police. As the phone started to ring, I reached for her hand with my spare one.

I saw the glint of sun on metal as something fell from her hand and plinked to the paving. Her fingers cautiously grasped mine as I recognised the pocket knife I kept in the glove box, now lying open on the ground beneath the car.

When did she pull the knife from the glove box? How did she even know it was there? What was she going to do with it?

I stared at her for a moment, torn between panic and curiosity.

She looked up at me – *so trusting!* – and I had to drag my attention away from her to focus on what the woman on the other end of the phone line was saying.

We didn't wait long before a police car was in the driveway. Two male officers got out and approached the front door.

"Have you been inside yet?" he asked us and I shook my head.

The one who hadn't spoken pulled out a boxy item that I assumed was a Taser, but the other kept his hands free as he pushed her front door open with his shoulder.

Caitlin shivered, despite the warm day, as both police officers moved out of sight into her house. I crouched in the driveway and slid an arm around her shoulders. She leaned in closer to me, her eyes fixed on her front door, now wide open.

It was less than ten minutes before the police officers re-emerged from her house, but the wait felt interminable.

From the doorstep, the talkative one called out, "You can come in. There's no one else here," as the quiet one went around to the garage and through the open back gate, looking thoughtful.

Caitlin didn't move. She looked too stunned to protest, so I lifted her out of the car and carried her into the house. She closed her eyes as we entered the lounge room, but after a few seconds her eyes were open again, looking for some evidence of what the intruders had done.

I saw nothing different, so I put her down in an armchair before sitting in the chair closest to her. She kicked her shoes off almost immediately, bringing her knees up to curl into a little ball where she sat.

The talkative police officer pulled up a straight-backed dining chair from the next room and plonked himself down in it, across from us. Behind him, the smashed sliding door lay in pieces on the floor, except for a few jagged shards up the top. A brick that I'd seen by the back gate, presumably used to prop it open, sat on top of the broken glass.

Well, I can see how they got in, and they left by the front door, I thought, eyeing the mess on the floor of Caitlin's kitchen.

I moved my gaze from the room behind him to the police officer himself. He was close enough for me to read his name badge now, which read *David*. . . I squinted at the large number of letters in his last name, but failed to make any sense of what they spelled out, before he spoke.

He had a handheld tablet out, stylus ready. He didn't ask for our names, so he must have known who we were already. "So, you arrived how long before you called the police?"

Caitlin was silent, so I shrugged and said, "Five minutes, or less."

"How long were you gone?" He looked at Caitlin as he said it, but she didn't say a word.

I spoke up. "We left the house maybe two hours ago."

He wrote something down, before looking at Caitlin again. "Can you tell me if anything is missing?"

I opened my mouth to answer this, too, but Caitlin beat me to it. She uncurled from her foetal position, planting her feet on the floor and leaning toward him. "How do you expect me to know that, when I wasn't stupid enough to go into the house until I knew the intruder was gone?"

Both of us were stunned by her angry outburst.

Before I could react, she pushed herself out of her chair and strode over to the kitchen table. She surveyed the broken glass on the floor, gripping the table for support. She shook her head, then turned, gritting her teeth, and walked past us through the lounge room to the bedrooms.

I leapt to my feet to help her as she went past me, but she shrugged off my hand with a shake of her head and kept walking.

I followed close behind, Officer David with-the-long-last-name a few steps behind me.

The doors to all the other rooms were shut. The only open door was the one to her bedroom, so that's where she headed. Her wardrobe doors were open and so were all her drawers. There were clothes everywhere, as if they'd been looking for something. On her bed, on top of the mess of clothes, lay a big knife and a matching pair of scissors I recognised from her kitchen.

She went to the wardrobe first, opening the doors wide. A blue dress hung at an odd angle, stopping the doors from closing properly. She reached up to push the hanger back into the wardrobe, but the dress slid right off it, puddling at her feet.

She reached down and held it up. The sound that came out of her mouth was halfway between a sob and a yowl The dress was slashed down the front in several places, so the fabric hung in tattered ribbons. If she ever wore the dress in its current state, it'd leave less to the imagination than her scanty hospital gown had.

I picked up a pair of pants on the bed, which looked like they'd been slashed with scissors. The entire crotch of the pants was cut out, from the waistband at the front all the way to the back. I dropped them again quickly before Caitlin could see them.

She started pulling items out of the wardrobe, one at a time, dropping them on the floor. Dresses, shirts, pants, skirts – almost everything she touched had been a victim of knife or scissors.

I edged away from the bed and bumped into the chest of drawers beside it. The top drawer was wide open, with something lacy hacked into pieces on top. Unable to help myself, I lifted the mess of white lace up for a better look. From the little that remained, it looked like they had once been a bra and matching knickers. Now they looked like some white elastic with scraps of lace dangling off at odd angles. What I'd give to have seen her in these when they were still intact. . .

The police officer stared at me, not saying a word, though he evidently wanted to say a few things. I dropped the ruined underwear back in the drawer.

Caitlin backed away from the wardrobe and sat down heavily on the bed, taking stock of the destroyed clothing strewn across it. I stumbled through the clothes on the floor to the passage outside and made it to the bathroom. In my mind's eye, I saw the drawer full of shredded lace and wondered why they'd come in and shred her clothes, but leave before she came home.

The silent police officer stood in the open bathroom doorway. He moved aside when I approached.

My eyes went to the floor of the bathroom first, but the only clothes were the pyjamas Caitlin had left there this morning when she'd taken a shower. They looked untouched.

I closed my eyes and splashed water on my face, grabbing a towel to dry myself where I stood. So I was standing in front of the mirror when I opened my eyes to see my reflection was obscured by lipstick smeared across the reflective surface – four words in bright red capitals:

FUCK YOU

LITTLE BITCH

What remained of the lipstick was on the bench beside the basin, next to a box of Caitlin's makeup that I'd never seen her use. The lipstick looked like the one she'd worn only last night. When it had graced her lips, it'd reminded me of strawberries. Scrawled across her mirror, now it looked more like blood.

When I turned to meet the eyes of the silent police officer, I was more confused than ever.

The bastards who hurt Caitlin weren't likely to cut up her clothes and make a mess of her bathroom mirror. Any message they'd have for her would be vocal, physical and brutal. Any red marks left in the house would have been drawn in her blood.

The officer looked grim. "There's a woman out there who really hates your girlfriend. She should watch out."

A woman? Who hated her more than those bastards? I found that hard to imagine, until I remembered.

When his wife heard what had happened to him, she was very distraught. Her name was Laura.

The dead bastard had a wife.

I wonder if she knew what he was really doing.

She was little and pretty, with short dark hair.

The woman driver, who spoke to Caitlin before she hit her and pushed her into the car, had short dark hair.

What if the bastard's wife not only knew what he was doing, but she'd helped him? She'd be pretty pissed off, especially if she thought Caitlin had killed her husband.

I stared at the police officer in horror for a moment, before pushing past him to hurry back to Caitlin. I stood in the doorway of her room, hesitating.

She still sat on the bed, not touching any of the clothes. She'd clenched her hands into fists and her teeth bit so deep into her lip I hoped she wasn't bleeding. She was fighting so hard not to cry, with Officer David with-the-impossible-last-name's eyes on her.

She didn't trust police officers, not after one of them shot her.

Oh, shit. I'd left her alone with one.

He left the room as I entered it, murmuring something about filing a report and how he'd be in contact soon. He handed me a slip of paper, telling me it was for insurance.

Caitlin nodded numbly.

I shoved the damaged clothes into a pile on one side of the bed, away from her, and sat beside her in the space I'd made. I cautiously slid my arm around her shoulders and tried to pull her closer, but she wouldn't budge.

"We'll get you an alarm system and security guards." I told her, dropping my voice to a whisper. "I won't let her hurt you."

Still she sat ramrod straight, her whole body tense, and I wondered if she was going to push me away, or even hit me. She seemed angry enough to do anything, even if it would hurt her later when she calmed down.

Shit, I was worried that she was going to hit me, not because I might get hurt, but because she might hurt her hand and need an ice pack. I suddenly remembered the knife she'd held in the car. Had she left it there? Where were the knife and scissors? I looked around the bed for them, but I couldn't see them. On the edge of panic, I tried to pull her toward me again.

"I won't let them hurt you," I promised her again. "I'll even take you shopping to buy more clothes to replace these."

She looked at me, her eyes filling with tears. Her hand groped for something behind me — I prayed that it wasn't something sharp — before her tears spilled over.

What would the woman who did this to an entire wardrobe of clothes do to Caitlin if she got her hands on her? I realised suddenly, my arms tightening protectively around Caitlin. Nothing. NOTHING. I wouldn't let her.

Her tears were short-lived this time. It seemed only a couple of minutes before Caitlin sat up again, something still clenched in her right hand.

She wiped at her eyes with her free hand, sniffling. "Did she get to the dirty clothes in the laundry?"

I thought about the untouched pyjamas on the bathroom floor. "I don't know, but I doubt it."

She stood up, a little shakily. "Then I better go do some washing, before I get a rubbish bag for all this."

As she walked away with small, careful steps, leaning against the walls and furniture where she could, I noticed her hands were empty.

I watched her until she was out of sight down the passage, before I looked to see what she'd been so quick to grab and keep hidden from me. On the clear patch of the bed where she'd been sitting was a crumpled ball of shredded black satin and lace. I smoothed out the remains of the slashed g-string and felt my face grow hot.

Oh God, I just agreed to take her shopping for sexy underwear.

Don't think about it. Make some phone calls. Check with whoever's on surveillance to see if it was Laura.

Keep her safe 'til tomorrow and then worry about how I'd manage to go underwear shopping with her without being a blind eunuch with a preference for guys. Fuck. . .

SIXTY SEVEN

Knocked out or just asleep?
Still dark.
Chris. The only name they gave me.
Tied up, restraining wrists and ankles.
Someone else here?
Water. Sipping slowly, swallowing painfully.
Let me go! Help me, you bastard.
Give me a weapon so I can hurt them, kill them.
No.
Tears.
Pills.
Hurt?
Hell yes.
A sip, a swallow.
Silence.
Won't let them win.

SIXTY EIGHT

"Please. . . don't let them. . ."

Fuck. Another one.

The nightmares had started maybe an hour after Caitlin had fallen asleep and this was the third time tonight. Hell, it wasn't even midnight yet.

"I'm here. I won't let them hurt you," I murmured. I smoothed my pyjamas, making sure they covered as much of me as possible. I had to be so careful. If it weren't for Caitlin, I wouldn't even own pyjamas.

She owned very little in the way of clothing, now – in the end, I'd had to bag up all her ruined clothes before putting them in the rubbish bin. Caitlin's tears had been more than I could take. Her wardrobe was as bare as one in a hotel room – no, more than that. Even hotel wardrobes had bathrobes. Hers was sliced into so many pieces I'd had to vacuum some of them up.

I moved closer to Caitlin, every movement controlled as I pulled her into a hug. "It's okay. They're not here. It's over now, just a dream. . ."

I felt her relax. "Nathan?"

"That's right. Just us here, no one else. You're safe at home." I loosened my hold on her.

"I. . . they. . ."

"I know. Just a dream. It's okay." I took a breath and let it out slowly as I let go of her. "Try to get back to sleep, okay?"

"Okay. . ." The bed springs crunched lightly as they compressed under her shifting weight.

I sighed and shifted so my head was back on my own pillow. The clock read 11:46. I wondered how long it would be before the next nightmare as I slid into sleep.

"Let me go, you bastard!"

1:03. Oh, shit, it was this one. Don't touch her 'til she's awake.

"No one but you and I here, angel. No one's got you. They can't hurt you any more." I spoke at normal volume, hoping to wake her with only my voice. I didn't want her clawing at my face again.

"I said, let me go, loser!" Her voice rose.

Fuck. The neighbours were going to hear this one if I didn't wake her up soon.

I touched her shoulder lightly. "Caitlin, it's Nathan. You're safe. I swear, you're safe. . ."

She turned on me and I felt her nails rake my cheek as I pulled away too slowly. I caught her hands in mine, as carefully as I could. She dug her nails into my palm.

"Let me go," she insisted, trying to pull her hands out of my grasp.

"Wake up, angel. No one's hurting you — least of all me.

Come on, you know who I am. . ." I shifted away from her, letting go of her hands. "Just another nightmare, Caitlin." My heart ached for her as I touched my hand to my cheek, relieved to find I wasn't bleeding, though that also meant she wasn't strong enough yet. Almost. . .

A gasp and a sob. "Nathan? Please. . ."

Thank God. I moved quickly to her side again and held out my arms to her. She burrowed her face into the buttons on my chest and I felt the thin cotton soak through with her tears.

"Wouldn't help me. So much pain and no help. . . bastard." I heard the words that were muffled by my pyjamas.

I sighed in relief. "I'm here now and I'm helping you. No one's going to hurt you again, I swear. Definitely not her."

Caitlin pulled away, sniffling. She stretched out, resting her head on her pillow again. "Sorry. Thanks, Nathan."

I was slower to relax back into repose. My cheek stung, but my eyes still closed.

"Who do you think you are?" Her angry voice woke me again. I prayed that the dream wouldn't go any further.

"Took my clothes. . ." she wailed.

Fuck. I opened my eyes. 2:14. Here we go again. No sleep for the wicked, or the rest of us, either.

SIXTY NINE

"Hello?" Caitlin's voice said softly behind the curtain.

"I'm here," I answered from the chair outside, beside a rack of stringy satin and lace. If I didn't look too closely at the lingerie beside me, didn't think about how little Caitlin was wearing and firmly focussed on the memory of her broken fingers covered in blood on the beach, I could almost keep it together.

She stuck her head out, clutching at the curtain so it didn't reveal anything I really didn't need to see, except her bare shoulder. "Is the shop assistant there? I need help and I don't know how much longer I can stand up. . ." She swallowed, looking worried. The dark circles under her eyes only served to make them look bigger and sadder.

I crossed to the entrance of the change rooms and looked. The music over the shop speakers was a lot louder out here, but it didn't improve the perky pop song any. The teenage sales assistant was busy with a couple of giggling teenage customers, so she ignored my frantic waving.

Maybe she just didn't hear me over the loud music. I headed back in to Caitlin.

Grabbing the chair I'd been sitting in, I said, "She's busy. I can help, if you like." I held out the chair, so its outline took shape through the curtain. "First, you should sit down." I slid it through the gap, closing my eyes until I felt her take the chair from me.

"Thank you," Caitlin replied. She took a deep breath, like she needed to say more. "But. . . I still need help with fastening things," she finished in a rush.

Fuck. "I'll go see if she's free," I told her as I headed for the entrance again. The giggly girls continued to ignore me. I returned. "Sorry, angel, she's not. Can I help?"

I could hear her breathing, but she didn't reply for a few slow breaths. "You remember how you helped me get dressed this morning?"

I laughed. 'Of course, angel. I'll close my eyes or keep my eyes down the whole time. Don't you worry." Think horrible thoughts. Twisted, broken fingers. The gunshot wound in her leg, bleeding onto the road. Keep a blank face.

I slipped behind the change room curtain, my eyes on the grey carpet. A quick glance up told me Caitlin was sitting sideways in the chair, resting her arm on the back of it, so she had her back to me. As long as I stayed behind her, I might manage not to stare at anything she didn't want me to see. Of course, I wasn't counting on the surrounding mirrors, making sure even the slightest glance gave me a panoramic view.

She held out the back of her bra. I sighed and started on those little hooks. One, then the other one. . . oh, shit, now the first one again. . . I hated these bloody. . . Done.

I risked a glance up. Strawberry-red satin lifting a lovely cleavage. I closed my eyes. Not strawberries. Think of blood.

"Nathan, could you. . ." I opened my eyes. I didn't have to – I could undo her bra with my eyes closed. I kept my eyes on her back while she slipped the red one off and pulled something black on instead.

Smooth skin, marred only slightly by the pink and white patches where her ulcers had been. Healing rapidly, she'd already recovered so much. Far from the shadow of herself that I'd seen stretched out on the sand, she was every bit as real and vibrant as the angel I saw tripping down the Terrace. I wanted to. . .

"Nathan?"

Black hooks on black satin. I tried to focus on that bit, not the curve of black lace tempting me in the mirror. Think of her screaming in the dark, when there was nothing, NOTHING I could do to calm her down. I could feel my face wincing at the memory.

"Please. . ."

Pink and patterned, the swell of skin above them like the top of a tight-fitting corset. Pink like the scars on her ankles, where I'd had to peel the bloodied rope away. . .

Black and white stripes, cutting into her flesh like a knife blade about to pierce the skin. . .

Blood-red with black edging, like an encrustation of fresh and dried blood on her skin as she lay barely conscious on the sand. . .

Plain black satin, as dark as the inside of a nightmare when I couldn't stop her from screaming. . .

White satin, pure and pale like her face had been on the beach, when I'd thought she was dead. . .

"Can I help you with anything?" the salesgirl asked behind me, treading on my foot as it stuck out behind the curtain.

"Oh, thank God!" I blurted out as relief rushed over me. I wouldn't have to conjure up any more horrible memories of Caitlin's injuries to stop myself thinking about her in her underwear.

A sharp intake of breath and I dared to open my eyes. Caitlin's reflection stared at me, looking shocked and hurt. Instead of a new bra, she wore a silky little black nightdress and she looked nothing short of incredible. It hurt to look at her – close enough to touch and yet untouchable.

"Miss, are you okay in there?" the salesgirl asked, sticking her head inside the curtain. She squinted suspiciously at me, kneeling behind Caitlin.

"Fine," Caitlin said absently, whisking a tear off her cheek before the girl saw it. She reached for the hangers, laden with what she'd tried on. "I'll take these ones, with the matching knickers, all in small." She split the pile and handed a small stack to her, the strawberry-red one on top. "And you can keep these." The larger pile went to the girl's other hand. The girl didn't move, still gaping at me. "He's helping me," Caitlin said angrily. "Now let me get changed into my clothes."

The salesgirl opened her mouth like a flustered fish as she backed out and left.

Good riddance.

I looked at Caitlin, who gazed pointedly back at me. I closed my eyes and heard the rustle of satin as she took the nightdress off.

"You looked beautiful in that one," I said suddenly, feeling like I had to say something.

Caitlin didn't say anything until she needed my help. "One last bra, please, Nathan."

I fastened it fairly quickly this time – I was getting the hang of those bloody hooks. Deep purple satin, the colour of a blossoming bruise. . . Fuck.

Satin draped over her arm, Caitlin left the change room as soon as she was dressed, while I struggled to my feet and stumbled along behind her. She laid the nightdress on the counter. "This one, too."

I wanted to apologise. I wanted to explain. Most of all, I wanted to see her wear any of her new purchases without having to dredge up horrific thoughts. I wondered if there'd ever be a day I could think about her body without imagining blood.

I didn't have a hope in hell.

SEVENTY

My phone vibrated, not quite silent. The screen glowed brighter than anything else I could see, for it was almost dark. Caitlin wasn't within earshot, so I answered it.

Navid's voice was panicked. "They're almost there – just coming into sight of her house. It's too late to get her out and it's now or never – get her hidden. Our team are still on their way. Get geared up and stick your earpiece in, now."

"As soon as Caitlin's safe," I replied, my heart plummeting at the thought that she was in danger.

"Just don't waste time. They're coming and backup won't be here in time to stop them from reaching you."

"How many?" I asked urgently.

"Three men," came the answer. "No sign of her."

Shit. "I'll take care of it. Let them in. Talk to you soon." I hung up.

I knew she was in the toilet, but I couldn't wait. Perhaps this was the best place to hide her and she'd be safe. I had a million thoughts running through my mind, but I couldn't focus when I considered the possibility that she might not survive. I couldn't think it and I didn't want to.

I heard the sound of cascading water and burst in, almost knocking her down with the door. She looked stunned as she tried to regain her balance, but I shoved my body up against hers, pinning her to the wall, as I kicked the door shut behind me.

My shirt slid over warm black satin with a froth of white lace at the top, highlighting the cleavage it made no attempt to hide. Oh God, she was wearing the new little nightdress. I dragged my eyes from her lace to her face.

A face full of raw terror and panic that I'd do anything to wipe clean. Her eyes didn't leave mine before she whispered imploringly, "Nathan, please. . . don't hurt me," as Caitlin closed her eyes. Surrendering. NO!

Painfully, I was reminded of her lying on the beach and that moment when I'd thought she was dead.

My heart contracted in my chest, aching for her, as I thought about how lost I'd be if anyone hurt her. If I lost her tonight. I tried to reassure her. "It's okay. You're safe," I lied through my teeth, knowing she didn't believe me.

I could feel her heart beating fast under my hand, reminding me that she was still alive. "I'm not going to hurt you," I murmured. Fuck. LET THEM hurt you. Not going to let THEM hurt you. . . Surely she knew by now that I'd never hurt her!

Her eyes stayed closed. She opened her mouth to draw a deep, shaky breath.

I moved almost by instinct. There was no thought. I just looked at her face, her lips, her closed eyes. . . and touched my lips to hers.

She stiffened and her eyes flew open. She just stared at me, her eyes filled with hurt and betrayal, as if she didn't know me, as well she might. Like I reminded her of them.

I broke away from her. "I'm sorry. . ."

"Chris. . ." she breathed, confirming my fears.

She brought her knee up between my legs as hard as she could. "You prick," she hissed in my ear as I doubled over. "You did that before and you hoped I wouldn't remember."

She tried to shove past me, but even in my haze of pain I remembered why I'd cornered her in here in the first place. She's getting stronger, I realised. If I could keep her alive past tonight, she'd recover. My heart leaped at the thought.

"I need you to stay here. The security guard's told me there are people outside your house and I need you to hide in here, where no one will guess you are. Just until the police arrive." I pushed her into the corner, pressing her shoulders toward the floor.

Her cheek pressed against the trickling cistern, her dry eyes were both furious and terrified as she looked up at me. "You can't leave me here alone – give me something to defend myself with or stay here with me!" Her hands were curled into fists and so were her bare toes, she was so angry.

I wavered, wanting to stay.

NO – don't think of that night on the beach. Concentrate on keeping her alive. Struggling to keep my focus, I crouched in front of her. "I can't. They might have seen me come in here. If I stay here and they come into the house before the police arrive, this is the first place they'll look, because they know I'll be here. Then they'll find you, too."

She bit her lip and closed her eyes. When she opened them again, her eyes held mine. No longer terrified, she'd harnessed the fury. FUCK. "Make sure you kill them all," she told me through gritted teeth. "None of the people who hurt me deserves to live."

I nodded once.

It felt like forever, but barely a minute had passed, the time it took for the cistern to fill, ready to flush again.

I had to get out of there to keep her safe. I opened the door and pretended to zip up my fly as I shut the door behind me. I ran for her bedroom, praying I'd have time to get my vest on and some extra clips for my standard issue semi-automatic before they arrived.

The rip of Velcro as I fastened the vest, as fast as I could. Spare clips shoved in every available pocket. A loaded gun in my hands.

Please, just let her survive 'til tomorrow.

Would I? I wondered as I fumbled to fit the earpiece in place.

"Time's up," said a voice in my ear.

I jumped a mile, before I realised I was alone. The voice was Navid's.

"Coming through the kitchen now. Ready?"

No. Nevertheless, I nodded. Now or never. I need to end this.

Don't let her die!

SEVENTY ONE

"Rounding the corner, you should see him in five, four. . ." Navid's voice buzzed in my earpiece.

I heard him before I saw him, so when he rounded the corner he met the muzzle of my gun in his face.

He backed up a little and his hands went up, too. He didn't even have a weapon out.

"Which one are you?" I asked roughly.

"I'm Pete," he said through his nose.

"What'd you do to Caitlin?" I demanded.

"The little girl?" He grinned lazily. "I fucked her more times'n I could count. Broke her fingers, too, when she tried to fight me. She screamed real sweet then."

Caitlin screaming. Nothing sweet about that.

The sound of her screaming still echoing in my head, I shot the smile off his face. Okay, I shot off most of his face. The dead body crumpled to the carpet. One down.

I felt nothing but a grim satisfaction.

"Fuck, Nathan. Alive?" I nodded, knowing Navid could

see me through the surveillance cameras. I'd try harder to resist killing the next one if I could. *"Leaving the kitchen now, he's headed into the lounge. . ."*

I stepped over the corpse and carefully continued up the passage. The clean-up crew could deal with it later.

I crept up on the next one from behind, my gun to the back of his head as he leaned over to look under a table. "Which one are you?"

A snort as he straightened. "I *was* Senior Constable Nick Dennis, before I got suspended after meeting you and your girlfriend."

"What'd you do to her?"

He grunted. "Nothing. It's what she'll do to you that matters."

I jabbed him with the gun. "What Caitlin will do to me?"

He snorted again. "Laura, fuckwit. It doesn't matter where you go or what you do, she'll find you and fuck you up worse than the little girl who killed her husband."

"Tell me where to find her," I said urgently. "I can get you into protective custody."

He let out a bark of laughter. "Not from her you can't. She'll pay whatever it takes to get whatever she wants. I'll lose my job as it is – I almost did when I shot you and her. Are you gonna shoot me?"

I pulled the gun back a little, so it wasn't pressed against his skull. "Maybe not, if you tell me where I can find her."

More laughter. "She'll find you and you'll wish she hadn't. Not me, mate." He lifted his own weapon. The barrel pointed at me over his shoulder and I ducked to the side. I was just in time to miss the shower of blood and brain that blew out the back of his head as he killed himself.

Instead, I felt nothing.

"Number three, in the bush with the red flowers. Unconscious is fine but we need him alive."

"Do you want to do this?" I muttered. "I'll take your place in the van."

"Love to, mate, but you know Sam will kill me if I don't come home in the morning. I have to pick up nappies on my way home." It took me a minute to make sense of that. His wife would kill him if he got killed? I shook my head and decided I didn't need to understand it.

The third man was outside, keeping watch by Caitlin's bedroom window. I looped around the house, out of his sight, so I could come up behind him and surprise him.

I stuck the gun in his ear. "Which one are you and what did you do to her?"

He didn't say anything, so I repeated the question and jabbed the gun to emphasise each word.

"Tom," he grunted. "Held her down for the old bugger. Did her a couple of times, but I don't like leftovers."

"Are you going to tell me where she is?"

"Little leftovers? Or the bitch she made a widow?"

I spat the words out. "The bitch who's responsible for what happened to Caitlin."

"Focus, Nathan." I ignored Navid's voice in my ear.

"You won't get Laura. She had her husband in a gimp mask for a week for asking her if the dishwasher had been loaded. Whipped him raw, too. If she did that to her own husband, fucked if you have a hope in hell. Good luck!" He lumbered to his feet, reaching for his weapon.

"Stop!" I ordered, still aiming my gun at him.

He dropped his hands to his sides again. "You think I'm

the last one who matters? She has the money to hire as many thugs as she likes. Tomorrow, she'll have replacements for the lot of us – all convicted rapists and child molesters, who'd pay for a bit of Little Leftovers. Don't know why – she's about as responsive as a corpse."

I wanted to kill him, my heart almost bursting out of my chest, I was so angry. "Not another step."

"Or you'll shoot me?" He smiled grimly. "It's nicer than what Laura will do to me, or to you when she finds you. She'll leave Little Leftovers for last."

I gritted my teeth. "Don't call her that. Her name's Caitlin."

He turned his back on me and started walking away. "Like I fucking care. She was just a little cunt to me and she's less than shit to Laura. She won't last long enough for me to learn her name."

The sound of the shot echoed between the brick walls of the front yard and the house like there was more than one. I fired before I realised I was going to. He fell face-first onto the paving as the acrid smoke wafted away in the wind. I left him where he lay. Like I fucking cared.

"Fuck, Nathan! You were supposed to keep him alive for questioning!" Navid complained. *"There's none left now. She should be safe for a few minutes by herself. Come to the van, so we can talk face to face."*

I started into the dark.

SEVENTY TWO

I tapped lightly on the van's side door. Navid opened it for me, a tight smile on his face and a phone jammed between his ear and his shoulder. "That's the lot, mate." He nodded in greeting. "All clear. You can stand down." He beeped the end of the call and stuck his phone back in his pocket.

"Any sign of her?" I asked tersely, slamming the door hard behind me. The icy fury I'd started with now burned white-hot and I had no one left to kill.

"Nope. Did you get anything out of them?"

I shook my head. "They said they hurt Caitlin and they'd prefer a clean death over the one she'd give them, so they wouldn't say a thing about her, except how shit-scared they were." I thought back to things I hadn't noticed at the time. "They were all limping, though, walking stiffly the way you do with a knee injury." I felt some satisfaction that Laura had already fucked them up before they died. Only now did I wish that Caitlin or I'd had some hand in that, but it was too late.

I looked up to find Navid's eyes on me. He looked like it pained him to say, "You should have left at least one of them alive, mate. You're going to get in trouble for killing them all."

I shrugged. "One of them killed himself instead of coming with us. He was police, or ex-police. The one who shot me and her. Fucking crazy."

Navid looked worried. "Him or you? Now we have no choice but to get the woman alive. You've killed the rest."

I nodded. "Yeah, she's next. Time to get the clean-up crew in here, I think, then we'll plan out her capture. It won't be easy." Easy to resist strangling her with my bare hands. I flexed my itching fingers.

Navid laughed. "We've been after that crazy bitch for months. If it was easy, we'd have her already."

I nodded again. "But first – Caitlin. I need to get her somewhere safe."

He shot me a sideways glance. "Didn't you already hide her somewhere safe? She gave me the shock of my life when she came sliding out of the ceiling, right in front of one of my cameras. Some very close-up curves." He smiled.

I stared at him. "I didn't hide her in the roof. Show me."

He checked the surveillance footage and replayed it, from maybe twenty minutes ago, when I'd headed for the third bloke in the bushes. A clear hallway, then a pair of black-clad legs dangled in front of the camera. She descended slowly, as if she was carefully letting herself down from the access cover by her hands. Her hair swung a little, too short to touch her shoulders. It looked like a black helmet, matching her dark clothes. She hung suspended from her fingertips for a moment before she dropped to a crouch in the passage.

My heart plummeted, watching her pull out her handgun and hold it out in readiness, as she rose smoothly to her feet. She strode down the passage, scanning from side to side, rolling out like a tank on patrol.

"It looks like she's doing your job for you," Navid said with a smile.

"That's. . . that's not Caitlin," I managed to say. I stared at him in horror as my heart froze.

We both dived for the door, fumbling with the lock, losing precious seconds to clumsiness. Released, I sprinted back to her house, Navid right behind me.

"How far away are the rest of them?" I panted.

"Ten minutes," puffed Navid, struggling to keep up as he pressed buttons on his phone. I heard him recall the team that should have been here by now, but I made no move to slow my pace.

I was out of breath by the time I reached the toilet, but I wasn't sure if the pain in my chest was from trying to breathe or trying not to shout at Navid for putting Caitlin at risk and not fucking telling me. I had to get her out and somewhere safe, before Laura found her.

The toilet door was still shut, as I'd left it. But, when I tried, the damn thing didn't open. There wasn't a lock – she must have somehow wedged it shut on purpose.

"Caitlin, angel, it's me," I called through the door, but I got no reply. The door was still stuck. I shoved with my full weight and it opened a little. I pushed and widened the gap further, now big enough to get my head inside for a proper look. She was there – lying face down, the soles of her shoes jammed against the door. I'd never felt so relieved.

Laura didn't get to her. I got here in time. Oh, thank God.

"Hey, it's okay. It's me." I knelt and moved her legs so that I could open the door fully. Strange – she was limp. I shook her shoulders, her nightie sliding off her and revealing her bare skin, but she didn't react. I turned her onto her back.

"My God!" The black tiles beneath her were slick with blood, and her face was a mess. Feeling sick, I felt for a pulse that wasn't there. And the smell. . .

Had all this been for nothing? Stupid, stupid, to have left her alone!

I should have stayed with her – that was what she'd asked me to do. Now she couldn't even have the satisfaction of being right. She couldn't have anything. I may as well have killed her. This was my fault.

I'd as good as killed her.

She was dead.

Shit.

I'd killed Caitlin.

SEVENTY THREE

I stood up slowly. I had tears on my face and I didn't want to turn around 'til I'd wiped them away. Navid would think I'd lost it. But I'd lost her. . . Fuck! I swiped at my face with the hand that wasn't covered in her blood.

When I turned around, Navid's hands jerked up in stunned surrender, like someone had jammed something explosive up his arse. I saw light glint on something behind him and realised it was a gun to his head that had him scared shitless. The fingers holding it were small and definitely female, the edge of a black sleeve barely showing at her wrist

Laura. You fucking bitch. "You killed her!"

Navid had a wife and baby waiting for him at home and I had. . . nothing. I didn't care what happened to me anymore. I was useless now Caitlin was dead. What else did I have to lose? Maybe the last shreds of sanity, is all.

I heard her hoarse whispered, "Yes," as Navid nodded emphatically, a puppet without strings.

I hoped her throat was sore because Caitlin had tried to choke the life out of her, fighting back to her last breath. Now it was my turn.

I lost all reason then and there. I shoved Navid out of the way and went for her. It didn't matter if I died, just as long as I took her with me. It was the least that Caitlin's killer deserved. All the shit she put that poor girl through. . .

She tried to hide behind him as she crooked her finger round the trigger. Navid and I both heard the click as her gun jammed. We exchanged a glance and moved together. He pinned her up against the wall, almost smothering her with his body, as I bashed her gun hand on the metal door frame, trying to get her to drop the weapon.

The psychopathic bitch wouldn't let go. She even tried to point the Ruger at me. I'd have laughed if I could unclench my jaw. The bitch's gun was useless and she didn't have a free hand to do anything about it.

I managed to pry my fingers between hers and the butt of the pistol, so the gun clattered to the floor. The noise distracted Navid and that was all she needed to slip from his grasp, sliding down the wall to the floorboards.

From her crouch, she dived between his legs for her useless weapon, but I kicked it away from her scrabbling hands as he flattened her to the floor. Shoving her down, he used his much longer reach to grasp both of her arms and twist them up behind her back. She muttered into the mat.

I couldn't hear everything she said, but it sure didn't sound complimentary. ". . . Fucking kill you. . ." was the only phrase I could make out.

I itched to kill her, too, for everything she'd done, but Navid was already shaking his head at me. We had to bring this bitch in alive, even though she'd shot Caitlin. He pulled out some handcuffs, looking up at me.

I swallowed and nodded.

She started struggling to throw him off as soon as she felt the touch of metal, but he held her down as he fitted the handcuffs tightly around her wrists and snapped them closed. Instead of giving up, she struggled harder. Her bare feet drummed on the boards like she was going to kick through the jarrah. Fat chance, bitch. That stuff was harder than my heart.

"Now, look," Navid said reasonably. "You're coming with us whether you like it or not. If you don't cooperate, I'll knock you out and carry you, like a sack of potatoes. Are you going to cooperate?"

"Fuck. . . you," she panted, her voice muffled by how her face was mashed into the hall runner.

Navid pulled a syringe out of his pocket. "I'm taking that as a no." He ripped the cap off with his teeth and looked at me as he pressed the point of the needle to her neck.

I wanted to be the one to stab her, just for the sheer satisfaction, but I knew it was better if Navid did it. Gritting my teeth, I nodded again.

She jerked her head up at the touch of the needle. "Nathan. Please. . ." Her eyes met mine. I saw betrayal and terror.

Oh, fuck, no!

I froze in horror. It was only for a moment, but in those precious seconds Navid pushed the plunger on the syringe with his thumb and she collapsed. He rose to his feet, leaving her body where it lay.

No. It couldn't be. I had to be hallucinating. Like the time I thought Caitlin was Alanna in the ambulance.

No. Don't think about that. Lock it down. Think about now and what you need to do.

I dropped to my knees beside the unconscious girl, my hands shaking. I reached out to touch the handcuffs at her wrists and saw the scars beneath the metal. No. . .

Gently, I turned her over. Her face was streaked with blood and grime, but it was unmistakeably her. I hadn't killed her. She was alive.

I lifted her torso so her head rested on my chest. "Get the cuffs off her." My voice came out quieter than I'd intended.

Navid looked confused. "But. . . she just tried to kill both of us. I'm not taking her in the car without restraints. What if she wakes up?"

"You're not taking her anywhere. Take the handcuffs off her. I need to get her cleaned up before she wakes up."

Unwillingly, he did as I asked. Gently, I brought her arms around so her hands rested in her lap, trying to rub away the red marks on her wrists. Her expression tightened in discomfort as she pulled her hands away from me, so I stopped.

With a sigh, I shifted, lifting her limp form in my arms as I stood up.

"Get some towels. A lot of towels. And some clean pyjamas for her. Bring them to the bathroom." I strode toward the shower, her body carefully cradled in my arms. I was filled with a desperate desire never to let her go again. "I'm sorry," I whispered to her, too late, as I touched my lips to her blood-matted hair.

Navid hadn't moved – he was staring at the wall. "Navid." He didn't turn around. "Navid!"

He finally turned around, then stared at me, or Caitlin. "But. . . she killed the girl we were trying to protect. What do you think you're going to do with her?"

I looked from the bloodied bitch's body on the toilet floor to the unconscious angel in my arms and shook my head. "No. Caitlin killed the bitch we wanted to bring in alive, in what looks like a fair fight." I tasted salt. Too late I realised that it was Laura's blood I'd licked off my lips. I shifted closer to spit the offending saliva on her faceless corpse.

Navid's mouth hung open. "But you said. . . the girl in the surveillance footage wasn't Caitlin. . ."

Caitlin couldn't hang from her fingertips, nor use her hands to slowly climb from a ceiling. She didn't move like a tank, either. "She wasn't. That was Laura. Somehow Caitlin managed to take her out and take her clothes, too. She left her own clothes with the body."

His disbelief wasn't easily dispelled. "How can this be the sweet little girl you've been guarding? How'd she beat the killer bitch we couldn't catch? Someone's going to have to debrief her to find out."

Caitlin was stronger than he knew. She'd survived this long against all odds – why be surprised at one more night? "It's over, mate. The three that were left – Nick, Pete, Tom – they're all dead. We don't need to debrief her. We know what she did and we don't need to know how. We're going to make all this go away before she wakes up and remembers what she did."

Navid looked in horror at Caitlin. "There's no way she'll

forget this. She killed someone and then we. . ." He swallowed painfully. He still held the syringe, but he'd put the cap back on. Good thing, too. It was shaking in his hand.

"She's blocked out the memories of a lot worse," I replied. "I'll tell her it was a dream."

Navid was shaking his head in disbelief. "That's a hell of a messed-up dream for a girl to have."

"Compared to some of her nightmares, this is nothing."

"Mate. . ." he started to say, but I cut him off.

"Can you get someone to take care of the mess?" I nodded in its direction. "I want the whole team guarding every entrance to the house — especially her room. I want you outside her door, all night. If anyone leaves his post, I want him replaced, even if for only a minute. And get her some ice for her hand."

He stared at me. "It's over. You said it yourself."

I slowly shook my head. "We got all the ones who hurt her. One of them said she paid them for what they did. She could have hired more." I swallowed. "Please. I can't stand to lose her again. One more night — just in case. They're all on duty tonight anyway. . . mate, please. I'm begging you."

Navid nodded. "Hell of a night." He chewed on his lip, as if he was trying to bite back what he really wanted to say. "I'll go direct our team — they're arriving as we speak. You take care of her, okay?"

Curtly, I nodded, too, carrying my precious burden back to where I could get her cleaned up. I wished I could wipe her memories away as easily as blood.

SEVENTY FOUR

Staring and standing beside her car, they
matched.
Bright red car, bright red lips.
Shiny black and silver wheels, shiny black
bobbed hair.
Her heavy-breathing friend.
A blow, couldn't breathe.
Pushed in with the pervert.
Her friend.
She drove away.
Kept driving.
Bastard in the passenger seat.
Her friend.
Forced down against taut thighs.
Face up.
Face faded as dark descended.
Red-tinted darkness.

<h1 style="text-align:center">SEVENTY FIVE</h1>

When I reached the bathroom, Michael, his earpiece barely visible, had a stack of towels in his arms and a fairly confused look on his face. We exchanged nods.

"Navid said you needed these?" he said.

"Spread a couple of them flat on the floor, one on top of the other, so I can put her down on them," I instructed.

I watched Michael smooth the towels across the tiles before I was satisfied. "Now, go get her some pyjamas or a nightie to wear. I don't care if you have to go out and buy it. Just leave them outside the door."

He nodded and left.

He didn't have anything else to say to me tonight. I didn't have anything to say to me either. All my attention was on Caitlin. I'd come so close to losing her, I was scared almost into speechlessness. But I couldn't touch Caitlin without talking to her – she flinched away from contact unless I spoke. No bloody wonder after tonight.

"Okay, I'll be really careful, just in case you've been hurt.

I'm going to try to get you cleaned up a bit. It's okay – it's just you and me. No one else."

I carried Caitlin to the shower. The plastic chair was still in the cubicle, so that's where I carefully placed her, the arms curving around her and keeping her upright.

My arms felt empty as I let her go. I shook myself out of my silly sentimentality and dropped to my knees on the tiles. I started checking her over. She'd been splattered with Laura's blood, dusted in something grey and then rolled on the carpet, so it was hard to tell if she was wounded. I decided to check her bones for breaks first, then look for anything else after I'd cleaned her up. Aside from the red marks from the handcuffs, her left hand looked fine. Her right hand wasn't so good, though, already swelling and tender from the pounding it had taken against the wall. A trickle of blood started at one knuckle, running down to her wrist. I took her hurt hand in mine and brought it up to my lips. "I'm sorry," I whispered again.

I felt stupid talking to her while she was unconscious, but it wasn't the first time, though it might be the last. I wondered what she was dreaming about, or if she heard me.

I closed my eyes, wishing there was someone else I could ask to do this. But there wasn't anyone else I trusted. I took a deep breath. "I'm going to take these clothes off you, angel. I need to check your injuries and make sure you're okay. Then I'm going to get you cleaned up. You won't need those any more – I'll get you into your own clothes as soon as I can."

Gently, I peeled the bloodstained pants from her legs, then pulled them off her feet, one at a time. I balled them up and threw them into the corner by the bin.

I took a deep breath and looked at Caitlin. There was dried blood on her knees and all along her shins. I closed my eyes, the images coming unbidden. She'd knelt in her nightie on the floor, slick with Laura's blood, as she pulled the pants off her and put them on. Fuck, what had she been thinking? Taking the clothes from a corpse?

Another deep breath that I held. Time for the vest. I swallowed, wishing I didn't have to do this. I had to check if Navid had broken any of her ribs. I told myself that if I thought of this as just another med practical and ignored her boobs like any professional doctor would, I'd be okay. Fuck. No, I wouldn't. Like a coward, I closed my eyes as soon as I touched the zip. Caitlin cringed, throwing her arms up to protect her chest, pushing my hands away.

I lifted my hands in surrender. "It's me and it's okay. I need to check if you're injured and get you out of these clothes. You're covered in blood, angel. I need to know that you're okay." Cautiously, I touched her zip again. "Just me, angel. I'm not going to hurt you." And I'm going to do my best not to perve on you, I swear. I clamped my mouth shut so I didn't say it. Right now, I'd apologise for it being dark at night if it would make her feel better.

Slowly, I pulled the zip down, then flipped it open to expose her blood-soaked shirt. Pretend you're back in the hospital, doing a chest examination on someone who's been in a fight. "It's okay, it's okay," I murmured as I checked her ribs. I breathed a sigh of relief as I realised that none of them was broken, though she had a fair bit of bruising already. "Okay, I'm going to take the shirt and vest off you completely so I can wash off some of the blood."

Carefully, I slid the vest down her arms, mindful of

catching her hands on the armholes, before I pulled the shirt over her head. Desperately, I tried to think of anything but what was in front of me. I turned away to bunch the whole mess up and pitch it after the pants, but it was soaked in blood, leaving still more on Caitlin's skin and mine. I'd never been so happy to see she wasn't wearing a bra, for it was one less thing to take off.

I pulled the showerhead from its cradle, pointing the nozzle at the floor as I turned the tap on. I waited for the water to warm up, wanting it the perfect temperature to wash Caitlin without waking or burning her. I kept one finger in the spray the whole time and turned the fine mist on Caitlin's body.

I fixed my eyes on the floor, trying not to look at her as the pink water cascaded onto the tiles. When the water ran clear, I dared to lift my eyes. Her shins were clean and a few seconds more took the last of the dried blood from her knees. I leaned over her, letting the spray stream down her back as I watched the water on the tiles go from red to pink to clear once more.

Lastly, I focussed on Caitlin's face. Blood streaked her cheeks and there were chunks of Laura in her hair. I couldn't leave Laura's blood on Caitlin's hands or any other part of her. There was no way I could convince her it was all a dream if traces still remained.

Gently, I cupped the back of her neck in my hand so I could tip her head back and rinse the gore from her hair. That done, I carefully directed the spray so it ran lightly down her face. She screwed her face up, but she didn't open her eyes.

"It's okay, angel," I said softly. "Almost done."

I turned the water off and reached for a towel to cover her with. I spread another across my arms and lifted her from the chair to the towels on the floor, laying her flat. I slid a folded towel under her head as a makeshift cushion, spread another towel over the top of her and returned to the shower. For a moment, I looked at her, lying unconscious and cocooned in the white towels as she had been in the sheets on a hospital bed. It was less than six weeks ago, but it felt like a lifetime. A lifetime that had nearly ended for her.

I stuck the shower head back in its cradle and turned the water on, hotter and stronger than I had for Caitlin. I dumped my vest on the floor and stood beneath the needle spray in my dripping clothes as tears rolled down my cheeks. I don't know how long I stood there, nor whether I was mourning or relieved. Or both.

Eventually, I came to my senses enough to realise that I had to get Caitlin up off the floor and into her own bed. I shut off the shower and dripped across the floor to the door. Just outside was a plastic shopping bag, so I yanked it inside and closed the door.

I dried my hands before taking a look in the bag. It looked like someone had gone up to Kmart and brought back some new pink pyjamas for Caitlin. I ripped the tags off and looked at her towel-shrouded body on the floor.

Now I just needed to get her into them.

I swallowed and leaned over her, not sure where to start. The pocket of my shirt sent a stream of water pattering onto the tiles. I jerked back, not wanting to wet her again. Fuck. I needed to take my wet clothes off and any clean ones I had were still in her room. Fucked if I was leaving her alone to go get dressed. But I couldn't go naked around her, either, in case she woke up. Fuck.

I stripped my wet clothes off quickly and wrapped a towel around my waist, praying it wouldn't come off. I wasn't sure what she'd do if she woke up to find me naked next to her.

I knelt on the floor beside Caitlin and slid a hand down her back, lifting her torso a little off the floor.

"Okay, I've found you some pyjamas. Let's get you dressed again," I murmured as I slid the top over her head. She started to pull away, but I kept talking. "It's okay, it's me, just getting you dressed for bed. . ."

I pulled the top down over her chest and stomach, taking the towel away as I did so. The top was huge on her. I told myself it was better than nothing. I couldn't have done any better – only in books and movies could a bloke buy clothes for a girl and get the size perfect, first try.

Right, time for the pants.

I pulled the towel down further.

Oh, shit.

She still wore her wet underwear. I wasn't game to find her fresh underwear – I didn't want to take these off, but I'd have to. Fuck.

Caitlin's a beautiful girl. I'm not gay. It was fucking hard and I was wearing nothing but a fairly flimsy towel. I tried really hard to think of something, anything, but the beautiful girl I was about to undress.

I kept the towel over her. I hooked my fingers into the waistband of her knickers and pulled them down, keeping my eyes closed 'til I got them to her feet. Equally quickly, I slid the pyjama pants up to her waist, trying to touch her as little as possible. I pulled the towel away when I knew she was dressed. I took the last towel and spread it across my chest before I lifted Caitlin up and carried her back to her bedroom.

I laid her on the sheets, my hand lingering on her hair as I let her head down onto the pillow. I wanted. . . fuck. I pulled the quilt up to her collarbone, hiding temptation from sight.

Navid knocked on the door. "Everyone's in place. Even if there's nothing to watch for – they're all dead," he said. He looked hesitant. "Can I see her?"

I jerked my head toward the bed, lifting a finger to my lips to indicate quiet. She'd have a heart attack if she woke up to find him that close to her again, after what we just did.

He stood over Caitlin and looked at her for a moment, before he whispered, "She's just a kid! How did she survive?"

I shrugged. "She's stronger than she looks."

He got down on his knees beside the bed, next to her. "But isn't she beautiful? No wonder girls like this cover their faces. With one look, she could steal your soul. I swear Persian girls are the most beautiful in the world." Before I could stop him, he ran his fingertips down her cheek.

She shrank away from his fingers, screwing her face up. "No. Nathan. Nathan?"

I jerked my head toward the door. "Get out," I hissed.

I dropped to my knees beside her bed and held her tightly. "I'm here," I breathed into her ear. "I'm here." I felt her body relax in my arms and my heart with it.

"Why don't you just seduce her and be done with it?"

Navid's voice startled me. Where he stood, his face was in shadow, his expression unreadable. "We've all seen how you look at her, how you act with her. You even sleep with her, every night. Some of the other guys find it hard to believe you haven't yet, but they don't know you. You wouldn't look at her the way you do if you'd already fucked her."

"It's not like that," I told him. "She'd run screaming if I so much as kissed her." Or fight as dirty as she had to if she was cornered and she couldn't run. I ached in more than one place at the memory of my lips on hers earlier that evening.

I like a girl with spirit.

A terrible line for a movie villain, yet no less true in my case. I hid a smile. But Caitlin wasn't just a girl with spirit – strike a match and I could set that spirit alight.

Oh God, what I'd give to see her burn with a passion that wasn't fury. . .

Navid interrupted my thoughts as if he'd heard them. "Give it a shot. What do you have to lose? You said it yourself. This operation is effectively over after tonight. It's not like you'll be seeing her for much longer." I could see his shoulders shrug.

What did I have to lose? I could lose HER. For the second time that night, I felt hollow, as if all my organs had suddenly been sucked into a vacuum in my chest, my ribs caving in under the pressure.

I snapped, "We almost lost her tonight because you couldn't count. Only three men and no sign of her, you said. The only reason we didn't fail is that Caitlin shot her. Now go stand guard to make sure there aren't any more mistakes."

"Just like you taking so long to help her. When she had to shoot the bastard on the beach herself," he shot back.

When I'd thought she was dead. Like tonight. "Get out," I managed to say.

He shrugged. "You might want to put some clothes on if you're not going to fuck her. You look pretty stupid in a towel." I heard his laughter as he left. He shut the door again, and we were alone. The loudest sound in the room was her even breathing, lifting my heart like a feather buoyed by each breath. She was alive. Oh thank God, she was alive.

They were all taken care of. All of them. Her house was safe, she was safe – even I was safe. For the first time in how long? Too long. I pulled on my own pyjamas automatically, my eyes not leaving her sleeping face.

I almost lost her, then I almost killed her. By what miracle was she alive?

I didn't care. I lay down beside her, wrapped my arms around her like I had in the hospital – it seemed like a different century – and tried to believe that this was really happening. Despite my stupidity, she was alive in my arms.

SEVENTY SIX

Hand sliding between shirt and skin.
Fighting. NO.
Please help me. . .
These hands won't hurt, sometimes help
Just let me. . .
Scared. Tears.
I don't want to. . .
Clinical hands. No passion.
So cold.
Couldn't get it up.
Clothes taken away.
So cold.
Shivering until handed a pulled-off sweater.
Still warm from someone else's skin.
Wouldn't look. Couldn't look.
Need Superman.
Need help.
Sorry.

SEVENTY SEVEN

In my nightmare, the dead girl in the toilet had a face and it was hers. My heart broke anew as I felt hers no longer beat, before I realised her eyes were open. "You bastard. . ."

Fuck, I hate zombies.

I woke up in shock to find that Caitlin had woken in the dark, too. Her breathing beside me was fast, panicked, as if she was choking back tears. I didn't dare touch her. Zombies, corpses, blood – what if she still wanted to kill me? She'd said as much before Navid knocked her out.

"Hey, are you all right?" I asked her.

Her words tumbled over each other, trying to tell me her nightmare as I tried to focus on what she was saying, pushing the image of her dead face out of my mind.

"Just a bad dream," I told myself as much as her. "It's all over now." And she was alive here, so close. . .

I turned on my side to look at her in the faint illumination filtering through the curtains from the street lights outside, to see and believe what I was telling myself.

At the same time, she shifted closer to me.

My lips met hers, her body against mine. I both heard and felt her sharp intake of breath. I froze for a moment, but she didn't move away or try to kill me. I should have backed away. Fuck, I should have. But I didn't.

This could be my last chance. Fuck it.

For the second time that night I kissed her, apprehensive at first, then with more feeling as I realised *she was kissing me back.*

If the last thing I did before she ripped my face off was kiss her, then I got a pretty good deal.

But if she wasn't going to kill me, I was taking advantage of her. She'd remember and she wouldn't forgive me for it, I struggled to tell myself, but even I couldn't hold that thought tonight. Her hands were under my shirt, on the bare skin of my back.

I kissed her lips, her neck, following her singlet strap as it slid off her shoulder and partway down her arm. I brushed my lips along the satin edge, from her shoulder to the swell of her breast. I took a deep breath and let it out, fluttering the thin layer of fabric. I gently cupped her breast in my hand through her top, hesitated, then planted a kiss where satin met skin before letting go of her. I felt her gasp, her rapid heartbeat and her ragged breathing as I waited to see what she'd do next.

She pulled back. Her hands held my face like a huge, hairy hamburger she was hesitant to touch. Her lips sought mine in a less ardent kiss than my last.

Her hands weren't touching me any more. Her lips were the only contact between us now, before that was broken, too. Resigned, I consoled myself with the thought that every kiss we shared now was one more than I had any reason to expect. Even the thought of more than that was a faint hope. Faint but alluring. . . Oh God, what I'd give for more than just a hope. . .

"I dreamed I killed someone, Nathan, because I'd prefer to die than let them hurt me again." Her voice was small and sad.

I dreamed you were dead and I won't let anyone hurt you again, I thought. I kissed her mouth, her lips salty with fresh tears. Don't cry, angel. What can I do to make you happy to be alive again? "Just a dream. Let me help take your mind off it."

I was slow to slide my arms around her, hoping to hold her close if nothing else. Of course, I hoped for more, too. Hoped she'd forget everything else and believe it was nothing but a bad dream. Dreamed she'd let me do some of the things I fantasised about, the first time I saw her. Not a hope.

Caitlin gave a shudder and I stopped. "No. I can't do this. No, Nathan. Maybe one day, when it's all over and there's no one left for me to be afraid of – but not tonight."

I felt the broad smile spread across my face, though she couldn't see it. "It is over, angel. They caught all three men tonight, trying to sneak into your house. I heard the names – Pete, Nick, Tom. The woman, too. It's all over and you're safe."

She shook her head and pulled away. "All of them? What about Mike? And Simon? If they're still out there, it's not over yet."

I felt sick. "I thought you said there were four. . ." I looked over at the laptop, closed on the desk. I wanted to switch it on and look through her nightmares, to work out what I'd missed. But I couldn't go snooping through her files while she was watching me. I scrambled to my feet "I'm going to go to the toilet." I dragged myself away from her, stumbling toward the bathroom without looking at Navid. I couldn't face him or the toilet, reminders of the corpse that had almost been hers. Could still be, if there were more of them out there.

I gripped the edge of the basin, my head swirling, trying to focus on whether I was going to throw up or not. When I managed to get a hold of myself enough to realise that I was not, I turned the tap on. I took my time washing my hands, trying to come to terms with the last few hours, still not entirely sure they'd really happened. I splashed water on my face, a cold shock that still couldn't clear my head. I did it again, slopping water down my pyjama top. Oh, fuck. I pulled it over my head and draped it over the side of the bath.

I dried myself before I went back to Caitlin's room. This time, I stopped just outside the door, trying to work out how to tell Navid that I'd fucked up.

"More nightmares?" Navid asked, not looking at me.

"Yes," I said shortly, low enough so that Caitlin wouldn't hear me. "Hopefully there won't be any more tonight." I stared at him, not sure how to start. "She says we didn't get them all."

He raised his eyebrows. "Are you shitting me or serious?"

"Serious, mate. I wouldn't joke about Caitlin's safety."

He pulled out his phone and started dialling. "It's Navid, sir. . . sorry, sir. . . no, apparently Nathan says we didn't get all of them. No, sir. . . sure." He held the phone out for me. "He wants to hear it from the fuckwit's mouth."

The fuckwit tonight was definitely me. "Hello?"

"Navid tells me you were quite the hero, taking out four of them in a gunfight," my boss said with a laugh. "The girl was good bait! A pity we didn't get any of them alive, but he tells me you have new information for me." The following silence was ominous.

"The girl says we didn't get them all."

He laughed. "Has she changed her story? Before, you told us there were three men left and the woman – Navid's confirmed, three men dead and one woman, with no casualties on our side."

I wet my lips. "One of tonight's kills was a police officer. His name doesn't match what I remember her saying." I took a deep breath. "She said there could still be two of them we didn't get. One of the kills confirmed it – the woman had the means to hire whoever she felt was necessary."

"So you're saying we still have live ones we can interrogate?" He sounded surprised.

"Live ones who aren't here and could still target Caitlin," I replied cautiously.

A sigh. "Fuck, we can't waste any more resources on just a hope. Navid's team will pull out in the morning – make sure you get her out of the house, so we can remove any surveillance equipment."

"But it's only been a week, sir. You gave me two." The 'sir' grated on my tongue but I gritted through it anyway. It couldn't hurt to be polite.

Silence.

"You told me I was assigned to her for two weeks. So Navid's team will be leaving, but I'll remain. Presumably, you'll permit me to call on his team in case their assistance is required. Correct?"

He laughed again. "Sure, Nathan. You can see your project through to completion. One more week and your contract is finished."

Finished. All this would be over in a week and I could go back to Uni next year. And I'd get to see Caitlin again. Maybe. . .

"Thank you, sir," I said as the phone beeped to indicate he'd already hung up.

I looked at Navid. "So you're all gone in the morning and I have to take her out of the house tomorrow?"

He nodded. "As early as possible. The boys'll be glad to wrap this one up – babysitting your girlfriend was getting to be a joke."

"She's not –" I began.

He nodded and waved me into silence.

I ventured back into Caitlin's room and shut the door behind me.

I sat on the edge of her bed, listening to her even breathing, not saying anything.

"Caitlin," I began softly, but she didn't answer. I wanted to touch her, but I clenched my hands to stop myself. "Angel. I swear we'll get them, too. I won't stop searching until I know you're safe." She still didn't reply. There was the other thing; even if she was asleep, I had to say it aloud. It wouldn't be the first time I'd confessed to her as she slept. "You're a very beautiful woman. Every man who sees you is attracted to you. I'd have to be blind not to notice."

Or concentrating really hard on something else. "I'm sorry if I got carried away and pushed you too far."

She didn't say a word. Asleep already, I thought. Lucky.

I thought of going to sleep on the couch in the lounge room, or getting some spare blankets and making up a bed on the floor of her bedroom for me. I couldn't bring myself to leave her tonight. Until I left her house for good.

Wondering where she kept her spare blankets, I wavered between waking her to ask and leaving to search the house for them. Wasn't there a blanket at the top of her cupboard? I stood up, trying to remember.

Her fingers on my back, a light touch. "Nathan?"

"Mmmmph?" I turned so I was facing her, even though I couldn't see her.

I could hear the bed springs shift as she moved. When she spoke, her voice sounded closer. "You think I'm beautiful? Even," she swallowed, "even with the scars?"

The scars will fade and you'll always be beautiful, I thought but didn't say. "Yes, Caitlin, you're very beautiful. The scars don't change that."

I felt the breeze of her breath on my skin an instant before her arms were around my neck, her cheek against my chest.

"Thank you, Nathan," she murmured.

I draped an arm cautiously around her. "Any time, angel." Any time you want, all you have to do is ask. . . I tried to bring my thoughts back to reality, here and now, but that was her body beside mine, so close I could feel her breasts move with every breath, me wearing nothing but my shorts. . .

"How about we try for some more sleep?" I asked her,

guiding her back to bed. She didn't let go of me, so I lay down beside her.

She pillowed her head on my chest. "Sleep well," she said softly.

I listened to her breathing slow, becoming even again. Even as I closed my eyes, I doubted I'd sleep with the tumult in my head.

At least if I had any more dreams tonight, they weren't going to be nightmares.

SEVENTY EIGHT

When I woke up, Caitlin was still asleep, her head resting on the pillow beside me, a slight smile visible on her face. No more nightmares, then, I decided.

I reached out to stroke her hair, then hesitated. How much of last night would she remember? What else had she remembered?

Last night, she'd kneed me, called me. . . names, I'd almost gotten her killed and she'd tried to kill me. And afterwards. . .

I'd kissed her, she'd responded and the feel of her skin, the taste of her, her hands on me, how much I'd wanted her, *how much I still want her now*. . .

Oh, shit. I sat up and started looking for my clothes, hoping I could make it into a cold shower before she woke up.

Part of me hoped she'd forget all of it, thinking the whole night was a dream. It wouldn't be the first time. Then she could go on, tolerating my presence because I was a friend who wanted to help her and I didn't want anything else.

Could I go back to ignoring how much I want her? Especially now I had the faintest hope that she wanted me. Or one day she would. . .

Last night, she'd shown me a small part of the fire she'd had before all of this. The inner fire that had gotten her through it. To imagine what she'd be like, not scared and not hurt any more. Just Caitlin. . .

I found myself staring at her. *I want you* was probably written across my face – and my shorts as well.

Her big, dark eyes opened.

Oh, fuck. I had to cover up before she noticed and ran away screaming. Or worse.

I smiled and sat on the edge of the bed, dumping my clothes in my lap. "Good morning."

She was silent for a moment as she sat up, pulling the quilt with her. Caitlin winced; her fingers looking thicker than usual. I'd forgotten the ice pack, so they'd swollen up from the beating her hand took last night. A beating I gave her. . . oh God. I swallowed.

"Good morning," she replied vaguely. "What happened to my hand?"

I thought quickly. "You must have been lying on it. You passed out in the toilet last night, angel – remember?" Of course she wouldn't. "Maybe you hit it as you fell. You were lying pretty awkwardly on the floor."

Awkward was an understatement. Pinned under Navid before he knocked her out as I looked on and did nothing.

Caitlin looked puzzled, then nodded slowly.

I changed the subject. "Did you have any more

nightmares?"

"No, no more nightmares." Caitlin's face lifted with a watery smile.

"Good." I hesitated, before I gave in and leaned forward to kiss her. Her hands crept around my neck as she kissed me back. I didn't want to stop. Her quilt slipped down and I was conscious of her breasts pressed against my chest.

She pushed me away, clutching at the quilt again. "Nathan, please, stop." She sounded breathless.

I leaned back again as she caught her breath. "I want. . . I wish. . . I wish I was brave enough to do this. I'm still scared, Nathan. I'm scared of. . . even with you." She looked up at me, her eyes filling with tears.

I wrapped my arms around her, quilt and all, and told her it was all right, that she knew I'd never hurt her.

As she cried, my heart sang. She wanted me. One day, next week or next month or next year, she'd be ready.

All I had to do was hold onto her and wait. Hoping she didn't remember. . .

SEVENTY NINE

"You should wear this." I dropped the red dress in her lap. I sat behind her to help fasten her bra, trying not to think about how well the colour matched the dress. I had a serious craving for strawberries.

Her hair was still wet from the shower. Caitlin sprayed something on her damp tresses as she brushed them. More strawberries, I realised as the scent of her conditioner spray hit my nose. "What for?" she asked.

"I'm going to take you out for lunch, then maybe we can see a movie, or you can buy some more clothes to replace what was damaged. Afterwards we can have dinner somewhere. After that, I'll take you home, if you like. Or, if you'd prefer, I can take you back to my house for a bit." I raised my eyebrows.

"I would like to see your house," she said, thankfully.

"Okay, so get dressed so we can go have lunch." I left the room, but stayed by the door. She still had trouble with zips and buttons and if I wasn't there to offer a hand, I'd come back to find her half-dressed and in tears, her hands in the freezer, looking for ice to dull the pain. She never asked for help. I'd have to offer, or see her hurting.

"Nathan, could I ask you a favour?" Her words were quiet and precise.

"Sure," I answered. She didn't ask for many favours.

"Tonight, I'd like you to get me drunk in a pub or a nightclub, please."

I was glad she couldn't see my face. I didn't know whether to be horrified or happy. My heart flew. She'd do this so she could find the courage she thought she didn't have. She wanted me to get her drunk so she'd sleep with me.

Before it fell. That'd be taking advantage of her.

No it wouldn't. She was a responsible adult making a choice.

And was twisted like a crushed aluminium can. She wasn't a responsible adult – the pain and the pain drugs messed with her head. If I took advantage of her when she was drunk, I'd never forgive myself and she might not, either.

She might not even do it – she might just want to get drunk, pass out and nothing would happen.

"Why do you want to get drunk?" I asked, glancing over my shoulder at her, but she didn't need my help yet.

This time she hesitated and sounded uncertain. "Because. . . I turned eighteen while I was still in hospital. I've never been drunk in a pub. . . and I want to. I know that you'll make sure I get to bed afterwards." Big, trusting eyes looked up at me.

If only she trusted me enough to let me do what I'd like

to with her. Nothing scary, nothing strange, nothing I'd have hesitated to ask any other girl I wanted. Until Caitlin. If only she'd let me. . .

"Okay. I'll take you to a pub tonight and buy you some belated birthday drinks," I told her.

And anything else you want, angel – all you have to do is ask. And if you don't. . .

I'll be the perfect fucking gentleman, as always, I resolved grimly.

EIGHTY

The bouncer took one look at her ID, recognised who Caitlin was and let us straight in. It was Friday night and the place was packed, but we'd managed to get a tiny little table with a good view over the dance floor that wasn't too far from the bar. I bought us drinks and we toasted her belated happy birthday.

She was happy enough, well into her first drink, when the DJ turned the music down to make his announcement.

"We have a local celebrity here tonight – a girl who we all thought was dead, but here she is, celebrating her eighteenth birthday here with us. Let's all say a big happy birthday to Caitlin Lockyer!" Cheers erupted as he pointed straight at us. "There she is! And we're all going to make sure she has a great time tonight!" More cheers, louder this time.

The music started up again and Caitlin suddenly became very interested in finishing her drink. People around us were staring and I could hear someone at the next table saying, ". . . found by some bloke on a beach where she'd been left to die. . ."

I offered to get her another drink, but it was a long wait at the bar. I found myself listening to the conversation going on behind me.

"Matt, don't. Her boyfriend's just at the bar, you're not going to get anywhere with her."

"I say he's her bodyguard, not boyfriend. Come on, mate, it's worth a try. The worst she can do is say no." I turned slightly to look at the blokes having the conversation, just in time to see Matt disappear into the crowd. His mate shook his head and drank his beer.

"Nathan?" The voice that knew my name was familiar. Memories stirred of tequila shots, chartreuse and taking home two hot Canadian students. Marcus, who'd never let me live down leaving him alone while I escorted both girls to my house.

I turned my back on the head-shaking stranger and came face-to-face with Marcus. "Hi, mate."

He grinned. "I knew it was you. Haven't seen you in ages! I've had the pick of the best while you've been away. Who's your target tonight?"

Feeling proud, I nodded toward Caitlin. "Red dress." And far more beautiful than any other girl I'd seen in this club. Not tonight. Not ever.

I saw Matt sidle out of the crowd and sit down opposite Caitlin.

"Looks like you have competition, mate," Marcus teased.

Matt said something and she gave a short reply, with a nervous smile.

I shook my head. My smile was as confident as ever. I was the only one who'd be taking Caitlin home. "No, mate. Caitlin's mine."

"Caitlin?" Marcus peered at her, looking worried. "No, don't, mate."

I laughed. Give up on my angel? Not a hope. "Why the hell not?"

"She's been in the news, mate. Kidnapped, raped and found by some bloke on a beach where they left her to die. She's not worth it." Marcus sounded really serious.

He didn't know her, nor what she was worth. "Because some other bloke's had her first? You know I'm not into virgins, mate. . ."

Matt said something else to Caitlin, but she didn't reply.

Marcus persisted. "Are you stupid? Not only is she Mission Impossible, but if you manage to get her drunk enough to get into her pants, there's no saying she won't call it rape in the morning. You're fucked, either way. Don't, mate." I heard the words, but I didn't pay them any heed.

Matt must have introduced himself to Caitlin, because he stuck out a hand to shake hers. She hesitated, before she offered him her badly bruised right hand. I watched him give a firm handshake, squeezing her fingers too hard.

I saw her lips frame the words, "Let go of me," as she winced in pain.

"Oh, shit." I left Marcus standing at the bar and started to shove my way through the crowd back to Caitlin. Before I could get there, the guy from the next table leaned back and punched Matt in the face.

Matt keeled over backwards, flat out on the floor. The half-dozen feet he'd almost landed on laid into the guy, too, so I couldn't even see where he was in the free-for-all. Caitlin stood up unsteadily but didn't know where to go to get away from the brawl that was rapidly escalating in front of her. She looked around frantically, too scared to release the scream I could see building as she jerked in each panicked breath.

I curled an arm around her, trying to support her. I could feel her body shaking as she watched the bouncer drag a bruised and bleeding Matt out of the night club. "Are you okay? Did he hurt you?" I asked urgently.

"He barely touched me," she whimpered, almost ready to cry.

"Look mate, it's the girl's birthday and if you don't want what he got, I think you should leave her alone." The guy from the next table who'd thrown the first punch had sat down again and his warning was directed at me.

I needed to leave. She was safe here, but I wasn't. I could feel her sagging against me — she couldn't stand up much longer. If she didn't sit back down, she'd need my help even more than she did now. Caitlin murmured something I couldn't hear. I leaned closer to her and asked her to repeat it. She tilted her head up, so her lips were close to my ear. "Don't leave me. You promised."

My heart froze in my chest. All my previously solid thoughts of leaving her alone again, even for a moment, sublimated to join the dry-ice haze wafting around the dance floor of the club. I closed my eyes for the briefest moment, struggling to breathe. You promised. You owe her, you bastard.

"Last warning, mate," our friendly neighbour told me ominously. From the looks on the surrounding faces, they all agreed with him and they'd probably back him up, too.

I couldn't take them all on. And I couldn't leave her alone.

"Do you want to stay here or go home?" I asked her urgently.

"I want to get out of here!" I could feel her panic.

"Let go of the girl." Friendly Neighbour stood, both hands clenched on the backrest of his barstool.

"Wrap your arms around my neck, give me a big, sloppy kiss, smile and act drunk. I won't let you fall and I'll get you out of here," I told Caitlin, letting go of her and throwing my hands up in surrender. She stumbled, as I knew she would, but she came up smiling.

"I love you, Nathan," Caitlin slurred, throwing her arms around my neck.

I stared at her in shock for saying words I never thought I'd hear, even though I knew she didn't mean them. It took me a minute to realise how much weight she had hanging on my neck, I was so euphoric. I reached out as if all I wanted to do was steady her, but really trying to stop her from breaking my neck. She kissed me clumsily, as if she didn't know how, and looked up at me with a blissful smile on her face before her knees buckled.

I had most of her weight anyway. It wasn't an issue to lift her off her feet and into my arms, commenting about how she'd had enough to drink for one night. Her smile remained pasted on her face as she looked up at me.

Smiles, claps and a few bawdy cheers followed us as I carried Caitlin out of the club. I could see Marcus shaking his head in disbelief as we passed. I shrugged, smiled and shouldered my way through to the cool darkness outside.

I tried to set her on her feet again when we reached the street, but her arms were still around my neck, so she swung around to face me. She was still smiling, looking up at me, but it was too dark for me to tell how this was different. She stretched up to kiss me again, hesitant at first and then. . . more like. . . last night. And I knew she wasn't drunk.

"Thank you," Caitlin said slowly as she pulled away from me.

Like some lovesick teenager who'd just slurped his first kiss, I wanted to savour the citrus taste of her tongue in my mouth. My adrenaline levels were higher now than they'd been at the thought of a fight in the club. I tried to calm down enough to sound sane. "Come on, I'll take you home now, if you like."

"Your place. You promised your place," she insisted. "And I'd like to stop at a bottle shop on the way. You said you'd get me another drink."

EIGHTY ONE

"You could have cleaned up after your little drinking party last night," Chris said as she walked into the kitchen, an empty bottle in each hand. She clinked them into the recycling bin. "Well, you're certainly back. Back in action, too, if last night was anything to go by." She smothered a smirk with her hand. "I heard you two come in, but I didn't hear her go. So, what time did she leave last night?"

I looked at her, bleary-eyed and yawning, as the watery sunlight trickling through the kitchen window turned her fair hair into a halo Chris didn't deserve. "She didn't."

"You let her sleep in your bed? What happened while you were away to make you so considerate?"

Irritated, I responded, "She's tired and she had a bit to drink last night. She needs some sleep before I take her home." Caitlin had smiled in her sleep as I'd tucked the quilt around her. My mouth had gone dry and I couldn't bring myself to wake her yet. So beautiful. . .

Chris whistled. "She gets to sleep in your bed and she

282

gets driven home! When did you become such a perfect gentleman?"

I tried to concentrate on making myself a coffee, in between thoughts of Caitlin. I didn't want or need to listen to Chris.

"You're not having breakfast? Or have you already eaten?"

"Can't you leave it, for even a second?" I didn't want to get into an argument – I wanted to have Caitlin's breakfast ready before she was awake. "What can I make her for breakfast? Do we have anything besides," I glared at the box, "cornflakes?"

"Breakfast, too? Was she *that* good?" Chris pressed.

Now I was pissed off. "Leave her alone! Just lay off her, okay?"

She let up. "All right." She paused long enough for me to take a sip of my coffee. "At least it's good to know you're not a paedophile."

"What?" I nearly choked.

"Well, you've finally left that poor kid alone. The one in hospital. How old was she – twelve, thirteen? It's about time you got over your crush on her."

"I didn't have a crush on her! She wanted me to be there!"

"Come on, the last thing she needed was to have you at her bedside, mooning over her."

"There are plenty of girls who'd love to have me sit by their bedside when they're in hospital!"

Chris took a deep breath. "Like the one in your bed right now? Maybe, but not a girl who's been abducted. After she's been raped and God knows what else, the last thing she wants is a man anywhere near her. Least of all you." She grabbed the cornflake box and turned around to put it away. She reached for the sponge and started wiping down the bench, refusing to meet my eyes.

"Nathan?" Caitlin was hesitant.

I saw Chris turn around at the sound of her voice, but I had eyes only for Caitlin. "Good morning, angel," I greeted her with a smile.

I couldn't take my eyes off her. Behind me, I knew Chris was staring, too.

One arm was wound around the door frame and the wall beyond, supporting her. Caitlin wore one of my jumpers, which reached almost to her knees, making her look like the child Chris had called her. The depths of her eyes told another story, though – one that wasn't suitable for children.

I took a step toward her, drawn closer by the irresistible black-hole hint in her eyes.

She gave a sheepish smile. Or perhaps it was rueful. "I can't seem to be able to turn the taps on in the shower." She held up her hand and her fingers looked red.

"I'll be right there." I jumped up, as if my chair was an ejector seat, and coffee splashed over my hand. I almost dropped the cup, but made it to the table in time. Shaking the coffee off my burnt fingers, I added, "Just as soon as I finish my coffee."

"Thank you!" Her eyes lingered a moment before she left.

Chris barely waited a few seconds for her to get out of earshot before she spoke. "You didn't!"

She was right and I hadn't. I'd come damn close,

though, and I wasn't telling her that, either. Caitlin. . . oh my God, Caitlin. . . it was worth every sleepless, screaming night just for last night. And there'd be more.

I responded with only a smile. One that said there's chocolate for dinner and nothing else.

"You're a bloody cradle-snatcher! And don't get any ideas – you aren't and you'll never be Prince Charming!" she shouted at me.

I tipped the rest of my coffee down the sink, then stalked to the door. "Just leave her alone!"

"You should take your own advice," she said with venom. "Go on, go help her – she probably can't even reach the taps!"

Bloody Chris – didn't know when to keep her mouth shut. After a night like last night, the last thing I wanted to do was argue – couldn't she see that? To stop myself from shouting back in kind, I left.

Just outside the door, I almost stepped on Caitlin, sitting on the floor. She didn't say anything. She just looked up at me with big, sad eyes and I held out my hands to help her to her feet.

I walked her to the bathroom, where she sat on the edge of the bath to watch me. I closed the door, then turned the taps on for her.

She came up behind me, her hands sliding under my shirt. "Why don't you set her straight? You could just tell her how old I am – it's hardly a secret."

"I know." My voice was muffled as she pulled my shirt over my head.

"Then why did you let her say what she did without defending yourself?"

"She likes to argue. That's why she wants to do law." I shrugged. "I don't want to argue with her. It would end in me telling her things she doesn't need to know – about you and about me." I closed my eyes, trying to squeeze my mental images out of existence.

Caitlin had taken her – my – jumper off, and the touch of her bare skin against my back was more than a little distracting.

"Would you like me to help you in the shower?" I couldn't resist saying.

"That would be lovely, Nathan." She sounded like she was smiling.

EIGHTY TWO

I offered to make her breakfast, but Caitlin said she wasn't all that hungry. She kept quiet as I helped her dress in some new clothes she'd bought yesterday, so we could both hear Chris crashing dishes around in the sink. I was more than happy to avoid the kitchen until Chris was out of it, but Caitlin insisted she wanted to speak to her. I grabbed the wet towels to hang them outside, telling Caitlin she could call me in if she needed anything. So I was outside with a clear view into the kitchen when she walked in.

Chris couldn't miss Caitlin entering the kitchen this time, a beacon of glowing white as the bright sunlight touched her t-shirt, but my sister didn't let on. Caitlin turned the kettle on and began hunting through the cupboards.

"He's not even making you breakfast?" Chris said suddenly over her shoulder, not looking at Caitlin.

Caitlin glanced at her, then looked away. "No, I talked him out of it."

She stared at her in surprise. "How did you manage that? It's difficult to talk him out of anything."

Caitlin laughed, her face lighting up in that irresistible way she had. "Difficult? He's as stubborn as a mule!"

Chris broke into a smile. "Well, yes." She laughed, too.

Caitlin stuck out her hand. "I'm Caitlin. Nathan seemed too preoccupied to introduce me before." Though she tried to hide it, her hand still hurt her and I saw her wince as the pressure of Chris's handshake bordered on painful.

"I'm Chris, his sister, as you've probably already been told." She saw the look on Caitlin's face. "Shit, are you all right?"

"No, but I will be one day," Caitlin said pleasantly as she pulled her hand away.

At that, Chris pushed Caitlin down onto one of the chairs and made coffee for her.

When Caitlin protested, Chris said bluntly, "It still hurts you to walk, doesn't it?"

"Not as much as it did at first, but it still does, a bit," she admitted reluctantly. My heart constricted in my chest – she tried so hard not to let the pain show, but I knew.

"Does he even know?" Chris said, half under her breath. "Look, I don't know what you've been through, what they've done to you or anything. Just don't assume he's some kind of Prince Charming because he rescued you. He's nowhere near perfect – he'll probably just end up hurting you, breaking your heart. He's good at that." She sounded bitter.

I frowned. What in hell did she know about broken hearts? I'd never hurt anyone. I'd never hurt Caitlin. . .

"Do you think badly of me for staying last night?"

Caitlin asked her quietly.

"No, it's him –" she broke off, then passionately began again. "What you want to do is your business, and you're not the first." Caitlin tried to say something, but Chris went on. "Not the first girl he's ever brought home, I mean. He'd come in late, not alone, and she'd be gone by morning. I've never seen – or heard – the same girl twice, except when they called to try to get in contact with him again."

I hid my smile. Alanna used to deal with those phone calls – some mad girls I'd slept with, who thought we had a future, though I'd made it perfectly clear there wouldn't be one. I was just that good in bed that they wanted more. It wasn't my fault they weren't up to par. Alanna used to give me an earful about it afterwards. Maybe Chris had heard it once or twice.

"It's been a long time since he brought anyone home, but I'd have thought he'd know better than to seduce you, or play on what he did for you – after all you've been through, you don't need him to hurt you as well!" Chris looked fiercely at me outside and I pretended to be very busy with the towels.

Chris sat down at the table by Caitlin, handing her a coffee. There was silence for a few minutes while they both drank.

Caitlin broke it. "I'm the same age as you. He told me about you, so I knew." When? When had I told her about Chris?

"Just don't let him hurt you," Chris repeated, staring at Caitlin as though she could see bruises. Oh hell, was there a mark where the needle went in? Was she looking at her fingers? I could've sworn the swelling had gone down. . .

Preoccupied, I didn't notice that Caitlin had been silent, her head bowed. "He said he never wanted to see me hurt." Her voice shook.

When I'd said that, she'd been unconscious in hospital. What else was she remembering? This could only end in tears. I swore and headed inside.

Chris had pushed a box of tissues across the table to her, but Caitlin hadn't noticed. The tears just kept on coming.

I took one look at Caitlin's face and dropped to my knees next to her, arms around her, letting her cry against me.

"What did you say to her?" I demanded of Chris.

"I. . . I don't know." She sounded puzzled, and I looked up to see her staring at Caitlin, a look of astonishment on her face.

Caitlin stretched her arm out to take a tissue and used it. "I don't think I want breakfast any more. I want to go home."

"Are you sure?" I asked.

"I'll be right," Caitlin said fiercely, to herself as much as to us.

EIGHTY THREE

Caitlin unlocked the front door and turned to me, pressing her lips briefly against my cheek. "See you tonight for dinner?"

I stopped dead. "Don't you want me to stay with you?"

She shrugged. "I'll probably just be writing more of my memories down and doing some washing. Maybe catch up on the sleep I missed out on last night." Her smile was enough to remind me of things that were better than sleep. "I feel bad that I take up so much of your time. Like the rest of your life is on hold for me."

Right now, her safety was my life. Nothing was more important to me.

I'd sound like a real idiot if I said it, though, so I smiled and said, "I definitely don't mind. Are you sure, though? I mean, what will you do if the last of the bastards come for you while I'm not here?"

Her surprise made me feel stupid. "Call the police, of course, like you did last time. After all, they were so efficient. I'm sure they'd be just as helpful again."

The police did fuck-all last time – that was us. I tried to find a way of saying it inoffensively, but came up blank before I realised that she didn't know – and I had to keep it that way. "I'm sure they will," I said, summoning a smile. "You know my number if you need me, too. So, dinner?"

Caitlin looked relieved. "Dinner. See you tonight."

She left me standing on the doorstep as she shut the door. Feeling stupid, I trudged back to my car.

After a few minutes' driving, I still didn't know where to go or what to do. On Saturday, Chris would still be home and I definitely wanted to avoid my sister today. My job was to protect Caitlin as much as she'd permit, so I didn't have work to do after she'd dismissed me for the day. My life was on hold while I protected hers, and I wouldn't get my life back until it was over.

I wasn't stupid enough to think it could go back to what it was, no matter how much I wished for it. Before Mum and Dad made names for themselves as successful investment advisers in Dubai. It sounded so simple – telling a wealthy investor that if he invested his money in businesses known to support terrorist activity, he'd lose it. It wasn't that simple, of course, as Dad had explained on his last visit.

"For our advice to mean anything, we have to know which businesses support violent extremist activity and demonstrate with extensive data the resulting losses," he'd said, lining up his points like ducks crossing a road. "With the numbers to back us up from Marion's PhD project and the glowing reviews of satisfied customers, it was just a matter of the right introductions. . ."

Alanna had laughed at him as she shook her head. Her laugh had been deeper than Caitlin's – more a throaty chuckle, I remembered fondly. "But Dad – you're forgetting that violent extremists use religion as their basis for action. Aren't the businessmen anxious to save their souls by investing in a religious cause?"

Dad's laugh had matched hers – maybe the last time it ever would. "The successful ones are more concerned with the state of their bank balance than that of their soul – plus they feel that taking money from people in the West is revenge enough."

He'd explained how he'd speak to the men and Mum would sound out the women, for wealthy wives had money to invest, too. If they hadn't been so successful, maybe Alanna would still be alive.

One too many investors had stopped giving money to some group who decided they didn't like their funding drying up. They hadn't gone after Mum and Dad – they'd threatened their children. A threat Mum and Dad had ignored.

"After all, you're all safe in Australia," Dad had laughed over Skype.

First Alanna disappeared. No word, no sign, nothing. Then the gory envelopes arrived at home, as I tried to hide them from Chris. She'd had final exams to focus on and so had I. She'd done well, of course. She'd channelled her worry into study and it showed.

Yet I'd failed, my thoughts on Alanna at the exams she should have attended with me.

Receiving the results of DNA tests, confirming the envelope contents were from Alanna. Grave-looking police officers, always offering sympathy as there was nothing else they could do that they hadn't already.

The message was clear – no one's safe, no matter how far away. Yet Dad said she'd turn up. Alanna always did, because she was so good, so perfect, a fighter to the last. . .

Mum and Dad refused to capitulate. Their business model was too good. There was too much money to be made in doing the right thing to give in to terrorists. The kidnappers would realise they had no choice but to release Alanna.

When are terrorists ever reasonable?

I got sick of the positive fucking spin. Endless repetition of, "Alanna will appear. She always does."

She did. The call came to my mobile, to come and identify her. I didn't tell Chris. I didn't call Mum or Dad, far away and far from concerned. I stood and stared at the corpse of my sister as the images seared themselves into every layer of my consciousness, never to leave me. Leaving only ashes and a smouldering desire for revenge. I'd resolved to make the bastards who took my twin pay in tears of blood.

The most terrifying thing is losing those you love.

Mum and Dad did mourn. We all did. We just didn't do enough.

One sister gone, I dreaded losing Chris next. I was the only man home – it was my job to protect them and I'd already failed. I couldn't fail again. Time to get fucking proactive. The ASIO team started asking questions so I started with them. I was going to help, whether they paid me or not. In the end, they gave in just to stop me from interfering in their operation.

Gotta catch 'em all.

Almost. God, almost. So close and so fucking frustrating. My hands tightened on Alanna's steering wheel. Mine now.

What if they got to Caitlin while I wasn't there?

I decided to go to the gym. I wanted to punch things.

I'd never worked so hard with a speedball. I lost count and didn't stop 'til I couldn't see, there was so much sweat streaming down my face. I mopped my face with a towel and moved on to weights.

Lifting Caitlin so often meant I wasn't completely out of practice, so I was pleased not to need to drop the weight down much. I did a few extra sets, just to make up for the time I'd been away.

I refilled my water bottle, nodding to some of the familiar faces I hadn't seen in a while. Mine wasn't a social gym – all the battles were personal, except when you worked with a personal trainer. The guys who grunted and sobbed as they did bicep curls with a barely loaded barbell didn't last long in my gym. They soon found somewhere else to train.

I finished up with intervals on the treadmill, starting out easy and then turning up the gradient. I ran 'til I ran out of water before heading home for a shower. Chris had already left the house by then, thank God. Showered and freshly dressed, I watched TV until it was time to go back to Caitlin's.

We had Japanese for dinner and Caitlin cried when she couldn't handle the chopsticks. I threw them out and fed her sushi with my fingers until she laughed again. Of course, that didn't happen until my eyes were streaming from finishing up the wasabi in one mouthful. She could've warned me.

She let me ditch the pyjamas, but not my shorts. I wasn't complaining. I still got to sleep with her.

And the next night. And the one after that.

I wished I hadn't spent so much time at the gym that first session, because everything fucking hurt like I'd been in a fight and lost. It got better, though. After three days, I upped the weights. It felt damn good. The gym had to replace the speedball and my six-pack was starting to return.

For two days and nights, I rinsed and repeated – gym, shower, clothes, TV, back to Caitlin's.

I could hear the child practising the piano again each day as I climbed out of the car. The same song, over and over, but it sounded smoother and more like music now. Everything coming together to turn something rough and awkward into something pleasurable.

Maybe tonight. . . I thought as I walked stiffly up the steps to Caitlin's front door.

EIGHTY FOUR

Caitlin smiled when she saw me. She let me in and offered me a drink. I took it and drank deeply, my bicep burning with fatigue as I lifted my arm.

"What'd you do today?" I asked, wondering.

"Writing down more memories. Getting reacquainted with some of my music. . ." Caitlin trailed off vaguely and my attention wavered until I realised she was looking at me expectantly.

"Sorry?" I asked, embarrassed at being caught out for not listening.

"I think I need to give a press interview," Caitlin said, looking frightened at the thought.

"Why?" I asked. "We've avoided the press as much as possible, with the help of the police, because you didn't want any publicity. Besides, what about the ones still left, who hurt you? What if they see the interview and come after you?"

"After that night in the night club, where everyone

recognised me, what's the point of me trying to hide? They already know what I look like. I won't be able to fade into my life again." She sounded near tears and I thought I understood why. "And. . . I owe it to you. Every request I've had for an interview wants the fairytale story, the one with a hero in it. And no one knows who you are and what you did."

Because I don't want them to, I thought, but didn't say. "You don't owe me anything. I was in the right place at the right time to help you. Anyone would have done the same."

"Like the helpful guy in the club who attacked that bloke, who almost attacked you? I don't want that to happen again. This isn't a story I want to tell, but it's not just mine, Nathan. I want to make sure people know what you did for me. I don't want to see you framed because you helped me." She sounded firm, but she looked like she was holding something back. I assumed it was tears, but there was more. "I. . . need your help to do it, Nathan. They want to interview not just me but you, too."

NO! That was my first thought, and the second, too. I'd lose my job, was the third, followed by, Did I really want to do this job any more, now that it's over? I could go back to Uni next year. . . I realised what else was bothering me and voiced it. "You don't like telling anyone what happened. How could you give an interview about it?"

She bit her lip and her voice was barely audible. "Because if I do this, I won't need to tell it again. Everyone will know and I'll only need to tell it once."

And there it was. No matter what I felt about it, no matter how much either of us didn't want to do it, we both would – so that I would know she'd never have to go through it again. I still couldn't get her face out of my mind, that day in hospital when she first started telling me what she remembered so I could take it down. The way she'd cried torrents without stopping, as if something inside her had ruptured and spilled out through her eyes. I'd do anything to know she never had to hurt like that again.

"If you really want to do this, I'll help you," I told her. "But we'll tell the press crew that there are conditions, to make this easier for you."

And I'd be there every step of the way, so I'd hear everything she had to say. I couldn't lose my job over that — I was still supposed to gather information. Even if it was in a TV studio. . . Fuck, how did I get into this mess?

EIGHTY FIVE

"Remember, we set conditions," I told Caitlin in a low voice as we drove to the TV station, two days later. "This isn't live, they'll tape it and cut it, so there's no audience. I won't answer many questions, but I'll be there for you – for photos, too, if you like." I had misgivings about any photos or filming, but it was part of the deal. "If they ask anything that upsets you, you don't have to answer. You can end the interview when you're ready. If it gets too much, we can end it."

"If I've had enough, end it," she murmured to herself as she clutched my arm. Together, we walked into the studio buildings. I was nervous as hell and I couldn't imagine how much bigger the butterflies were in Caitlin's tummy. She'd promised to tell the story she hadn't even told me.

The receptionist's eyes widened when Caitlin gave her name, murmuring about makeup as she hurried off, waving frantically for us to follow her.

Caitlin's expression tightened. I could feel her fear

through her fingers, pressed firmly into my forearm, but she didn't falter as she followed. At least she didn't draw blood this time.

A round, little woman dressed all in black directed proceedings in the dressing room. "You – makeup," she barked at me, pointing at a chair in front of a mirror framed with lights. It might have looked like a starlet's dressing room in a movie, if three of the light globes hadn't blown. I sat down cautiously, resolving to raise merry hell if they turned me into a drag queen or a baby-faced teen idol.

Another black-clad girl started swiping a sponge across my cheeks, as if she was trying to sand the stubble back into my skin. I'd shaved this morning, so it wasn't like it was too bad today.

"Right, get her undressed. We'll try the blue first. . ." I looked at the room reflected in front of me. The round woman stood with her hands on her hips as three other girls circled Caitlin like a flock of magpies – a combination of sweet song and sharp beaks.

Hands plucked at her shirt. Caitlin shrank away, her arms curled across her body. "No, please. . ." Her eyes were wide with terror and turned to me. "Please. . ."

I stood up and shooed the magpie girls away as I strode through them. "Let me help you, angel," I said softly. I took her shaking hands in mine and touched my lips to hers.

"Need to get changed," twittered one of the girls. I didn't turn to see which one.

My eyes never leaving Caitlin's, I shifted my fingers to her shirt. I smoothly undid the buttons and slid the shirt off her shoulders. There were gasps as the girls saw the scars on Caitlin's back, but I ignored them for my eyes were busy holding hers. I eased it down, baring her arms and her bra, and I heard a muffled sob from one of the nameless girls. "Angel, you don't have to do this if you don't want to. You don't have to tell this story to anyone. I can take you home if you want." I took her hands again and kissed her fingers.

Caitlin's eyes were dark, dry wells. Her tone was equally deep. "No. I can do this." She pulled her hands from mine and gritted her teeth as she undid her pants, letting them slide to the floor. Her pink underwear matched her scars perfectly.

In the mirror behind her, I saw the shaken round woman say, "Not. . . not the blue. Too much skin. The mulberry, I think. . ." Even her voice shook.

One of the girls nodded, wiping her eyes, as she hung the blue dress up and reached for something in purple. The room was so silent I heard her every footstep on the vinyl until she passed the purple dress to me.

I helped Caitlin slip the dress over her head, the skirt falling to just below her knees.

"May I?" asked a quiet voice beside me.

Caitlin nodded silently to the girl, who wiped her eyes once more and started to adjust Caitlin's dress so it sat perfectly. Caitlin stood like a statue of fortitude, frozen and unflinching, yet still I worried.

"Are you sure?" I asked.

This time, Caitlin nodded only once. "Yes, Nathan. I know what I can take. Get some makeup on, because the interview questions will be harder than just getting dressed. I need you." Her fearful eyes lingered on mine, showing the terror the rest of her body hid beneath her stiff stance.

I sat back down, watching her reflection carefully until

Caitlin was led to the chair beside mine. I reached out and took her hand, smiling at her.

"Done," said the makeup artist with considerable relief. I looked in the mirror at her work. I was relieved to see I still looked like me. If it weren't for the Vaseline she'd brushed on my lips, I could ignore the fact that I was wearing makeup at all.

"You need to change your shirt," the round woman told me, her voice quieter than her first command. "For you, the cornflower. . ."

I turned to see what sort of flowers I was expected to wear, but the girl held only a light blue striped shirt. I shrugged out of my own and put on the proffered one. The fabric felt thick and crisp against my skin — like my good suit shirts that I only wore on special occasions. I guess this was one of them. The day Caitlin told the country what had happened to her.

I looked to Caitlin, her eyes closed as the girl took a brush to her eyes, darkening lids and lashes with careful strokes.

Reaching for Caitlin's hand again, I was quick to press my lips to her fingers before she could pull them out of my grasp. Of course, I got Vaseline all over them and felt stupid, so I started to apologise.

"It's okay, Nathan," Caitlin cut me off, then was silent as the makeup artist painted her lips the same purple-pink as her dress.

"There you go, sweetheart," she said, standing back and smiling with considerable pride.

Caitlin's eyes fluttered open.

My breath caught in my throat. "You look beautiful,

angel."

Her slight smile was enough to lift my heart. "Thank you, Nathan." She stood stiffly, holding still to have her dress arranged around her once more, before she held out her hand to me.

I took it and we were ushered into the studio to tape the interview.

A bloke wearing a headset told us to sit down, pointing at the armchairs arranged in a semicircle. Caitlin sank down in relief on one. One of the magpie girls swooped in to tweak Caitlin's dress and hair so that everything was perfectly in place.

Caitlin didn't let go of my hand, so I sat beside her while the dolled-up interviewer sat on her other side. The interviewer looked vaguely familiar, but for the life of me I couldn't remember her name.

She'd evidently been warned not to attempt to shake Caitlin's hand, so she just sat and smiled at us while people scurried around the two women, making sure they looked their best.

Caitlin looked pale, which only served to draw more attention to her big, dark eyes. I caught sight of what she looked like on camera on the screens in front of us – a hauntingly beautiful woman I ached to make mine. I looked over at her and she turned those eyes on me. *Help me,* they said, as she looked more vulnerable than she ever had before.

"I'm here for you," I promised her.

The interviewer cleared her throat and we looked to her. The questions began.

As she asked Caitlin the first question, my stomach

clenched in the worst case of stage fright I'd had since primary school. I forced my face into sympathetic blankness as Caitlin told what she remembered, being kept in the dark, men hurting her. I let the words wash over me, trying not to visualise the vague events she'd described in more detail on Alanna's laptop. She wasn't asked to elaborate. Instead, the interviewer asked how she felt and prompted her when Caitlin appeared lost for words.

"I wanted to kill them all, but I knew I couldn't," Caitlin said at one point. "Sometimes I just wanted to die so that the pain would end." Her eyes filled with tears then, but she squeezed my fingers and, with iron self-control, she didn't cry, blinking the tears away. "And then, I woke up and Nathan was there. He told me it was over and they weren't going to hurt me again. It seemed too good to be true so I didn't believe him at first." Her watery smile left me wishing I could comfort her.

As if her words were some sort of cue, it was my turn.

"How did you find her?" the interviewer asked me.

I took a deep breath, trying to unlock my jaw to answer. I'd prepared a response for this and I had to get the words out.

Do it for Caitlin.

I looked at her beautiful, brave face and found courage I didn't know I possessed. The power to open my mouth.

"I couldn't sleep. I went for a walk on the beach. I saw someone lying on the sand and when I approached she didn't move, so at first I thought she was dead."

Caitlin's huge eyes were on me, worried. Still, she smiled.

"I. . . I asked her if she was okay, but she didn't answer."

Now her eyes held sadness.

"She was very cold and barely conscious, so I called an ambulance and got a first aid kit from my car while we waited for help to arrive."

Caitlin pressed her lips together, giving the slightest nod.

This was the hardest part. Slowly, slowly. . .

"She woke up before the ambulance arrived. She was so scared." I swallowed as I looked at her, remembering what I could never forget.

The interviewer's voice broke through my memories. "What was the first thing you said to her?"

I'm sorry. Oh God, so sorry.

"I told her it was over and that I was there to help."

One look at Caitlin's watery smile made me continue.

"She asked me to stay with her in the ambulance and the hospital, because she was afraid to be alone."

The image came to my mind then of what she'd looked like when she'd said that and I stared at her now, trying to replace the hellish image I remembered with the vision I saw now. "She's amazing," I blurted out. "No matter how much pain she was in, she never stopped fighting to live, to get better. Anything else would mean they'd won."

Caitlin looked so deep in thought she didn't seem to know what she wanted to say. Her lips formed words, but no sound came out. She tried again and I barely caught the words, her voice was so quiet. "End it."

I dragged my eyes from Caitlin to the interviewer. "This interview is finished," I told her, as Caitlin and I stood up together. I moved closer to Caitlin, so I could support her before she walked too far.

She stood still for a moment, her arms resting on mine as mine held her. She looked up at me slowly, a smile on her face. She brought her lips up to mine and kissed me. Her gaze never wavered from my face, even as her heels touched the ground again and the kiss ended.

"Beautiful," came a voice from behind us. I turned my head a little, to see a cameraman flip two emphatic thumbs up.

Caitlin sagged in my arms, squeezing her eyes shut, more exhausted than I'd realised.

"I'll take you home, if you like, angel," I said softly. She nodded wearily, leaning heavily on me as I escorted her out.

End it. The words echoed in my head as I desperately hoped they didn't inspire the same memories in Caitlin as they did in me.

EIGHTY SIX

"An interview. You gave a fucking television interview."

His name was Paul Mott. It said so on his door. An ordinary name for an ordinary bloke, the boss who was yelling at me for fucking up this entire operation from start to finish. This time, in person and not by phone.

I'd failed. I didn't get all of them. Caitlin would never be safe and I'd never stop worrying.

"It won't be broadcast until Friday," I replied. "You still have time to pull the interview. You can contact the TV station and ask them not to air it." I kept my face blank, fighting a smile.

"Tell the news that they can't show an exclusive interview they paid for? Fuck, Nathan, they'd have a field day with that one." He glared at me. "How much did they offer you?"

I met his gaze squarely. "I don't know. I didn't ask for or accept any payment. I believe they offered money to Caitlin and she accepted it." Money to support her through her studies. A tiny amount of compensation for what she'd been through. Millions couldn't make up for her time in hell.

"What questions did they ask you?"

My breath hissed through my teeth. "They asked how I found her."

"And you said?" His voice was dead flat and dangerous.

"Nothing about the police, shots fired or even the other bloke on the beach. I didn't say which beach or how we knew she'd be there. I said I stumbled across the poor girl, lying on the sand, all alone."

"You know you can't be working for us when it airs. You're no use to us as some hero everyone's seen on TV. Any hope you had of continuing your contract died the minute you walked into that TV studio. And the moment you opened your mouth. . . you voided the contract, anyway."

My face was stony. "I was already photographed with her at the hospital. I had to go in, to find out what she'd say about what she remembered. She said. . . less than I did, and that's saying something. Half the interview is her describing her feelings about what they did to her! Fuck, that's something no one should hear. I answered questions to back up her vague story so they'd believe it. That's all." I looked at him, about as angry as I'd ever been at any boss, no matter what the job. "The contract ends tomorrow. Let me keep her safe for one more day." And try to find a way to get her to let me stay for longer than that.

"If it was anyone else, I'd say fix it or I'll fire you, for it's not fucking hard." His eyes burned with anger. "But you can finish up tomorrow, along with your contract. I don't want any more fuck-ups, so you'll be handing over all your gear – weapons, body armour, the works – today. I don't want to see you back here."

I nodded, knowing I couldn't ask for any more. "Do we have any more leads on the rest of them?" Please tell me so I know what to look out for to keep her safe, even when it's not my job any more.

He sighed. "Our team has been through Laura's house from one end to the other and nothing. We have her computer files, but no one's managed to break into those yet. The only records she kept on paper are in a diary she had in her handbag. She occasionally made reference to contact with someone she called 'Al Himar,' but we haven't managed to work out who he or they are. Once we have access to her computer, we'll call in the translators and see what they make of it. If we don't close this operation properly, we'll look like right asses."

"What if they come after Caitlin tomorrow when I'm unarmed?" I asked.

He snorted. "Let her take care of them. She has a pretty good track record so far – maybe better than yours."

I didn't laugh. I wanted to cry. Instead, I just tightened my jaw and left. I had a gun to hand in and a shitload of worry to carry, with nowhere to offload it.

EIGHTY SEVEN

I arrived early at Caitlin's. It was still mid-afternoon, but I didn't want to stay away from her any longer. My head was too filled with dread for her safety when we were apart.

I dragged myself up her front steps, trying to pull myself together into some semblance of company for her, instead of the wet dishrag I felt like.

It was piano-lesson day, it seemed. The child I'd heard practising the piano for the last fortnight had played a very simple song, but the virtuoso who played what I barely recognised as the same song must have been the child's teacher, demonstrating how something so simple could become a complex masterpiece. For the second time that day, I felt like crying. Caitlin and I were right there at the child's skill level – our relationship working well enough to appear to be music. Would she survive long enough for us to take it further, to be the symphony we could be together? I wanted it – God, I wanted it, almost as much as I wanted Caitlin herself.

I couldn't wait any longer. I knocked on her door, dying to see Caitlin again.

The piano-played song ended in silence. The music lesson was over for the day, it seemed. Oh God, please don't let anything else be over. Not yet.

I heard Caitlin's steps creak on the boards in the hall before she opened the door. "Nathan – you're early!" Her eyes lit up and she threw her arms around me, delivering a delightful kiss.

My heavy heart lifted a little and I felt my smile return. "Angel," I murmured, not wanting to let go. She was the only light I could see, even with the sun still in the sky.

She laughed as she pulled away from me. "Come on in. I was thinking about an afternoon snack and the cheese looked really good. . ." She took my hand and pulled me inside, leading the way laughingly to the kitchen.

From the fridge she pulled out something small enough to hold in her hand and proffered it. Nestled in her palm was a small cheese, coated in black wax. "Jo and I bought it this morning and I wanted to share it with you." She flitted around the kitchen, pulling out a cutting board and a wicked little knife. Caitlin stretched up onto her toes to reach the crackers in a high cupboard above the bench, but her balance was perfect.

She took the knife and touched the point to the wax.

"Let me help you with that," I offered, worrying about her hurting her hands by handling a knife and hard cheese.

Caitlin shook her head, still laughing. Her fingers were quick. With a few deft strokes she'd peeled the wax from the little cheddar and laid it naked on the cutting board. I watched her carefully as she started to slice the cheese, but

Caitlin didn't show the slightest sign of any pain.

She's really recovering, I realised. My heart lifted a little more.

Caitlin held out a cracker, topped with a freshly cut slice of cheese. She popped another in her mouth, smiling as I took her offering.

I crunched my way through what was good cheese. Better still was the cheese-flavoured kiss Caitlin followed it up with.

Her smile was almost infectious. "What would you like to do tonight?"

I found my grin again. "I'll leave that entirely up to you. Dinner, maybe?"

"I was thinking about going out to the hawker's. I want to try with chopsticks again. . ."

I needed to ask her out for tomorrow night. Plan a special dinner and maybe something else after, anything to get her to let me stay again tomorrow.

I opened my mouth to suggest it and the phone rang.

Caitlin looked surprised and picked up. "Hello?" Her eyes widened as she listened. "Is your wife feeling better? She had a cold last time I spoke to you. . . the kids didn't get it, too, did they?" She listened for a little longer, nodding a little.

"You want me to. . . hang on." She put the phone down on the bench and hit the speakerphone button. "Sorry, Detective McGuinness, I'm in the kitchen so I just stuck you on speakerphone. Now, what was that about me coming in to identify someone?" Our eyes met and my mouth wouldn't close. Caitlin didn't need the memories of dead bodies on top of the other horrible memories she had.

Who did she know who'd died?

"Some of these bodies were found last night in a place that links them to your kidnapping. We'd like you to take a look at them and see if you recognise them. We've already identified four of them, with one family member coming in tomorrow to confirm the last identification. We'd like you to come in on Monday to. . ."

Caitlin was shaking her head and I understood her denial completely. She shouldn't need to do this.

"Detective, I can't come in on Monday. I fly out tomorrow night. . ."

WHAT?

Caitlin's eyes were on the cheese as she carefully cut another slice.

". . . so the latest I could come in would be tomorrow afternoon. How about right after lunch? Or is that too early?" She turned her eyes expectantly to the phone, as if she could see through the plastic and phone lines to the detective himself.

"We have a relative coming in at two, so maybe. . . at three? Would that be too late for you? It's probably best that you don't meet him, especially if you identify his son as one of the men who. . ." He coughed.

Caitlin glanced at me and then away before I could say anything. "That's probably a good idea. Can I bring a friend along with me. . . for moral support? I just. . ." Her fingers slid between mine, squeezing lightly.

I looked at Caitlin to find her questioning eyes on me. I nodded in response. Of course. Any support she needed and I'd be there.

Even the detective sounded sympathetic. "Of course.

Whoever you need. I realise this is difficult for you. Is there any chance you've remembered more than you told me the last time we met? That kind of information could be really useful. . ." He trailed off.

Caitlin's eyes went to the cheese as she sliced a fair bit more. I felt each stroke of the knife seemed a bit harder than the last. "I'll bring along what I have. It's just as much of my memories as I could recollect. Not really in the kind of format you're after, but I've tried to group them into people, places and days. . ."

He was silent. I could hear him clearing a dry throat before he could speak. "Of course. Thank you. Anything you have for us would be wonderful. We really appreciate any new information you can provide. See you tomorrow " He waited for Caitlin's goodbye before he hung up.

My mouth was still open and I didn't know what to ask first.

Of course, Caitlin did. "Nathan, would you please come with me to the police station tomorrow? I don't want to do this alone."

My answer was immediate – without thought. "Of course. I'll hold your hand, no matter what."

She smiled and took another slice of cheese, savouring the taste with her eyes closed.

"Are you really flying somewhere tomorrow?" I blurted out, my voice sounding really forlorn.

Her eyes snapped open. "Yes. Jo told me this morning, while we were shopping for clothes. If you're really lucky, I may show you later." Caitlin winked, as she pulled down the shoulder of her shirt. I caught a glimpse of satin and lace before she covered her bra again. "The trip is my birthday present. She and Dad arranged with all of my friends to pay for me to have a holiday – she's coming, too. She wouldn't even tell me where – except that we'll be going clothes shopping, so she told me to pack light for warm weather, with underwear for two weeks, and I'll find out at the airport tomorrow." Caitlin looked so excited I couldn't bear to be anything but happy for her. She did deserve a holiday.

"Just you and Jo?" I enquired, not game to ask what I really wanted.

She laughed. "Yes, that's what Jo said. A girls' trip, now we're both old enough to travel alone." She looked sympathetic. "I'll be back in two weeks, Nathan. It's not like anyone will be following me – even I don't know where I'm going."

I didn't know what to say. I wanted to go with her, but there was no way in hell I was going to say it. I pasted a smile on my face. "So I only get you today and tomorrow? How would you feel about getting into the vodka tonight after dinner and we'll see what happens? I'd better make sure you enjoy yourself, so you don't forget me while you're away on holiday."

Caitlin's kiss was long and lingering. "I'll never forget you, Nathan. You saved my life, remember? And then stole my ice cream." Her smile was impish. "C'mon, let's take the cheese and crackers to the lounge room. Jo lent me some DVDs of her brother's, a TV series she said was really funny. It's about some secret agent who works with computers. . ." The cutting board in one hand and the box of crackers in the other, she led the way out of the kitchen.

Some hours later, when the episodes on the DVD faded to warning messages in a dozen different languages, I looked around. The coffee table was littered with the takeaway hawker food we'd eventually ordered, along with the empty vodka mixers we'd drunk afterwards. Caitlin snuggled closer to me, letting out a little contented sigh in her sleep. Smiling, I shifted her into my arms and staggered to my feet to carry Caitlin off to bed.

I considered waking her to ask about the very pretty underwear she'd tempted me with earlier, but I decided against it. I settled for sleeping with her in the somnolent sense tonight. I didn't know when I'd get another good night's sleep, what with worrying about her while she was away from me.

At least I knew that anywhere else would be safer than here.

EIGHTY EIGHT

Caitlin was so worried about getting to the State Mortuary on time that we arrived way too early. It was easier to humour her than argue. I'd never seen her so nervous – not even before the interview. In the waiting room, she hopped from chair to chair, convinced that she wasn't comfortable in what looked to me to be identical seats. When she settled in one for more than a minute, I shifted to the one beside her and slung an arm around her shoulders.

"It's okay, angel," I murmured, pressing my lips to the top of her head. I could feel her bouncing a little with a rhythm only she could hear.

She didn't reply, for her eyes were fixed on a lost-looking old bloke, standing by the reception desk. I hadn't seen him come in, but Caitlin couldn't stop staring at him.

The poor old guy noticed her staring and his eyes grew wide as he looked at Caitlin. The receptionist saw him and stood up, moving around the desk to stand by his side. "I'm so sorry for your loss, Mr Dennis. Would you like me to call you a taxi, or did you drive today?" She walked with the man out the doors to the car park outside. She returned after a few minutes, looking sad.

He must have lost his wife, poor bloke, I thought.

I looked at Caitlin. Her eyebrows were down and her forehead was wrinkled. I stretched out a hand to smooth the skin, stroking her hair, too. "Don't worry, angel. We'll be out of here soon."

Her smile was tight as it turned up her mouth, as if she were trying to convince herself as much as me. "You're right, Nathan. It'll be okay." I didn't want to think what would happen if circumstances conspired to make it any less than okay.

Footsteps sounded on vinyl and the detective I'd last seen trying to interrogate Caitlin in hospital stepped up to the reception desk. The receptionist said something to him, too soft for me to hear, before he turned to look at us. "You're early," he said with some surprise.

Caitlin pressed her lips together, looking at the floor, so I answered, "Caitlin really wanted to get this over with and I was worried about parking, so we made sure we had plenty of time to get here."

"And she brought you for moral support," he went on, as if I hadn't spoken.

"Yes I did, Detective," Caitlin said with a sweet, sad smile. "I couldn't do this without Nathan." She held out her hand, a CD case clutched between two fingers. "This is what you asked for – my memories."

I looked longingly at the CD, wondering how to ask her for a copy, but I didn't say a word.

"Thank you," he said in wonder, tucking it into the

folder he held stiffly at his side. "Shall we?"

My arm tightened protectively around Caitlin as she stood up and I did the same. She leaned against me for comfort as we followed the detective deeper into the building.

He led us to a waiting room for the bereaved – the same place where I'd waited to see Alanna one last time. It was my turn to hold on to Caitlin for comfort, but the pain wasn't as bad as I remembered. As if she'd filled the gap somehow.

Caitlin's eyes looked up at me in surprise for a moment, before she settled closer into my embrace. Maybe it worked for both of us right now.

The detective sat on the couch across from us, a manila folder in his hands. He cleared his throat. "I have some pictures for you. Can you tell me if you recognise any of these people?" He opened it and held up a photo.

Laura in life. "She pushed me into her car, the red Mercedes," Caitlin said in a flat tone. He scribbled notes quickly.

Laura's photo disappeared into the bottom of the file. The next one was of a man, his eyes closed in death. "The police officer who shot Nathan."

He shot you, too, angel, I thought but didn't say. And later, he shot himself when he tried to shoot me again.

The next photo showed a live man. I recognised it from the surveillance footage of the inside of Caitlin's house. Pete, the one who broke her fingers, before I shot his face off, I thought with some satisfaction.

"I don't know," Caitlin said softly. She looked at the detective in consternation. "I didn't see all of their faces. I remember other things about them in the dark. Their hands, the size of them, what I. . ." She took the photo from him and looked more closely at it. "He broke my fingers. After I broke his nose." She sounded proud of it, too.

I smothered a smile.

The next photo was of a dead man. The one who tried to walk away, outside Caitlin's house. Tom, after I shot him in the back of the head as he heaped insults on her injuries.

Caitlin shook her head. "I don't know."

"Last one," the detective said as he pulled out one more photo of yet another waxy male corpse. This one had a bullet hole through his forehead, but the blood I remembered was gone.

Caitlin's expression hardened. "He was in the car. And on the beach that night."

He slipped the photo back in the folder, leaving only Tom's photo out. "So, you've identified all of them except for this one." He shook the photo. "What else do you remember about them?"

Caitlin screwed her face up, trying hard to remember. "I bit someone's hand. I remember spitting out the mess." She pulled a face in distaste. "He had some chunky rings on that cut my face when he hit me." Her voice was so devoid of emotion I could barely believe it. It was as though she'd locked the tears away for later.

The detective looked as disconcerted as I felt. "Well, that's why we're here, so you can identify the bodies if the photos aren't enough. Have you ever seen a corpse before?" He looked intently at Caitlin, ignoring me entirely. If he had the surveillance photos, then he knew what my answer would be.

Caitlin looked up at him, affronted. "I'm studying medicine. Of course I've dissected a cadaver." She followed him without hesitation, her head held high.

I followed more reluctantly, hoping to avoid my memories of this place.

In the cool room, the detective opened up drawers, each occupied by a sheet-shrouded body. The hands were visible on either side, though, and that's what Caitlin studied as she walked along the row of corpses. She stopped and pointed. "That one. You can see the ridges and tan lines where the rings were and there's a chunk missing on the side." Her face was firm as she waited for the detective to reach her. She flipped the sheet from the man's face and it was Tom, as dead as his picture. With a shrug, she covered him again. "Are there any more?" she asked, her face a mask of indifference.

He looked shaken. His composure was no match for hers. "No. . . no, that's all of them," he said with a sick smile. "Thank you for your time. I'll walk you out."

He hurried us out, looking like he couldn't be finished fast enough.

Caitlin looked pale as we left the mortuary, but she had her teeth clenched and her expression was fierce. She was remarkably composed for someone who'd just been looking at corpses.

"Are you relieved?" I asked. "They can't hurt you any more."

"No," she replied curtly. "They'll never touch me again, but that's not all of them."

"Are you sure?" I responded.

"There's one more man who hurt me. One they haven't got yet." She looked straight ahead as she said it, not looking at me.

For the first time, I struggled to keep up with her, as she marched back to the car. "But is he really a risk? The one they haven't got yet?"

She stopped to look up at me, her look incredulous. "He hurt me. He wasn't the worst of them, but he still hurt me. I'm not safe until they have him."

"Excuse me. . ." I turned to see the lost-looking old man approaching.

There was no one else around, so I answered. "What is it? I'm sorry for your loss, mate, but we're in a hurry here."

Caitlin had stopped moving. She was a frozen statue at my side, clutching at my arm. I felt a frisson of fear.

He raised his gun and pointed it at us. "You killed my son. Give me the girl."

"I don't know what you're talking about. . ." I began.

"I do," Caitlin cut me off. She glared at the old man.

"Give me the girl," he insisted.

All warmth drained from me as she let go of my arm and took a step toward him, lifting her hands to the height of her shoulders. Another step and another as I watched, helpless to stop her.

"No, don't hurt her. . ." I barely recognised the desperate voice as my own.

I watched him lower the gun as she steadily approached. I wished Caitlin would look at me, to let me beg her not to do this. My voice died in my throat, terrified that she'd die before my eyes.

She stood close enough to press her body against his,

but he held the gun between them. I couldn't see if it was still pointed at her. I couldn't see her hands or his.

The moment stretched forever.

He broke the silence. "You killed my son."

Caitlin shook her head. I heard the quiet murmur of her voice but not the words. Would they be her last? Please, no!

She lunged across the narrow space between them. If he'd had his gun pointed at her, it would have dug into her soft flesh.

I heard the shot and was cowardly enough to close my eyes. I couldn't bear to watch Caitlin die. The slither and slump of a body hitting the bitumen.

I could have cried when I heard the most heavenly sound in the world. "Good riddance, Simon." I opened my eyes in time to see her spit on his corpse, the gun still clenched in his hand. She turned to smile at me. Pure spring sunshine. "Now it's over and I'm safe."

I stumbled toward her, my arms out to hold her, to make sure she was real. She let me hug her before she straightened up and pulled away.

"I have to get to the airport, Nathan," she said.

I looked at the body on the bitumen before my eyes bumped back to her. "But. . . you just. . . he's. . ."

Her hand slid into my pocket and pulled out my phone. "You have friends to call, to clean this up. That's what they're good at, isn't it? Tell them you have the last one."

I stared at her, speechless. How long had she known?

"I need to get to the airport. May I borrow your car? I'll leave it at my house, with the keys on the table inside the front door. You know where I keep the spare house keys. You can get a lift with your colleagues, right?"

"I'll drive you," I whispered.

Caitlin shook her head. "You have a dead body to deal with. I can drive home and Jo will pick me up from there."

I pulled the keys wordlessly from my pocket and held them out. Alanna wouldn't have hesitated, so neither did I.

She dug into her handbag and pulled out a stack of folded paper, a little crumpled and crushed around the edges. "This is what you wanted. My memories, as complete as I could make them. If. . . if you still want to see me when I return, I'll be back in two weeks." She smiled sadly as she traded the papers for my keys. Her lips lingered on my cheek. "See you then."

I waved in stunned wonder as I watched her drive off in Alanna's convertible before I dialled Navid. I had a shitload of explaining to do.

Simon. Safe. It's over. Oh, Caitlin. . .

EIGHTY NINE

When I reached home, five exhausting hours later, I pulled out the crumpled papers and sat with them, my eyes closed. If I read these, I'd know. Know what happened in full, know how much she remembered and how much she'd managed to forget. Every painful moment of violence, abuse and neglect until I managed to help. I'd know what I was responsible for and how much guilt I'd have to live with, for the rest of my life.

I could wait. I had enough to be miserable over.

My angel was winging her away across land and sea, away from me, and it'd be two weeks before I'd see her again. At least I knew she was safe, I told myself. Her nightmares were over. And mine had barely begun.

I placed the papers carefully on my desk before I went to bed. Every time I opened my eyes, I could feel them burning a dark hole in my head, but I didn't touch them.

In the morning, I dug out the keys to the red Mercedes Caitlin hated so much. I drove it to a car dealership and haggled half-heartedly with a used-car dealer until he gave me a cheque in exchange for the keys and some signed forms. I trudged all the way home in a daze. It might have taken three minutes or three hours. I didn't care.

I offered the cheque to Chris, telling her I was keeping Alanna's car and I'd sold mine, so I owed her half the money.

She snorted. "Keep it. You need it more than I do." She chewed her lip, as if she was dying to say something. "Where's Caitlin? Did she finally kick you out?"

I couldn't summon the energy to get angry at her. "No, she's off on a holiday somewhere with a friend. Girls' trip and I wasn't invited. I'm not anatomically equipped for days of clothes shopping and cocktails."

She looked sad. "It's for the best, you know. She's not good for you."

Of course she was. She was amazing and perfect for me — everything I'd ever wanted. Everything I didn't have. I didn't say it — she wouldn't listen, anyway. I clicked on the TV and took a big bite of my lunch sandwich. Sawdust or salami or spinach — I didn't taste it and I didn't care. It was as dry as dust in my mouth, anyway.

I didn't look at the papers when I went to bed that night. A white beacon on my desk, waiting to drag me into the darkest depths of despair. I wondered if there was any such thing as a white hole — like a black hole, only camouflaged in colour and light. Or carefully covered by a sheaf of pristine pages, lying in wait.

We ran out of milk so I ate my cornflakes dry. Soft and stale from sitting in the cupboard so long, untouched, I remembered how much Caitlin hated them. And why. I threw up the gooey orange mess into the sink, washing it away with a hissing stream of water. Wishing I could wash memories away like cornflakes. Like blood.

The pages taunted me day and night. Sitting in a patch of sunlight through the window, glowing in moonlight much later, hidden by darkness and ever lurking.

I should've just rung Navid and handed them over. Never reading, never knowing. But I owed it to Caitlin to read what she gave me, to know what she went through. The least I could do.

But not yet.

I watched TV. Light blended into dark and I didn't leave the house. I focussed on nothing but advertising – endless repetition of a dramatic voice, telling me that Caitlin would tell her story. The time, the day and the haunting picture they'd plastered over the papers. Her haunted eyes as she whispered, "End it." Over and over until I tried to reach out and touch her through the LCD screen.

I wanted to steal an old TV from someone's verge, one with a dodgy picture that wasn't so clear and real. I didn't want to feel like I was in among the action. If I couldn't touch her, it was more torture than entertainment. The minutes ticked 'til the Friday when they'd show the complete interview. Or as much as they chose to.

Friday night came and Chris was out. I spread out across the couch with a beer and waited.

I tuned out through a story about cyber-bullying. My beer was empty and I went to get another one when the story switched to some con-artist who wouldn't say anything but swearing to the cameramen as they stalked his house. What else do you say to stalkers who won't leave you alone?

"Up next – miracle girl Caitlin Lockyer tells her story!" A quick flash of her duckling photograph from the newspaper and an ad for cornflakes appeared. Fucking cornflakes.

I went to get another beer, but we were out. I opened one of the lemon vodka things Caitlin had left here when she stayed over. When we'd. . .

"End it," her voice said from the lounge room and I ran back to the couch, only to find that it was an ad. A dancing dishcloth cleaned someone's house to upbeat music as I thought about ringing the TV station to complain about the wait.

I didn't do it. I drank a gulp of vodka, remembering the taste of it on Caitlin's tongue.

I decided to order a copy of that photo in the morning.

"They hurt me. They came in the dark and. . . hurt me. I couldn't understand it – why they'd want to, why they came back again. Only to hurt me. . ." Her forlorn voice cut deep and I listened.

She never used the words rape, break or cut, though that's what they did. Only hurt. All she ever said was that they hurt her, a word that haunted me more than the precise ones she avoided.

Please don't hurt me. . .

My heart went out to her, wherever she was, and for the first time I saw the interviewer's tears, too. Yet Caitlin never cried – not a drop. She'd cried herself out in my arms and she had no tears left to shed when she talked of hurt and dark.

I stared at her angry-looking protector, knowing it was

me in makeup, as the figure on the screen talked of how amazing she was and how she never gave up.

If I'd known then what I knew now – that she could kill a man for what he did to her, no fear left for she'd spent it all long before. . .

Our kiss had the interviewer clapping and crying at the same time. I didn't remember her making a sound – maybe they taped her response later. My strong suspicion was confirmed when she asked one more question that I know I never heard.

"What were you thinking most, in the pain and the dark?"

Caitlin's whispered response was taken completely out of context. "End it."

And the interview ended.

No, she wasn't thinking that she wanted to end it, I fumed. She was thinking what she said, so many times in her sleep: Keep fighting. Don't let them win.

"Up next, a live performance from meteoric Melbourne band, Chaya, performing their debut single, Necessary Evil, followed by an exclusive interview with their hot lead singer, Jay. . ."

I clicked the TV off.

You didn't know her. You made her sound like a helpless little innocent, instead of the fierce fighter she was. No matter what kind of hell she'd been through, there was nothing that could stop me from going to meet her again when she came home.

Fuck it. I was going to read the whole thing in the morning. I owed it to her.

NINETY

I finished my toast and sat down to read what Caitlin had given me. It was what I both hoped and dreaded – a detailed description of everything she remembered of her kidnapping, captivity and afterwards.

Every memory was preceded by a line of key words across the top in bold, a chilling summary of what was to come. Names, feelings, sounds and specific injuries.

My heart grew cold as I read, wondering how she'd come to write those lines. As if she'd thought, "I dreamed he broke my fingers and raped me," then searched for those words to add to the memory of breaking and brutality. . . oh God.

There was far more than I thought she'd remembered and my first instinct was to call her, to start asking questions. I hesitated a moment, before I realised I should read it through to the end before I started asking anything else. I couldn't call her – I didn't know if she had her phone or even if there was mobile access, wherever she was. My questions would have to wait.

One page had her handwriting across the top, above the line of bold words:

Not in the police transcript

Of all the pages, this one I kept returning to, as if rereading the words would somehow change the past they described. I ripped the page free of its fellows and read it again:

Beach – Stars – Sand – Shots – Surf – Chris – Nathan – Numb

I was floating. No pain – nothing holding me down, anymore. Something cold touched my face and I opened my eyes slowly. I recoiled from the dark shape hovering over me.

"It's okay. I'm just washing your face," said a voice I barely recognised.

I shivered in what felt like a cold wind. It couldn't be. I looked around fearfully. I looked up, and saw the contrast of pinprick stars on the darker black of the open sky. "Where are we?"

"We're at a beach, out of there, away from them." His voice sounded different, that was why I didn't recognise it immediately. More abrupt, more certain. More authoritative. "There's something I have to do here."

"You got me out. Thank you, Chris!" I felt a surge of joy well up, bringing tears to my eyes, barely able to believe it was possible.

He was silent, and I looked at him to see the reason for it. I was shocked to see he held my hands in his – I couldn't feel his touch, and they didn't look like my hands – they were twisted and swollen, dark with blood to well past my wrists. As he held my hands, he said,

"Can you trust me?"

"Okay." I was surprised that he'd bothered to ask, after all that had happened.

He suddenly turned to face the dunes, looking worried. "Wait here. I'll be back." He got up and jogged off into the dunes, leaving me alone. ". . . First aid kit. . ." were the only words I could discern as he took off.

I tried to move, but my body wouldn't respond. There was no feeling left in my legs, and my hands were numb from the wrists down. I tried to call out, to tell him to wait, not to leave me alone like this, but even my voice wasn't strong enough. Just as I started to panic, I heard footsteps approaching me across the sand.

I struggled to sit up, realising too late as I managed it that I was wrapped in a blanket, which slipped off my shoulders, exposing most of my top half to the freezing wind. I clumsily attempted to pull it back up again with my numb, mangled fingers, but failed miserably.

Somehow, I collapsed on the sand again, my head spinning. So cold already, I barely felt him rip the blanket away from me and toss it aside.

I should have fought, but it was like moving through cold water and I was so tired, so tired! "Sadistic prick," I mumbled.

I couldn't even feel the pain any more. I heard a voice, but I didn't care enough to focus on what it meant. I closed my eyes, drifting into sleep.

A sharp pain woke me and I cried out, opening my eyes as I struggled to sit up, convinced I'd been stabbed.

He pushed me back down, his voice an unintelligible sound that I couldn't focus on, but I fought him now, desperate to see if I'd dreamed it.

Then he was gone.

A gun in my hands. I couldn't feel it, had to touch it to my face to be sure I had it.

"End it," I murmured.

A gasp. No.

Tugging, snapping, took it from me. The gun was gone.

Shots.

"Wake up, angel."

Nathan, saying, "It's over."

"Chris. . ." I mumbled.

"It's all right, he's dead," Nathan replied.

NINETY ONE

I read it for what might have been the hundredth time, then dropped the page and closed my eyes. I wanted to erase my memories. I wanted to erase hers. I wanted no one to know what I'd done. But some things can't be undone.

I opened my eyes, looking for where the paper had fallen, and realised she'd written something on the back, too:

Nathan, this is as much as I can remember. If you'd like to talk about it, I'll be at 47 Adelaide St in Fremantle at 4:30 pm next Saturday — two weeks after I gave you this.

I thought it sounded strange, but I'd go just to see her again. I had so much I wanted to say. Starting with "sorry."

Coward that I am, I wasn't sure if I could say it all. I started writing it down instead.

See, Caitlin? I could document my worst nightmares, too. And mine are as real as yours.

I sealed them in an envelope, wishing I could seal them as securely inside my head.

The week dragged like an insomniac snail, the only bright spot the day the newspaper photo of her arrived. A framed memory of Caitlin smiling at ducklings, as happy as

I'd ever seen her. Now I'd never forget, either. I turned on the bedside light when I woke up in the dark, just so I could see her face again.

On Saturday afternoon, I drove up and down Adelaide Street, looking for the right number. After three tries, I gave up, parked the car and started walking. I couldn't find the number anyway.

So, at 4:30 pm, I stood outside an old church, which was where number forty-seven should be. A large wedding party posed for photographs on the steps. I stopped on the footpath, not wanting to get in the photographer's way. I searched the wedding guests for her, scanning faces.

The bride was Caitlin's opposite – tall and blonde with bloody big boobs, wearing a blue and white dress with lots of coloured pearls. Her husband looked at her as if he was hypnotised by bliss.

I bet they'd never had anything but smooth sailing, from first kiss through to wedding night – they couldn't have had as hard a time of it as Caitlin and I had. I could count the number of kisses we'd shared and I didn't dare even mention the possibility of sex...

At the happy couple's feet, a grumpy little flower girl in a miniature version of the bride's dress sat pouting at her toy fish on the steps. Most of the guests were Italian – plenty of dark hair, but none of them as beautiful as Caitlin.

I couldn't see her anywhere. I took a walk around the church, wondering if I was missing something.

The church door was open, with a sign beside it saying, *Reconciliation Today*. I stepped in through the door, wondering if Caitlin had gone inside.

It was dark in the foyer and while I waited for my eyes to adjust, I felt her fingers close around mine. She guided my hand into some cold water, then helped me draw a cross across my chest, my fingers still dripping.

Before I could ask why, she smiled and said in a low voice, "It's a reminder of your baptism, when all the bad things you've done are forgiven." She paused. "Were you christened, Nathan?"

"I think so," I answered, worried. "I was too young to remember and I don't think I've been in a church much since."

She smiled again. "Then perhaps it wouldn't hurt to spend a moment longer in this one?"

Maybe she was going to kill me and she didn't want me to die unforgiven, I thought in mounting panic. Did I have the right to deny her that? I couldn't deny what I'd done.

A calm spread across my mind as I didn't care any more. She was entitled to any compensation she wanted to exact from me. I owed her far more than I could ever give.

She led me inside the church proper, into one of the pews close to the back. Her steps were light again, almost dancing like the first time I'd seen her. She wore a white cotton dress with light blue flowers on it.

"Were you christened?" I asked her.

She laughed. "Oh yes, first communion, confirmation, the works. Dad made sure I was brought up a good little Catholic girl."

She knelt down, looking at the front of the church, instead of me. As my eyes adjusted to the dim light, I realised we were alone in the church. I ached to touch her, but I couldn't bring myself to do it. I didn't want to disturb her.

I reached into my pocket and pulled out the envelope that held what I needed to tell her. The words I could never seem to say. I leaned down and slipped it into her bag, praying that she didn't open it until I was out of reach. Maybe after she'd read it and cooled down a little, she'd speak to me again. Maybe even forgive me, at least a little.

I jumped at a sudden sound. Someone came in behind us, walked up the aisle and then stepped through an open door to the side, closing it behind him. He didn't even glance at us. I hoped he hadn't seen me with my hand in

Caitlin's bag.

I looked askance at Caitlin, but she still knelt, looking at the front of the church or praying, for all I knew.

"He's going to reconciliation, Nathan," she said suddenly. "He'll express how sorry he is for the bad things he's done and the priest will tell him that God forgives him for them. Sometimes, you have to do a penance for them, too." She still wouldn't look at me.

I felt chilled. She was going to kill me and my last words would be in that letter. "Oh, confession. You want me to go in there with a priest and confess all the bad things I've done?"

"If you like." She grinned at me suddenly, looking like the cat who'd stolen the fillet steak. "I have."

I started to shake my head, knowing one of the last things I wanted to do right now was tell some stranger about the bad things I'd done. I could barely tell her what she already knew. A sudden thought distracted me. "What sort of things do you have to confess to?" I asked.

"When I was at school, we were taught not to ask anyone that question, because it's not polite," she admonished me, turning back to look at the front of the church. I thought she'd finished, but after a pause she continued, "Killing people isn't exactly condoned and I think lying to police and perjury are considered sins, regardless of the reasons for them."

"I haven't..." I began, than changed what I was going to say. "I don't have anything I want to tell a priest."

"You never told anyone about him, did you? You said I killed him, in self-defence." Caitlin's eyes were dark pools pointed at me. "I don't think it's a god's forgiveness you want," she said carefully. "At school, the teacher drummed into us that reconciliation wasn't so much about what you'd done, or what you'd failed to do, but how you were sorry for it and intended to make amends."

I didn't know what to say. I'd known this time would

come and I dreaded telling her the truth. That's why I wrote it down, so I'd know I said it all, even if I couldn't get the words out of my mouth. They'd flowed through my fingers far more easily.

I'd kept putting it off in the hope that maybe it wouldn't happen. Maybe she'd never remember it all. Fucking stupid hope.

She'd never forgotten any of it.

I fell to my knees. "Caitlin, I'm so sorry."

She turned her big, dark, sad eyes on me. They shone in the last rays of sunlight streaming through the high window as they filled with tears. "Chris. Why did you do it, Nathan?"

I took a deep breath. It didn't help. "It was my job to watch them kidnap someone and get out with the witness. But I didn't... couldn't..." My voice failed and I tried again. "I didn't know what they'd done to you until that night on the beach. Then it was too late. I'd let them hurt you like that and I hadn't done a thing to stop them."

"Why did you kill him?" Her voice shook as she said it.

I hesitated, not even sure of the answer to this myself any more. "I thought it was for Alanna, or even for me. Maybe it was for you. I... just... couldn't let him live... knowing... what he did... and what I didn't. How I'd failed." It felt like my entire digestive tract was so heavy it had dropped out of me onto the floor at my feet, taking my voice with it, leaving a gaping hole where my guts used to be.

She knew.

Her voice was sad and calm. "Why me, Nathan? Why did they choose me?"

I couldn't meet her eyes. "I couldn't take my eyes off you. *She* saw and picked you. Out of the hundreds of people walking down the Terrace that day, they picked you. And I couldn't stop them."

A tear stood bright on her cheek, but she wiped it away.

"I think you have a lot to answer for. What you put me through can't be undone, but you helped me recover from it. You even saved my life. Maybe one day I'll be able to forgive you for it." Suddenly, she rose and walked out of the church.

"Wait. Please." I hurried to follow her out.

When she stopped, it was so sudden that I almost bumped into her.

"I'm sorry. I'm so sorry." I couldn't say it enough.

She turned to face me, so close I could feel the warmth of her body, not quite touching me. She slid an arm around my waist to steady herself, as she stretched up onto her toes. She reached up with her other hand to my throat, her fingers moving up in a slow caress to my cheek, where she stopped. The heel of her hand was under my chin, her fingers curved up around my cheek. "Forgiven," she breathed, before she gave me a lingering kiss.

My heart ached in a void, daring to beat in hope.

Tell her about the letter.

She stepped back and looked up at me, a sad smile on her face. "Goodbye, Nathan."

In despair, I wondered if there was anything I could say to change her mind. "I love you," I whispered, realising I meant it.

She didn't hear. Her light, dancing step carried her into the evening cafe crowd and out of my sight. Caitlin never looked back.

I couldn't leave. I couldn't make myself move. I couldn't stand to shift from the spot where Caitlin had kissed me so sweetly for what might have been the last time.

She knew.

Dusk faded to darkness and still I stood, wishing, hoping, praying that she'd read the letter and return. She said she'd forgiven me!

Out of the darkness, I heard a live band in one of the nearby pubs start their first set, covering a Powderfinger song.

"Who will lift you up..."

Lifting her up when she was unconscious, on the beach, on the road outside the ambulance, in the hospital... Even now my arms felt empty without her.

"... your fool..."

Bloodied handprints on the quilt... a silent scream... running. NO. Don't think it.

"... watch your back..."

Her pulling me down as the gunshot echoed in the dark night... She'd saved my life.

Oh God, she knew in the TV interview and she never said anything, either. Two weeks ago, with the police... fuck! She was protecting me...

"... at the end..."

End it. Her whisper in the TV studio. Her lying on the beach, her eyes on me as she held a gun to her own head. Agonising memory that haunted my nightmares. Who would be there to protect her if they found her? She'd turn the weapon on herself before she'd let them take her back...

"... fall down at your..."

... trying to help her... in hospital, on the beach, on the road by the ambulance as the blood pooled beneath her...

"... fall down at your..."

Here in the church... begging for her forgiveness... when I should have been begging her to stay with me.

"... FALL DOWN at your feet?"

Did he have a fucking stutter? On my knees on the dull grey concrete outside a church, I was angry at a stupid singer I couldn't even see.

The letter. Fuck, the letter.

I staggered to my feet.

I had to find her.

I needed to know.

The nightmare may be over for Caitlin,
but for Nathan it's just begun.

Awake or asleep – Nathan's angel has
the answers.

Caitlin will tell her own story in
Necessary Evil of Nathan Miller.

ABOUT THE AUTHOR

Demelza Carlton has always loved the ocean, but on her first snorkelling trip she found she was afraid of fish.

She has since swum with sea lions, sharks and sea cucumbers and stood on spray drenched cliffs over a seething sea as a seven-metre cyclonic swell surged in, shattering a shipwreck below.

Demelza now lives in Perth, Western Australia, the shark attack capital of the world.

The *Ocean's Gift* series was her first foray into fiction, followed her suspense thriller *Nightmares* trilogy. She swears the *Mel Goes to Hell* series ambushed her on a crowded train and wouldn't leave her alone.

Want to know more? You can follow Demelza on Facebook, Twitter, YouTube or her website, Demelza Carlton's Place at:

www.demelzacarlton.com

9 781925 799576